TO DANCE IN LIRADON

Adrienne Clarke

SOUL MATE PUBLISHING

New York

TO DANCE IN LIRADON

Copyright©2012

ADRIENNE CLARKE

Cover Design by Rae Monet, Inc.

Published in the United States of America by
Soul Mate Publishing
P.O. Box 24
Macedon, New York, 14502

ISBN: 978-1-61935-220-9
eBook ISBN: 978-1-61935-127-1

www.SoulMatePublishing.com

The publisher does not have any control over and does not assume any responsibility for author or third-party Web sites or their content.

For Juliet and Callista,

my real life heroines.

Acknowledgements

My dream of becoming a writer has been supported by many people who I am grateful to have the opportunity to thank here.

First, my husband J.D. who believed in me when I didn't believe in myself, and my friends Laura and Heather who offered endless words of support and encouragement.

I am especially thankful to my friend and fellow writer Catharine Leggett, whose thoughtful comments and suggestions made To Dance in Liradon a much better novel.

I am also grateful to my former agent, Anita Bartholomew, whose enthusiastic support for my work gave me the confidence to keep putting it out there.

And finally, thank you, thank you to my mother, the first reader of my work and the first person to tell me I could be a writer. She was one of the few people who never asked, "Is it published yet?" But only, "When can I read it?" Her unconditional support means more to me than I can ever express.

Chapter 1

"But I do not love Connell," Brigid said.

Her mother leaned heavily on the windowsill and stared into the wasted garden that showed not a glimmer of green. "You think too much of love. Love is like a house of gossamer and silk—far too fragile a thing to build a life on. It will not put wood in the fire or food on the table, nor," she said, a note of fear entering her voice, "will it protect you from Lord Osin."

Brigid shivered. The mention of the lord's name seemed to suck all the warmth and comfort from the little cottage. Although nearly two miles away, the impenetrable stone walls of Lord Osin's manor loomed dark in her thoughts. Unable to find work in the village she took a position in the manor kitchen, and for the better part of a year she'd done her best to stay out of Lord Osin's way. But lately he took pains to seek her out, offering her a sweet or a piece of ribbon. It was the way he began with all the manor servants who caught his eye.

"I don't understand why it must be now," she said. "I am just turned seventeen. Surely there is still time for me to . . ."

"Meet another? Find this true love you're so desperate to find? Your father and I were wrong to tell you so many stories. You'll wait forever if you hope for a knight on a white horse to ride into our poor village and take you away with him."

"I don't want a knight on a white horse," she protested. "I just want . . ." She could not find the words to express the longing she felt when she went to bed each night and woke up in the morning. But it was not a Faerie tale; it was as real as the coarse, black bread on the table, and just as necessary.

Her mother turned away from the window as though unexpectedly troubled by the view. All the softness in her heart-shaped face, so like Brigid's own, fell away, her words arrows intent on their mark. "I know you've heard the whispers in the village, felt the women's eyes on you on market day. They will never forget. You're a good girl, and even without a dowry you would be the pride of any man, but you are tainted. God forgive me, but we should be grateful that a decent, hard-working man like Connell would take you at all."

She stared at the floor, her eyes burning with too familiar tears. Yet underneath the sadness she felt a surge of anger that would shake the cottage to rubble if she were to let it go. It's not fair, she thought. All she'd done was a pick a flower. Was she to be punished forever? "I'd go away if I could," she said finally.

Her mother lowered herself onto the cold, dirt floor from which her threadbare skirts offered no protection. When she grasped both of Brigid's hands in her own, Brigid felt the rough calluses that covered her skin like the bark of a tree. "There is nowhere for you to go. And even if there were, I could not bear to lose you. Marked or not, you are my own beautiful girl, and I want to see you safe and protected. If you were to marry well, perhaps, in time they would come to see you as . . ."

"One of them," she said bitterly. "As if the cold doesn't bite my toes at night just as it does theirs, as if my stomach doesn't twist with hunger when the crops fail, as if I do not cry when I think of Father dead and gone. I was only a child. Perhaps I got lost in the wood and only fancied I saw the Faerie Queen; it might have been a beggar woman or one of the Willows, and Father only . . ." She felt the gentle pressure of her mother's fingers against her lips.

"Do not speak of it, Brigid. They do not like it, and we have troubles enough without angering the Fair Folk. Alainn Ros has seen enough suffering this winter."

Her mother was right. The Fair Folk's desire for human company had grown stronger of late. First, Morded's wife, stolen the day after her wedding, and then the Cooley babe . . . Brigid would never forget the sound of Orla Cooley's screams when she awoke to find her baby gone and a rotting stump of wood in his place. Brigid's mother had delivered Orla's baby. She was the first person to hold the child and to place him in his mother's arms. She was the one who sat with Orla Cooley for three days and three nights to make sure the young mother didn't harm herself.

"Be a good girl and fetch us some more wood. A nice cup of tea and a cosy fire will cheer us up, and I'll have some of your favourite oatcakes waiting when you get back."

Brigid nodded, but the promise of food and warmth did nothing to lift the heaviness inside her. Only last night she was a child with her whole life before her, and suddenly she was to be a woman, forced to take a husband she did not love.

Her mother followed her to the door of the cottage that was beginning to rot around the edges, but before she could open it the older woman grabbed hold of the sleeve of her gown, suddenly reluctant to let her go. "Don't go too far into the woods."

Brigid hadn't left the house in nine years without hearing these words. But it was too late. She'd strayed from the path and now it seemed she must pay the price for that long ago afternoon forever. No one would let her forget she was taken by those who 'must not be named.' "Faeries," she said once she was out of her mother's earshot. The forbidden word tasted delicious on her tongue, like fresh honey from the comb.

She kept her eyes on the beaten path leading to the outskirts of the forest. Better not to dwell on the trees' velvety darkness that drew you inside like a lover and closed behind you like a sworn enemy. The forest surrounding Alainn Ros grew thick and fast. Even in the depth of winter the leaves of oak, willow, and ash remained lush and plentiful while the village fields turned dry and barren. The forest's seeming immunity to the ravages of storms or drought made the villagers fear it. They did not trust anything that did not suffer, whither, and die as so many of them did. Only her father was unafraid, building their modest cottage on the edge of the forest while the rest of the village settled as far away from trees as possible. He used to take her for long walks and picnics inside the forest so she could learn its stories. "Everything has a story," her father was fond of saying. "If you listen closely enough, even the moss beneath your feet has a tale to tell."

She'd lied to her mother when she spoke of the Faerie Queen. The memory of their meeting was as bright and true as the sun she watched come up that morning; so close she felt she could reach out and touch it.

Brigid was eight years old when it happened. She and her father were walking through the forest gathering flowers for Brigid's mother, who lay in bed with the fever.

"The bright colours will make her smile," Brigid's father told her as she ran along beside him, her short legs trying to match his long, powerful strides. The prettiest flowers required searching out. Sometimes a gem lay hidden beneath a fallen branch, or off on its own, a brilliant centerpiece surrounded by weeds.

The separation happened so quickly. One minute she was laughing with her father, looking at the places he pointed out, and then she was alone in the forest. The sun disappeared and the trees seemed to reach out to one another so she couldn't see the sky for the leafy branches overhead. The sudden silence was startling. No birds sang; no cricket brushed its legs together. And then she saw it: A glorious purple bloom with a golden centre raised its velvety head from a patch of ordinary green grass a few steps away. How happy Mother would be to see such a flower in her bouquet! Yet for a moment her feet didn't work. They seemed rooted to the ground beneath her, until finally, she took one step and then another, and another. She reached out her tiny hand and grasped hold of the vivid green stem, the snapping sound reverberating throughout the forest.

"How dare you take what does not belong to you?"

Brigid whirled around, the flower still tight in her grasp. Before her stood a tall slender woman, her simple dress covered by a voluminous green velvet cloak. Her bright hair streamed down her shoulders like amber fire in dazzling contrast to her milky skin. Brigid knew her at once, the heroine of her father's stories. The Faerie Queen. She could be no other.

The woman stretched out one of her long white hands. "Give it back to me and perhaps I shall forgive you."

The Faerie Queen's voice, though soft, held the power of the trees overhead and the earth underfoot. To refuse her was unthinkable, and yet, when Brigid looked at the flower, she could not bear to let it go. It was meant to make her mother smile.

"I should like to keep it if I may," Brigid said.

The Faerie Queen stared as though she were looking into Brigid's very soul, and then her flawless features opened up in burst of laughter. "Are you asking the Faerie Queen to give you one of her treasures?"

"I guess I am." She dropped a curtsy as it seemed the proper thing to do, even though the hem of her wool skirt was covered with holes. The ladies in her father's stories were forever curtseying, and the knights bowing low.

"What shall you give me in return?" the Faerie Queen asked.

"I don't know. I haven't anything to give." But then she smiled and reached into her pocket. She still had half of the current bun her mother had given her for breakfast. She thrust the treat towards the Faerie Queen. "Mother makes the best buns in the village—everyone says so."

For a moment it seemed the Faerie Queen would refuse, but then quick as a deer she seized the bun as if she were starving. "I accept your gift as partial payment, but I think I must have something else as well."

"But I have nothing else to give."

The Faerie Queen cocked her head to one side. "You are a pretty thing. You walk the ground lightly and you have a sweet voice. Would you like to come dancing with me? I'll give you a dress made of stars and all the sweets you could ever want."

Brigid closed her eyes. She loved to dance more than anything. For a moment she saw herself bejewelled and sparkling, spinning effortlessly underneath a bright sky; there was no cold or thirst or hunger, and no fever. Mother. She opened her eyes. "I can't come with you. It sounds lovely, but I have to go home and give Mother her flowers."

The Faerie Queen regarded her through slanted sapphire eyes. "Very well, then. We shall just agree that you owe me a favour."

Brigid nodded happily. "Yes, of course." It was a fine thing to do someone a favour if you could.

"Fare thee well, child," the Faerie Queen said. "I'm sure we shall meet again."

Brigid curtseyed until her knees ached. "One last thing, if you please. Do you know the way back to my father?"

The Faerie Queen raised one eyebrow so that it disappeared behind the gold circlet she wore around her head. "Another favour? I'm afraid this one shall cost you."

Brigid nodded. What good was the flower if she couldn't find her way back again?

"Close your eyes," the Faerie Queen commanded. "What do you hear?"

"Nothing."

"Still your breath, and let the pictures in your head slide away. Listen to what's underneath the silence."

She tried, but it was hard to do. And then she heard it, the gentle trickle of running water.

"Follow the sound. It will bring you back to the path and your father. But hurry, the forest is no place for a child." And then she began to laugh, the sound surprisingly harsh and deep.

Brigid ran towards the sound until she saw the sky peeking through the trees, and felt the path beneath her feet. When she saw her father, she ran into his open arms, the Faerie Queen's laughter still ringing in her ears.

"We thought we'd lost you forever," her father whispered into her hair.

"But I've only been gone a short time," she said.

"Nay, my sweet. The sun has risen and set twice since we came into the forest. Your mother and I have been searching everywhere."

She showed her father the flower. "The Faerie Queen gave it to me so I could give it to Mother."

Her father smiled, but fear spread across his face like a stain. Three days later he was dead.

Chapter 2

Brigid gathered firewood until the burlap sack made her shoulders ache with strain. Despite her mother's warnings, she liked being alone in the forest. Surrounded by trees and earth and stone she felt free. The urge to dance was so strong she often abandoned her sack of wood or basket of mushrooms and spun around in circles until she collapsed on the green moss, softer than the finest rugs at Lord Osin's manor.

The forest didn't care if she married well or not. When she returned to her mother's hearth, there would be more talk of the roof that needed mending, their shrinking store of grain, and of Brigid's future husband, the solution to all their troubles. She'd rather be cold and hungry with her true love than rich and fat with someone she didn't care for. But she couldn't think only of herself. Although her mother was the best midwife in the village, the frequent bouts of weakness in her arms made the work increasingly difficult. To say nothing of the fact that many women in Alainn Ros were reluctant to have their child delivered by the mother of a girl touched by the Queen of the Faerie. Her mother needed meat and cheese and good bread to make her strong, not wasted turnips and watered down porridge.

Brigid made her way back to the cottage, the smell of her mother's oatcakes wafting out to greet her. In spite of her worries, she was hungry. But no sooner had she collapsed in front of the fire than a knock came at the door.

"Who could that be?" she asked.

Her mother ran her hands from the top of her head to the bottom of her apron in one neat, tidying motion. "Hush, child. I've a very good idea who it might be, and we must make him welcome."

The oatcake in Brigid's hand felt as heavy as a stone. The fire, the tea, and the oatcakes were not for her enjoyment alone. Her mother was expecting company. She even placed a jar of wildflowers on the scarred kitchen table, although it did little to brighten the drabness of the tiny cottage. She expected to marry eventually, but why did it have to be so soon? The final moments of her childhood seemed more precious than the jewel-encrusted bowls Lord Osin reserved for the King's visits to the manor.

Her mother swung open the cottage door. "Good evening, Connell. "How good of you to visit us."

Connell nodded gravely. "'Tis my pleasure, Mary. I have brought you a gift from my mother's kitchen. I remember from market day Brigid's fondness for squash."

"Oh yes, it is her favourite dish. She hardly cares for any other. Please come in and join us for tea. Brigid, 'tis Connell come for a visit, and see what he's brought you, a lovely yellow squash."

Brigid rose from her seat, embarrassed. Connell's presence in the cottage disturbed her, but her mother's behaviour troubled her more. Could things really be so desperate that they must grovel at the miller's feet as though he were the lord himself? All of the formality seemed silly given that Connell and Brigid had known each other since they were babies.

Before Connell was old enough to help in his father's mill he used to play tag with the other children on the village green. But once he was strong enough to carry a sack of grain, she saw him less and less. Even as a boy he was as quiet as a winter's morning, his serious grey eyes intent on whatever task was at hand, his eyes never glazing over in daydream like Brigid's often did. Connell approached a game of draughts with the same steady determination he applied to cleaning the mill wheel. But he had always been kind to her, even taking her part when the other boys teased her for looking "fey." When his father died of heat stroke, Connell took over as the village Miller and there was no more time for games.

The transformation from boy to man would have been easy for Connell. Although he was only one and twenty, he seemed to have put all thought of play firmly behind him. He cared little for music. Brigid never saw him in the village square where the villagers often gathered to play tunes in the evening, and he never took part in any of the dancing, not even on feast days. On the few occasions she met him in the village, he spoke only of the fineness of that year's grain, or the weather. She'd no doubt Connell was a good man, but he was also a dull one. He would not dance with her in the forest, or anywhere.

"Thank you, Connell. It is very kind of you."

Connell sat in the chair her mother held out for him; it was the only one in the cottage whose legs didn't wobble. "I'd be glad to bring you as many as you'd like. It's been an especially good year for us. The carrots are nearly as big as a man's arm."

Unable to think of a reply, Brigid pushed the plate of oatcakes towards him.

"I wish I had your mother's skill in the garden," her mother said to Connell. "It seems as though nothing grows for me anymore."

It was true. Her mother's green thumb had turned black. Each year, their small, dry plot of earth yielded less and less. Lately, she and her mother enjoyed little more than watery porridge and boiled turnips with a few onions mixed in. Their meagre diet hadn't diminished Brigid's youthful energy, but her mother grew as thin and pale as a wraith.

"Would you like a cup of tea, Connell?" Brigid asked. "It's strong enough, but I'm afraid we've no sugar to give you."

"Thank you, I will, and I never take sugar," Connell replied, smiling shyly.

Brigid's hand shook as she gave him his tea. She wished her mother would stop hovering and sit down. For the second time that day, she wondered at how different everything had become. Not so long ago her cottage seemed the safest place in the world. Although not the least bit luxurious, it was always warm and comfortable. Neighbours often dropped by for a cup of tea and one of her father's stories by the fire. Michael O'Flynn was the best storyteller in the village, and even those who said it was a sin to speak of banshees and hobgoblins couldn't resist the rich, honeyed voice of Brigid's father on a cold winter's night. She'd rather have her father's stories than bread to eat or milk to drink. Nothing filled her up, or gave her that warm spread of contentment in the seat of her belly like her father's tales of the Sidhe, or the Fair Folk as the villagers were wont to speak of them. Every night, she took her place beside him at the hearth, and listened until her eyes began to close and her limbs felt as heavy as sacks of flour. Finally, her father carried her to bed and while she slept, the Gods of her father's stories—tall, beautiful, and proud—strode through her dreams on steeds the colour of freshly fallen snow.

Connell cleared his throat, rousing her from her memories. "How goes your work at the manor?"

She shrugged. "Well enough, I suppose. Lady Osin is a fair mistress."

"And Lord Osin? Connell asked, a shadow crossing his open, gentle face.

Brigid felt her mother behind her, heard her sharp intake of breath as she anticipated what her daughter might say. The lord's reputation for meddling with female servants was well known in the village. Only last year the shoemaker's daughter, Aolin, whose dancing raven curls and full-bodied laugh endeared her to everyone she met, was forced to leave her post as first chambermaid after her swollen belly made it impossible to scrub floors and empty chamber pots. Lord Osin was nothing like the gods of her father's stories, being neither tall nor handsome, nor gifted at music, but he behaved like them in some ways. He would not be refused in anything. He took what he wanted with no care for anyone, not even his gracious, sad-eyed wife.

Brigid's mother placed a warning hand on her daughter's shoulder. "I believe Lord Osin is rarely at home. Is that not so, Brigid?"

Brigid stared at the hearth, whose lively fire suddenly gave her no comfort. "He is often hunting or away on some other household business. I spend most of my time in the kitchen or serving Lady Osin."

Connell nodded, apparently satisfied, and Brigid sipped her tea. Did Connell ask about the lord because he'd heard stories? Brigid imagined the village gossips would be glad to think the worst of her. She could almost hear them whispering of her efforts to seduce the lord with "her Faerie ways."

Finally, Brigid's mother sat down beside Connell. "Will you attend the Easter feast night?" she asked, eager to steer his thoughts away from Lord Osin.

Connell put down his drink and looked directly at Brigid when he spoke. "Yes, I shall go, and although I'm not one for dancing, I hope that you will save me a dance."

The thatch roof of the cottage had never seemed so low. She could feel it pressing down on her as she spoke. "Of course, I love dancing more than anything. Perhaps you shall see me win the cake."

The corners of Connell's mouth turned slightly downwards, and Brigid fought the urge to place her hands on his sturdy chest and push him firmly out the door. Did he disapprove of everything that was not work? Dancing was common in the village on most Sundays and holidays, but it was also an activity that earned the disapproval of the village priest, Father Diarmaid. A long-standing tradition in the village, dancing for the cake was an even greater offense because it encouraged competition. It was one thing to join in the occasional country dance, but to show off the lightness of one's step in a contest was not the behaviour of a good Christian. Brigid suspected the priest considered her love of music and dancing further proof of the Fair Folk's early influence on her. He didn't miss an opportunity to tell her he thought she might profit from "resting herself a little." But she wouldn't give up dancing, no matter what the rest of the village thought. She spoke truly when she told Connell she loved dancing more than anything.

As if reading her thoughts, Connell said quietly, "Your skill at dancing is surely a thing to be admired. If you win the cake, I shall be glad to have a piece in celebration of your victory."

Brigid smiled, but didn't quite believe him. If they were to marry, she doubted he'd be so tolerant. She'd spend her days digging alongside Connell's mother in the garden, baking pies and loaves in the kitchen, and if she were lucky, the older woman might teach her how to weave and dye cloth. Any girl in the village would be grateful for such a fate, so why should she be any different? But every morning she awoke with the feeling that something important was going to happen. When she was dancing, the feeling grew stronger and brighter, like kindling slowly catching fire.

Brigid's mother put her hand on Connell's arm. "Brigid's a fine cook as well as a good dancer. Her pastry is so light a single breath might blow it away."

Brigid frowned. "I fear it is a mother's love speaking. My pies are as heavy as the stones at the bottom of the well."

Connell surprised her by laughing. "It would hardly be fair for you to be good at everything."

She crumbled the remains of her oatcake between her fingers. "You are kind to say so."

Her mother held out the nearly untouched plate. "May I offer you another oatcake?"

"Thank you, no, but they are very good," Connell added quickly. "I'd best be going home. I need to be up before the sun."

"I must be up early as well," Brigid said. "There is to be a feast at the manor tomorrow evening and I will be needed for much of the day."

"A servant's life is a hard one," Connell said, rising from his chair, "but perhaps you shall not have to work at the manor for long."

Connell spoke lightly, but she understood the significance of his words. "Not yet," a voice inside her whispered. She got up from the table and followed Connell the few steps to the door. "Thank you for coming, and for the squash."

"Brigid, why don't you walk with Connell down the hill a little ways? 'Tis not fully dark yet."

"No, thank you, Mary. I'm fine on my own. The air is still cold, and I won't take Brigid away from your good fire."

Brigid smiled at Connell gratefully. It would be so much easier if she could dislike him altogether. But every time she thought she'd made up her mind, a breeze of uncertainty would blow through her body, ruffling her feelings into a new state of disorder. "Good night, then."

"Good night, Brigid. Rest well."

Brigid closed the door behind him and turned to face her mother. The resentment she felt tightening her spine at Connell's unexpected arrival melted away, leaving her bent and weary.

"Well, that didn't go so badly, did it?" her mother asked.

"Nothing's changed. I can't force my feelings to where they do not go of their own accord. It's like trying to dance without music. Perhaps we can wait a little longer?" she asked hopefully.

Her mother sighed. "Easter is less than a fortnight a way. Mark my words, Brigid. Connell is a good man, the best in the village, and if you won't have him, another girl will."

Brigid's eyes went to the brightly coloured squash on the table. Perhaps she could learn to love him.

But when she lay in her bed that night, listening to the rise and fall of her mother's breathing, she could not suppress the yearning that seemed stuck deep inside of her, beating its steely wings against her chest like some wild creature. "If you're coming, come soon," she whispered to her true love in the darkness.

Chapter 3

Brigid awoke the next morning alone. She'd slept so deeply she didn't hear mother leave in the night. Clare Ryan must have had her baby at last. Clare was one of the few people in the village Brigid could call a friend, but they'd grown apart since Clare's marriage. Aed Ryan was a good man, but very superstitious. Born a twin, the Fair Folk claimed Aed's brother when he was only a few weeks old. Clare would never be unkind enough to tell her so, but Brigid knew Aed was not over fond of her presence in his home. She missed Clare, but believed it better to stay away than to be the cause of any unhappiness in her friend's marriage.

Her hands and feet were stiff with cold, but she couldn't be bothered to light a fire. The sooner she got to the manor, the sooner she'd be properly warm. Lady Osin insisted on having a fire in every chamber; it was perhaps one of the few things she could insist on. Although it was common for a lady of her rank to travel with her husband on errands for the King, or on some manor business in the Great Town, Lady Osin remained at home with the servants. For all her silk gowns and fine linens, Lady Osin seemed a lonely woman. Brigid might not be well liked by the other villagers, but at least she had the love and companionship of her mother.

She wrapped her mantle tightly around her shoulders and left the cottage. The walk to the manor was not far if she took a short cut through fields, but today she decided to take the road through the village. Perhaps she would look in on Clare and the new baby. Surely Aed wouldn't mind a short visit from her too much? When she reached the edge of the village green, she stopped to watch some of the children playing Hoodman Blind.

Not so long ago she used to be at the centre of such games, always plotting some new diversion for her friends. But that was before her she met the Faerie Queen in the wood, before her father's death changed everything. The villagers blamed Brigid for his death, and for the abundance of rain that had ruined the crops. A single encounter with the Faerie Queen had turned her into an outcast. As if the loss of her father wasn't punishment enough, every day she felt the hard, accusing stares of the other villagers pierce her skin like a quiver of arrows. Eventually her playmates came to share their parents' dislike. The other children no longer wanted to play her games or have her join in theirs.

At first, she refused to accept their abandonment. After she'd helped her mother light the fire, fetched the day's water from the well, and chopped the vegetables for supper, she ran to join the other children, longing for their forgiveness. This seemed to go on for days, until finally one glorious morning her friends seemed to relent.

"You're blind," Tanner's son said, grabbing her hood with large freckled hands and twisting it around so that it covered her face. Delighted her exile was over, she put both hands in front of her face and lurched her body forward. She'd only taken a few steps when she tripped over a broken horseshoe, and fell face forward into something soft and squishy. Sheep dung. The sour smell struck her nostrils before seeping into her skin. She struggled to free herself from the hood, but her hands were stuck in the muck.

"Here, let me help you." Strong hands encircled Brigid's waist and pulled her upright. Once on her feet, she raised her filthy hands to her head, but her rescuer pushed them away. "You'll only make it worse." He turned her hood around, but as soon as her face was free she wished it covered again.

Connell stood before her, his face suffused with pity, and Brigid felt a hot rush of crimson staining her face and neck. She could not even thank him, certain that if she opened her mouth to speak she would humiliate herself further by bursting into tears.

"You'd best go home now and let your mother see to your dress. If she sets to scrubbing it right away, the stink won't have a chance to take hold."

She smiled a little, recalling Connell's worlds. How practical he was, even as a child. Strange, she thought suddenly, that he appeared out of nowhere to help her that day. He'd stopped playing with her and the other children nearly a year before. Brigid avoided Connell after that. The sight of him reminded her of her shame. Not that Connell seemed to take any notice.

The child who'd been made the Hoodman stumbled heavily into Brigid's legs. Startled, the girl took several steps backwards and tore the covering from her face.

"Good morning, Emer," she said. "I think you've strayed too far from your playmates."

Emer looked at Brigid through lowered lids, and her painfully thin body crumpled into an awkward curtsey.

The movement struck her like a blow. The child curtseyed to her, an ordinary peasant, like she was the Faerie Queen herself. It didn't matter who she married, Brigid thought bitterly, if even the village children were afraid of her. The visit to Clare forgotten, she turned her back on the child who was already running back to her friends, and continued on her way.

In contrast to the village's tiny cottages with their low ceilings and walls of mud and straw were the towering stone walls that surrounded Lord Osin's manor. The first time the porter allowed her to pass through the enormous oak gate fitted with two iron locks, she felt a thrill of pleasure. The manor's great hall, with its long, elegant pillars supporting an impossibly high vaulted roof, reminded Brigid of the Faerie palaces in her father's stories. She delighted in the manor's large open spaces that seemed to make it easier to breathe, so different from the dark, cramped quarters she shared with her mother. But her feelings about the manor had changed greatly since that visit. She'd learned the walls of an unhappy house press in on you even when they are covered with silk tapestries and fine oil paintings.

She passed through the gate and made her way to the massive arched doorway that led to the great hall. Inside, she was greeted by a cacophony of sound; a group of female servants tore around the lords' table, crashing into one another like tempests in a teapot while the bailiff stood over them barking orders, and in the attached kitchen Brigid could hear Cook's shrill voice demanding assistance amid a loud banging of pots and pans. All was proof of Lord Osin's return. When Lady Osin was at home alone, her wants were few, but Lord Osin feared the quiet as much as Death himself. He wanted fine food, hunting parties, and all the amusements that riches could buy. From the heap of gleaming silver cutlery on the high table and the number of fine goblets, the manor was surely expecting guests. Perhaps there will be music, she thought with a sudden surge of delight. She stopped to imagine the sweet sounds of a travelling minstrel until Cook seized her by the hand and dragged her into the kitchen where she was put to work chopping onions.

"Not a moment too soon," Cook grumbled as she set a large caldron on the fire. "I would have had you here at first light. If the two of us had fifty hands between us, it wouldn't be enough."

"Surely there are more to help?" Brigid said. "Where are Aisling and Branwen?"

Cook frowned over the pot of water heating on the stove as though she saw something unpleasant reflected there.

"Aisling's in bed with the fever, and not fit to be seen, and Branwen . . . she's gone."

"Gone! When? Why?"

"Last evening. And as to the 'why', you and I need not speak of that."

Brigid could guess at Branwen's sudden departure. She'd been a 'favourite' of the lord's the last time he was home, and the last few weeks Branwen's already ample waist had grown steadily thicker, a fact that Brigid doubted Lady Osin could have missed, despite the looseness of the girl's kirtle. The lady could sit still and silent for hours with her needlework, but she missed little. Had Lady Osin turned her out then? It was hard for Brigid to imagine her doing so, but nor would she suffer watching a lowly servant grow heavy with her husband's child while she remained barren.

"What will happen?" Brigid asked. "To Branwen, I mean. Where will she go?"

Cook shrugged. "If she's lucky, one of the lads in the village will marry her."

"And if not?"

Cook pounded her large, red-knuckled hands into a mound of pastry. "Well, she won't be the first girl to bring a babe into the world alone, although it usually goes hard for both mother and child."

"What else needs doing?" she asked, still thinking of Branwen.

"You can start another pie, but mind you don't get flour in your hair. You'll be needed to serve, and Lord Osin likes to see a pretty face when he takes his meat, especially yours."

Cook looked up from her pastry, and something in Brigid's face must have revealed her anxiety. The older women reached out one floury finger and stroked it down the length of her nose. "On second thought, perhaps a little flour on your rosy cheeks would not go amiss."

Brigid smiled. At least there was someone who did not wish her ill.

She spent most of the morning completing the less complicated tasks of rolling dough, chopping leaks, and crushing handfuls of ginger and cumin into a stone pestle. Pleased with her work, Cook allowed her to shape the large slab of sweet almond paste into the beasts of the forest while she finished decorating the venison pies. Every few minutes, Cook would peer anxiously over Brigid's shoulder to check her work.

"That deer's antlers are too big for its body," she remarked. "And the swans should have more curves in their wings."

"They're meant to be eaten," she complained after Cook ordered her to redo a series of boars' heads. "Surely our lord will not notice such a trifling."

"Lady Osin specifically requested the marzipan. It's one of the lord's favourites. Tonight's feat must contain all that the lord desires and more besides."

She hopes to keep him home by giving him better food and drink than he would have anywhere else, Brigid thought. Even though everyone knew that a pretty face was more likely to capture the lord's attention than the richest morsel or the sweetest wine.

"There, now." Cook stepped back to admire her handiwork. "That is a fine pie, is it not?"

Brigid nodded her approval. Cook had decorated the edges in an intricate pattern of leaves and foliage, and three pastry woodcocks strode across the top.

"I'm sure Lord Osin would not get such a pie anywhere else."

Cook shrugged. "If it pleases our lady, I shall be content enough. But there's much yet to be done. Be a good girl and fetch me a half dozen chicks from the Dovecote. I've need of another dish, and I've a lovely recipe for dove gravy."

Brigid wiped her sugary hands on her apron, and went into the courtyard. The dovecote was a small round brick building with dozens of tiny openings to attract the nesting birds. Brigid could hear their soft cooing as she approached, and felt a tiny stab of guilt for taking them away from their home.

"Here now." Brigid put her hand through one of the narrow openings until she felt the downy softness of feathers. She only managed to seize hold of three of the birds and gather them in her apron when she heard a low whistle behind her.

"Good day, Brigid. I wondered when I'd have the pleasure of seeing you again."

She turned around slowly, so as not to disturb chicks. "My lord," she said, dropping an awkward curtsey. "Welcome home."

Even in her worn wool gown, Brigid could not help being struck by the ridiculousness of the lord's clothing. Tall and fleshy, his thick torso was ill suited for the tight-fitting tunics he favoured, and the dyed hose made his legs look like brightly coloured sausages. But far more disconcerting were his black eyes that moved slowly down the length of her body, his gaze lingering on the slit of her overgown that revealed the kirtle she wore underneath.

"Did you miss me then sweet, Brigid?" He smiled suddenly, the gesture mobilizing his features so that even the curve of his brow seemed ready to pounce.

A hunter's smile, she thought, searching for a reply that was respectful, but would give no encouragement. "The household is always cheered by your presence, Lord Osin. I know my lady was anxious for your safe return."

Lord Osin frowned at the mention of his wife's name, and Brigid wondered if she'd been too familiar in her reply.

"Two days I've been at home without even a glimpse of your pretty face. Why are you not more with us? Lady Osin speaks well of you. Surely she can offer you a place amongst her personal servants?"

Careful now, a tiny voice whispered inside her.

"Lady Osin is so kind to me, and I should be fortunate to be of greater service to her, but my mother is often unwell and has need of me at home."

The lord waved away her words in a gesture of dismissal. He had no interest in ailing mothers. Perhaps if he saw that she had none of Branwen's flirting ways, he would look elsewhere for his amusement.

"I must take my leave of you, but I expect, no, I require, that you serve me this evening."

"Yes, my lord," Brigid murmured. But Lord Osin had already turned his back on her and was striding towards the kennels to see his beloved hounds.

Brigid returned to the kitchen where Cook stirred a fragrant pottage over the fire, the servants' mid-day meal. The older woman put down her spoon and gave Brigid a look as sharp as the boning knives on the table behind her.

"It took you long enough! Where are my chicks?"

"Our lord bid me to tell you that he no longer cares for dove meat."

Cook sighed. "Well then, do you think our lord still has a liking for stuffed grouse?"

Now that Lord Osin had ordered her to serve him, she'd have to remain at the manor well into the evening and miss supper with her mother. At least she'd be able to bring home some of the leavings from the lords' table, but Brigid knew her mother would prefer her company. After a birth, she could do little more then sit by the fire with a cup of ale beside her. Still, a piece of marzipan in the shape of a deer should bring a smile to her face.

Soon it was time to begin putting out the seemingly endless array of dishes she and Cook laboured over. Brigid wondered how she could be thought presentable enough to serve. Dove feathers clung to her filthy apron, and her face was hot and sweaty from standing over the fire.

Cook handed her a plate of quail eggs. "Now then, don't forget to smile. The tastiest morsel will be found wanting if it's served with a sour expression."

"I shall do my best," she promised.

In one deft movement, Cook removed Brigid's soiled apron. "You needn't try hard. Tired as you must be, and none too clean I might add, the lord won't find a prettier face than yours, not even if he were to visit the Fair Folk themselves." Cook clapped a rough hand against her mouth. "Take no heed of an old woman's foolish talk," she said loudly, and Brigid realized she was speaking more to any Faerie that might be listening than to her. "I meant no offense." She took Brigid by the arm and pushed her towards the great hall. "Away with you."

Brigid entered the hall, startled to see only Lord and Lady Osin seated at the high table. After Lady Osin's elaborate instructions to Cook, she'd expected to see a duke, or at least a couple of courtiers, but husband and wife sat at either end of the long oak table inlaid with gold and silver leaves, distance yawning between them. The benches at the tables lining the walls of the hall, usually reserved for Lord Osin's huntsmen and lesser noble visitors, were empty.

Without a bard's instrument, or a minstrel's song to fill the air, the hall was silent save for the soft crunching sound of her footsteps as she walked across the straw-covered floor. She approached the high table that glowed with candles, her eyes downcast, hoping to attract as little notice as possible.

Most nobility treated servants as though they were invisible, but not Lord Osin. She felt the weight of his gaze on her as she placed the heavy pewter platter in front of him with trembling hands.

"Thank you, Brigid. I am pleased to see you looking so well. All meals should be taken in the presence of such beauty. It is as necessary to my pleasure as salt on the meat."

Brigid curtseyed, taking care to avoid his black eyes. "Thank you, my lord."

Lord Osin laughed, and Lady Osin's graceful posture stiffened so that her shoulders seemed melded to the back of her chair.

"So shy, little Brigid? You are like a deer with your quiet ways, and so easily startled. You must learn to accept a compliment. Is this not so Lady Osin?"

Her breath caught in her throat. If she were to lose Lady Osin's favour, it would be impossible for her to remain at the manor, and she and her mother desperately needed her earnings. *But if you were to marry Connell* . . . the voice inside her whispered.

Lady Osin inclined her graceful head in Brigid's direction, her expression an uneasy mixture of caution and anxiety. "Brigid is indeed a lovely girl, but she should not be faulted for her humility. It is a most Christian virtue."

Lord Osin tore apart a piece of bread with his fingers before turning to Lady Osin. "You think and speak too much of virtue."

Brigid felt her already warm cheeks grow hotter on Lady Osin's behalf. Why did he speak to her so? Could he not see that he was fortunate in such a wife? Her grace and kindness, to say nothing of her skill in running the manor in his absence, brought more dignity to his household than the spoils of his hunts.

"I'm sorry if you are displeased by my conversation. What does my lord wish me to speak of?"

Lady Osin's composure remained undisturbed, but the air between husband and wife was heavy with unspoken grief. Brigid waited until Lord Osin lifted his knife before scurrying back to the kitchen.

Cook rose from her rickety wooden chair. "How goes it? Are Lord and Lady Osin pleased with the quail?"

"I'm certain they'll find no fault with the food once they get around to eating it," Brigid said.

Cook resumed her seat and began to massage one of her outstretched legs. "They have much to say to one another, do they? Most of their meals are taken in such silence you could hear the tearing of the bread."

Brigid looked wearily at the dishes still to come. She wanted nothing more than to be away from the manor and safely back at home in her own cottage.

She carried out the roasted Capon with black sauce and placed it before Lord Osin, who took no notice of her, carving his meat with large, decisive thrusts. But when she turned to leave, he threw his knife onto the table with a violence that startled even Lady Osin.

"Come here, Brigid."

She returned to the table. "Yes, my lord."

"Sit with us a moment."

"But, my lord," she protested.

"I command you to sit at my table."

She cast an anxious glance at Lady Osin before taking her seat. If Lady Osin was disturbed by the request, she did not show it.

"Brigid," he began, "you are no doubt aware that Branwen has left us?" The lord did not wait for her to reply before he went on. "Lady Osin is in need of someone to attend her until a suitable replacement can be found, and it is my wish that you perform the duties of chambermaid and, of course, anything else that my lady requires."

"My lord, I am honoured, but surely someone better can be found. My needlework is poor and I've no skill at mending."

Lord Osin resumed eating and Brigid realized the matter was closed. She stared at Lord Osin, repulsed by the dribble of meat juice that ran down his chin. "But who is to help Cook?" she asked, her voice barely above a whisper.

"You needn't concern yourself. Lady Osin will see to it."

Brigid stood up from the table and curtseyed to Lady Osin. "It will be my honour to serve you."

"Thank you, Brigid. We shall speak more of your duties on the morrow."

His conditions met, Lord Osin seemed content to ignore her for the rest of the meal. Brigid even overheard him compliment Lady Osin on her handling of the household accounts. But even so, Brigid could not rid herself of the feeling that a plan was now in place. Personal servants had far more contact with the manor lord than lowly scullery maids.

Finally, after she helped Cook to scrub out the pots strewn over every surface of the kitchen, it was time for her to go home.

"Surely, you will sleep in the hall tonight," Cook said when she saw Brigid put on her mantle.

"It's not a long walk, and I prefer my own bed."

"The night has grown dark. You won't be able to see to put one foot in front of the other."

"'Tis a full moon tonight," Brigid said. "That will be light enough."

"All the more reason to stay. The time of the full moon belongs to the Fair Folk."

Brigid smiled. "My mother has sewn handfuls of yarrow into the hem of my gown. I shall be safe enough."

Brigid left the comforting warmth of Cook's kitchen and re-entered the great hall, transformed now into a huge sleeping chamber for the household staff. She stepped carefully over the small bodies of the pages huddled against one another for warmth on the straw-covered floor. Where had the children come from? She hoped they had not been abandoned and left to the care of Lord Osin. She could not imagine a worse fate for any child.

The smell of unwashed bodies combined with the lingering scent of grease from so many rich dishes hung unpleasantly in the air, and Brigid was glad when she was finally outside breathing in the night air, cool and sharp. She put her hands in the pocket of her gown, a sprig of St. John's Wort brushing against her fingertips; more of her mother's protections. But it was not the Fair Folk she feared. Lord Osin filled her thoughts. How long did he mean to stay at the manor? If it were only a short time, she might find ways to avoid him. And then, as if summoned by her fear, Lord Osin's stocky figure stepped out from behind the gatehouse. He must have been waiting for her in the Porter's lodge.

"My lord," Brigid said, the words tumbling over one another. Her legs trembled beneath her, making a curtsey impossible.

"Why so frightened, Brigid? I am not a stranger to you, and yet you cower as though I were a robber come upon you in the wood. Have I not always been kind to you?"

"Yes, my lord. You are very kind. I am just . . . surprised."

Lord Osin reached out his hand and let it rest against her cheek. The sensation should not have been unpleasant, the lord's hands being soft, white, and unblemished, so different from Connell's hands that were red and raw from hauling heavy sacks of grain. And yet the lord's touch made the bile rise in her stomach. His hand was heavy on her cheek, his fingers too thick and fleshy. She longed to push him away, but feared making any movement that might spur him into further action.

Finally, the lord took his hand away. "Why do you not stay in the great hall with the rest of the servants? Surely your mother will not be expecting you so late."

"I don't mind the walk," she said. "And my mother will not sleep until I am safely home, so with my lord's leave, I really must—"

Lord Osin moved his hand to the cloth she wore around her head, his fingers searching for the fastening that held it in place. "Why do you wear your hair covered? You have such beautiful hair," he muttered. "I have never seen such brightness. Not even the ladies at court with their jewelled combs and pearl nets have such lovely hair."

Released from its covering, her hair spilled down her back. A hot fiery ball of panic exploded inside her chest, pushing out every other feeling, even the need for obedience that she had been born to.

She tried to pull away, but Lord Osin held her fast by the hair.

"Please, I must go," she said.

"You shall go when I say you shall go. And here I thought you were a clever girl. Do you not understand that you live and breathe at my pleasure? Have you not thought how I might help you?" He released his hold on her hair and spoke softly, almost gently. "Your mother receives a widow's pension. If I am of a mind to make it so, there is no reason she might not be given more." He watched her face carefully. "Or less."

Brigid stared at Lord Osin. How could she have been foolish enough to think she was different? That she could find a way to refuse one for whom refusal was as impossible a notion as hunger?

Lord Osin pushed his face so close to hers she could smell the meat and wine on his breath. "I was right. You are very like a deer. The look in your eyes. . . it is the very same as that of the doe I took down this morning. As proof of my kindness and generosity, I shall give you leave to think on what I've said. Perhaps when we see each other again, there will be a new understanding between us?"

Lord Osin did not wait for a reply. In one swift movement, he swung open the manor gate and shoved her towards it. "Goodnight, Brigid."

Chapter 4

Brigid awoke the next morning, her eyes tired and sore from a night spent staring at the cracks in the roof. Would the lord really take away her mother's pension if she refused him? What if she went to Lady Osin and begged for mercy? Would she care enough to intervene on her behalf? Such a thing was impossible. Lady Osin had been kind to her, but that did not mean she would take kindly to further proof of her husband's faithlessness. Brigid would be just another peasant girl Lord Osin used to humiliate her.

Connell. If she were a married woman, the lord would be inclined to leave her alone, if only because once she left the manor she would no longer be in his way. Besides, it wouldn't be long before another servant girl came along to satisfy his need for pursuit.

Less than a fortnight ago, she told her mother she wasn't ready for marriage, and now it seemed a wedding couldn't happen fast enough. She considered every possible obstacle until her head ached. Connell would have to ask the lord's permission to marry her, and then the banns would have to be published . . . But what if her mother was mistaken? Perhaps Connell's kindness to her was only sympathy for her misfortune. Connell's generous nature was well known in the village. He was the first to offer aid to a neighbour who'd suffered some loss or injury. When one of the mill hands broke his arm falling out of a tree, Connell paid the boy's wages to his family, and gave him room and board at the mill until he was fully recovered.

Brigid no longer trusted her instincts about anything. When Cook offered her a place at the manor, she'd been more than grateful. After all, no one in the village was likely to hire her, not even the cottars who worked as swine herds wanted her among them. But Lord Osin's way of looking at her was far worse than the villagers' fearful glances. To him, she was not a woman cursed, but a beast of the forest, one that belonged to him.

Brigid rose quickly from her pallet and pulled on her worn kirtle and overgown. She needed to go to the forest— only there could she think clearly.

She ran a hand through her hair, wishing she thought to plait it the night before. Her tossing and turning tangled the fine strands into a mess of knots. She made a half-hearted attempt to smooth the worst of it, but then let her hands drop to her sides. Why should she take pains with her appearance? If Lord Osin saw her dirty and dishevelled, perhaps he would direct his attentions elsewhere.

After washing her face and hands in the wooden basin, Brigid put on her mantle and made ready to leave, but just as she opened the cottage door, her mother came in carrying two pails of water.

"Mother, you should have waited for me to fetch those."

"There is no need for you to take on all of my chores. You do quite enough as it is, to say naught of your work at the manor. Besides, I feel well enough this morning. Soon it will be Easter, and this year we'll have more than a feast to be grateful for."

"I know you wish me to marry, but Connell has not yet spoken. Perhaps we mistook his kindness for something else . . ."

Mary seized Brigid's hand. "I am not mistaken, not about this. I may have lost some of the strength in my hands, but my eyes are as sharp as they ever were. Connell is a good man, and he looks at no other girl the way he looks at you. I shouldn't be surprised if he decided to marry you the day he brought you home covered in sheep's dung."

"I came home alone that day. I remember it well."

Brigid's mother shook her head. "You were not alone. I watched the two of you from the hill. Perhaps he hung back because he didn't want you to see him, but I did. He waited in the bushes until he saw me take you into my arms."

Connell's long ago kindness confused her further. If he cared for her, then why in all these years had he spoken so little? Because deep down he felt like the others—that she was tainted and unlucky.

"Shall I fetch anything for you before I go? Lady Osin is short of servants and I promised to go back to the manor today."

"I'll be fine. Will you be back for your supper?"

Brigid nodded. "We'll have a feast. I brought home some scraps from last night's supper. There's some venison pie and a lovely bit of marzipan." She kissed her mother on the cheek and left the cottage.

In spite of all the reasons she had to fear it, Brigid loved the forest that seemed to have no beginning and no end. She felt more at ease surrounded by its untamed wildness than she did in the village where Lord Osin imposed his will on every bail of hay. The forest would not be ruled by Lord Osin or any man.

Once inside the trees, Brigid began to breathe easier. She did not fear the ancient, sturdy oaks with their gnarled hollows, the stately, silver-white birch, or the haunting, slender willows. Tree and stone and moss were not to blame for the fever that had taken her father's life, or for the treatment she and her mother received afterwards. It was the villagers who'd turned away from her in the village square, and who'd averted their gaze when Brigid used to go to church. It was the villagers who told their children she was not fit to join their games. When it came to the Fair Folk, the villagers saw nothing but their own fear. Brigid had walked with the Faerie Queen and paid the price with her father's death. She was cursed, and any pity the villagers may have felt for her was outweighed by their need to protect their children from suffering a similar fate.

The cruel game of Hoodman Blind had made her realize once and for all she was not wanted. If she no longer had playmates, she'd have to find other ways to spend her time. The woods offered both solace and adventure. The trees became her friends. She confided in them things she could not tell her mother, like how she longed to leave Alainn Ros and go to a place where no one knew her, a place where she would be greeted with warmth and familiarity, instead of fear and suspicion.

On fine days she walked along the stream, stopping occasionally to admire the fish that darted below the surface. If it were not forbidden to fish in the lord's streams, she would have tried to catch one to bring home to her mother.

Her favourite place for solitary games was the sacred well. There was nothing remarkable about the well itself except for the alder that grew beside it. The tree's branches reached out protectively over the opening. The curbstone had turned green from its thick covering of moss and lichen. No one in the village ever drew water from the sacred well, not even when the one in the village was flooded. There was talk in the manor court of boarding it up, but no one in the village would agree to do it for fear of offending the Fair Folk.

The villagers would not come near the well, but some said that on nights of a full moon, the Willow Women cast what few possessions they had into the water in the hope of finding their way back to Faerie.

Despite the fact they lived in a hut in the middle of the forest, the Willow Women defined life in Alainn Ros more than the church or the manor. The villagers feared their presence in the village more than God's wrath or Lord Osin's taxes. Stolen by the Fair Folk when they were young and beautiful, the Willow Women had been cast out of Faerie and had somehow found their way to Alainn Ros. No one knew their real names or where they came from before the Fair Folk had taken them. They were called Willow Women for their resemblance to the trees, pale and slender, with long, wispy white hair. From behind, they might be mistaken for young girls, but up close their vacant eyes stared out of faces as dry and ravaged as empty cornhusks.

Brigid was both repulsed and intrigued by the Willow Women, with whom she felt a kind of kinship. The villagers had not forced her to live alone in the forest, but neither would they suffer her among them for long. Anyone who spent time with the Faerie was tainted and unholy. Brigid thought of Morded's fiancée and Orla Cooley's baby. If they were to receive the same treatment as the Willow Women, Brigid hoped they never returned to Alainn Ros.

Brigid passed the well, taking her usual path along the stream until she came to a small clearing inside a circle of trees that contained a pool of still, clear water. She'd discovered the pool by accident during one of her early morning rambles. A white swan had flown across her path, and she followed it into the clearing where it settled on the water's surface without causing a single ripple. She never saw the swan again, and she wondered if Lord Osin had captured the bird and had had Cook turn it into some new and exotic dish. She shuddered to think of it. Better to eat her mother's watery pottage.

Brigid knelt at the water's edge and bent forward until she could see her reflection. What did the villagers find so strange about her appearance? She knew they found fault with her long, silver-blonde hair so she'd taken to wrapping it up on a length of plain cloth. But there was nothing she could do about the violet colour of her eyes, so dark her mother said they appeared almost black in some lights.

"Such a combination of light and dark is surely strange," she'd overhead Blacksmith's wife whisper to her husband one day in church. It was true that no one in the village had such pale hair (the colour of liquid moonlight her father had said fondly) or dark eyes, but no one had seemed troubled by her appearance until news of her encounter with the Faerie Queen spread through the village.

Still, the face looking back at her was undeniably human. The pool showed the curve of her mother's cheek and her father's wide brow. Her dark eyes appeared anxious, but not over-bright, and her skin was not unnaturally pale.

Entranced by the water's stillness, Brigid leaned in closer. The trees reflected in the pool grew taller and greener, the berries of the rowan bush redder, and the leaves of the birch trees glittered as though they'd been dipped in silver. Brigid felt the wind come up, ruffling her hair and the skirts of her gown, yet the pool did not show a single ripple. She had the strangest feeling of being there in the forest, yet somewhere else as well. The sound of a hare darting through the underbrush broke her concentration, and she looked up, dazed and slightly afraid.

Brigid tried to make her mind as calm and still as the water, but Lord Osin's heavy red face with his cruel hunter's smile tore through her thoughts like a wild boar. She tried again, this time willing the pool to hold her thoughts of Lord Osin like a jar holding a spider. She gazed into the water, hoping for some image to take shape, but all she saw was her own reflection staring back at her. She kneeled on the ground until her knees were damp and sore and her neck ached with strain.

Brigid struggled to her feet and brushed the dirt from her gown. What did she think was going to happen? That the pool would show her some wonderful vision of the future and make all of her worries disappear? Father Diarmaid said divination was a sin, one of Satan's tricks to lead people astray. Now she would be late to the manor and lose Lady Osin's favour, the one person who might be able to help her.

She heard a sudden snapping of branches close behind her and froze like a deer. "Who's there?" she called, but the forest only deepened its stillness.

"Don't be afraid, Brigid. It's only me." Connell emerged from behind an overgrown hawthorne, a large straw basket over one arm.

Too surprised to speak, Brigid could only stare at him. It was unusual to see Connell away from the mill, and stranger still to see his calm regular face shadowed by the wild tangle of trees overhead. "What are you doing here?" she managed finally.

Connell held up the basket he carried. "The Willow Women have a fondness for Mother's honey scones."

Brigid searched his face. Was he teasing her? No one went to the see the Willow Women.

"Will you come with me? Or would you rather I walk you home? The forest's no place for a woman alone."

Ignoring this last, Brigid took a decisive step forward. "I'll come."

They walked in silence for some time before Brigid worked up the courage to ask, "Why do you bring the Willow Women food? No one else in the village would trouble themselves, not even Father Diarmaid, who says it's our Christian duty to help those in need."

"The Willow Women need food like anyone else, so I bring it to them."

Brigid wondered how Connell's world could be so

simple when hers seemed almost unbearably complicated. "And you are not afraid?"

"Why should I be afraid?"

"I guess of being cursed. Isn't that what everyone says?"

Connell turned his serious grey eyes on Brigid. "Every village has its Willow Women, people who are old and unwell and in need of kindness. Tales of the Fair Folk are fine for a cold winter's night, but in real life, we must see things as they are."

Brigid returned his gaze, surprised. She'd never heard Connell say so many words at once.

The Willow Women's hut looked as though it had sprung from the forest floor. Covered in thick green moss with no windows to break the line of green, it would be easy enough to miss the humble dwelling altogether if you weren't looking for it.

"Are they expecting you?" Brigid whispered nervously.

"Wait for me here if you wish."

"No. I want to come with you."

Before Connell could raise his hand to knock, a tall slender woman opened the door. At first glance her appearance hinted at beauty, but looking closer, Brigid saw ruined features from which beauty had long since fled. Eyes, which might once have been brilliant green, had turned pale and watery, and the delicate bones of her face were concealed by folds of sagging flesh.

"Welcome, Connell," the woman said in a voice like a long sigh. "We hoped we might see you this day." She looked past Connell's shoulder at Brigid. "And you have brought a companion."

"She wanted to meet you," Connell said simply.

The woman nodded, unsurprised. "I am Eanna. Please come in."

Brigid followed Connell inside. The room was bare except for a low wooden table around which several silken cushions the colour of new leaves were scattered. Brigid wondered if Connell had brought them the cushions, although she could not imagine that even Connell's mother, whose gift with needle and thread was well known, could make anything so fine.

"Where are your companions?" Connell asked.

Eanna looked around her vaguely, as if expecting them to suddenly appear. "Perhaps they are gathering mushrooms. I have such fondness for mushrooms." Her gaze settled on Brigid. "They will be sorry they missed you."

Connell handed Eanna the basket. "This is for you."

Eanna bowed her head so that her long wispy hair swept the floor. "You are good."

The words were spoken in the same way you might say that the earth is brown or the sky blue.

"Won't you sit with me a little? We've had no visitors for . . . a long time."

Connell and Brigid each sat down on one of the cushions and Eanna drifted down beside them, fixing her watery eyes on Brigid.

"Will you tell me about it?" Eanna asked, her voice as eager as a young girl's.

Brigid shifted uncomfortably on the cushion. "Tell you about what?"

"The Faerie Queen. She showed herself to you."

No one in the village spoke of the Fair Folk out loud for fear of offending them. Not even Brigid's mother had asked her about her meeting with the Faerie Queen. And yet, in spite of all the warnings, Brigid longed to tell Eanna everything.

"Please," Eanna said.

"I saw her when I was lost in the forest. She asked me to come dancing with her, and she promised me a dress made of stars."

Eanna clapped her hands together in delight. "And did you?"

"No. My mother and father would have missed me."

Eanna cocked her head to one side, the gaiety leaking from her face. "Yes, there is that."

Silence settled between them until Connell cleared his throat. "I should be getting Brigid home."

Eanna seized both of Brigid's hands and held them to her withered lips. "Did she tell you the way in?"

"The way in?"

"The way into Faerie. Did she tell you?"

"I don't think so."

"Are you certain?" Eanna asked, her voice now closer to a shriek than a sigh. "Nothing? I'd give anything to find the way back, anything at all." Eanna removed the threadbare shawl she wore around her shoulders and thrust it towards Brigid. "Take it, and tell me what she said!"

Brigid pushed the shawl away, frightened by the agonized expression in the other woman's eyes. "I'm sorry, but she didn't tell me anything."

Eanna drew her knees up to her chest and began sobbing like a child.

Connell put a strong hand on Brigid's shoulder and helped her to her feet. "I'm sorry you are unwell, Eanna. I shall come back and see you another time."

Eanna raised her head for a moment, the expression on her face resembling a raw open wound. "Promise?"

Connell surprised Brigid again by bending down and placing a gentle kiss on Eanna's ravaged face. "I give you my word."

On the way home, Brigid's throat ached from all the things she longed to say to Connell, but somehow all she said was, "I would rather starve than live as they do."

Connell studied her for a long moment. "No, you wouldn't."

When they reached the edge of the forest, he offered to accompany her to the manor, but she said she was late already and could move faster on her own. While she admired Connell's generosity, she was eager to be away from him. She couldn't help but think that his kindness to her was very like his kindness to Eanna.

She shivered at the memory of Eanna's shrivelled, tear-stained face suffused with gratitude when Connell had kissed her. The Fair Folk would have shown Eanna a greater kindness if they'd killed her instead of casting her out into a world that didn't want her.

Chapter 5

Thoughts of Eanna stayed with her all the way to the manor, but when she approached the gatehouse, her sadness was replaced by a thrill of fear. Would Lord Osin seek her out and demand an answer to his proposal?

Brigid entered the manor grounds quickly, seeing no one save the Porter and Lady Osin's page, a shy, slight boy of about seven or eight, who hid his face in his hands when he saw her. When she opened the heavy wooden door to the great hall, Brigid cast a regretful glance in the direction of the kitchen. She realized how much she'd come to enjoy the warmth of the fire and Cook's easy conversation. Now that she was to be a chambermaid, she'd spend all her time in Lady Osin's rooms.

Brigid climbed the stairs that led to the upper floor of the manor slowly, as though she were an old woman instead of a young one. Please don't let the lord be at home, she prayed.

When Brigid reached the top of the stairs, the front room of Lady Osin's private chambers was empty. Modest by noble standards, the room was simply furnished with a damask silk-covered sofa and a writing table made of sturdy, polished wood. In the corner of the room, a large wooden chest held Lady Osin's embroidery tools and other personal items. Unsure of how to make her presence known, she gave what she hoped was a delicate sounding cough. A few moments later, Lady Osin appeared from behind a gold brocade curtain smoothing the crown of her snowy white veil.

"Good morning, Brigid. I am pleased to see you."

Brigid curtseyed, shamefully aware of the sprinkling of leaves and dirt that clung to the bottom of her gown. "I am deeply sorry for my lateness, my lady. I went to the forest to gather more wood for my mother, and I fear that I lost track of time."

Lady Osin waved away her apology with one of her soft, white hands.

"Your mother is fortunate to have such a dutiful daughter. I hope one day to have the comfort of a daughter's company, or a son's," she added quietly.

"I'm certain you shall, my lady."

Lady Osin smiled, her thin lips trembling slightly.

She knows she's barren, Brigid thought. It would not be proper for her to admit to such a failure, but she knows it all the same. And Lord Osin likely never lets her forget it.

"How may I be of service to you?" Brigid asked tentatively, aware of how little she could do. She knew something of herbs and medicine from watching her mother, but as for sewing and embroidery, she couldn't thread a needle without drawing blood.

Lady Osin gathered her silk skirts, the colour of doves' wings, and sat down on the sofa. "Come and sit by me. I should like to hear something of the village. What news is there?"

Brigid took her place beside Lady Osin, her spirits sinking further at Lady Osin's request. There were few enough in the village who would even look her way, let alone include her in their gossip. Still, Brigid searched her mind for something of interest. "Clare Ryan had a baby. My mother delivered him the night before last."

Lady Osin picked up her embroidery, a finely detailed picture of a unicorn, whose snowy white head lay on a young gentlewoman's lap. "That is good news indeed. This is the Ryan's first son is it not?"

Brigid nodded, wishing she'd chosen some other piece of news to share with Lady Osin, whose face reminded her of the painting of the Virgin Mary that hung in the village church. Their eyes shared the same look of restrained sadness. "And of course it will soon be Easter. Everyone will be looking forward to the feast, and to the dancing."

Lady Osin smiled, the rare expression accentuating cheekbones so high her eyes appeared almost slanted. "I have heard you have a talent for dancing. It is said you move so lightly, it is as though you have eggs underneath your feet."

Brigid laughed. "I am surprised to hear such kind words. Most of the village think my skill at dancing a curse or some other kind of wickedness. Father Diarmaid certainly thinks so. At Michelmas, he stared so hard at my feet, I thought he was saying a prayer to make them fall off my ankles!"

As soon she spoke the words, Brigid took a deep breath as though to draw them back into her mouth. "Forgive me, Lady Osin, I should not say such things of Father Diarmaid. I am so unused to speaking to anyone other than my mother that I . . . please forgive me."

"Hush, Brigid. I was fond of dancing myself not so long ago. And what Father Diarmaid doesn't know cannot harm him. But tell me, why you are unused to conversation? Surely you have many friends in the village?"

Brigid studied a crescent-shaped stain on the arm of the sofa. "I am not well liked."

Lady Osin lifted her eyes from her embroidery and gazed briefly at Brigid's face before returning to her work. "Pleasing features are thought to be a good thing for a woman to possess. A pretty face rarely finds fault, and yet great beauty is likely to inspire as much hatred as it does admiration. In truth," she went on, her fingers moving deftly back and forth across the screen on her lap, "great beauty can lead to a woman's ruin if she attracts the wrong kind of attention."

Brigid held her breath as she listened to Lady Osin. Did she know of Lord Osin's attentions to her?

"Tell me, Brigid. Is it true that no one cares for you? Surely you must have at least one admirer in the village?"

"There is someone. My mother thinks he wants to marry me, but I . . ."

"You are not sure of him or of you?"

"Both perhaps," Brigid admitted.

"Is he a cruel man? Do you think he would beat you? Or be unkind to the children you might have together?"

"No! Connell is a good man. If his character were etched on stained glass, you could stare at it until your eyes grew blurry and find little fault with him."

"So the fault lies with you?"

Brigid pressed the small of her back against the silk cushion behind her. "I should be grateful that Connell wants to marry me . . ."

"And yet?"

"Perhaps it sounds foolish, but I thought when it was my time to marry, I'd feel differently."

Lady Osin rose quickly from the sofa, letting her embroidery fall to the floor. She crossed the room and stood in front of the room's only window, a narrow, rectangular opening covered with dirty glass. "Brigid, I tell you this as one woman to another. Marriage is a strange and unpredictable thing. No one is ready for it, but it is nearly always necessary. Do not turn this man away in hope of some undiscovered feeling you cannot name. None of us have that luxury, not even I."

"I shall not come to the manor anymore once I'm married."

Lady Osin swept back to the sofa, put one of her delicate

hands under Brigid's chin, and tilted the girl's face towards her. "No, Brigid. You shall not."

The sky was turning to soft grey when Brigid left the manor. Since she was a child, twilight was her favourite time of day. As the village fell quiet, fluttering between light and dark, she felt a surge of energy in her tired limbs. Twilight was when her urge to visit the forest was strongest. Even after the morning's strangeness, she felt the familiar longing for leaves overhead, and the smell of dark, rich earth filling her nostrils. But she would not go to the forest. She would go home to the dimly lit cottage, eat a bowl of pottage with her mother, and perhaps a slice of marzipan, and then she would light a candle, dampen the fire, and prepare for bed. And so the days would repeat themselves until something happened to make everything worse.

Lady Osin's words about marriage had not gone unheeded. If Connell asked her to marry him, she would accept, and perhaps in time the strange longing deep inside of her would disappear.

Chapter 6

The whole village attended the Easter feast. Good meat and drink summoned the villagers to church in a way the finest sermon never could. Whatever else Lord Osin could be faulted for he was not stingy when it came to village celebrations. Although Brigid suspected that the credit for the abundance of delicacies that weighted down the long wooden table at the back of the church belonged to Lady Osin.

The villagers' delight in the good ale, the softness of the bread, and the richly spiced meat, seemed to soften the edges of their dislike for Brigid. Baker's wife even nodded to her in an almost friendly way as she helped herself to a large slice of almond tart and several sugared figs.

Mary, always quick to detect the slightest change in her daughter's favour, nodded at Brigid approvingly. "There. Mark my words, the others will soon follow, especially once you're . . ."

Brigid turned away before she heard the rest. She had spent the better part of a fortnight worrying over every possible turn of events, visions of Connell, Lord Osin, and her mother, dancing around in her head until it throbbed from exhaustion. What if Connell had no intention of asking her to marry him? Or what if he did want to marry her, but had been persuaded against the idea? Connell's mother did not whisper about Brigid behind her hands the way some of the other women did, but nor did she seem to have much liking for her, either. Surely, she would want better for her son than the wild dancing girl who consorted with the Fair

Folk. Or worst of all, what if Connell thought she already belonged to the lord? The latest addition to his chattels? This last thought kept her up at night, tossing and turning until she'd worn a deep hollow in her pallet. She recalled Lord Osin's grasping hunter's hands trembling in their eagerness to remove her head covering. If he had his way, she'd be his creature. No matter what happened, she'd never give in to his demands. She'd ask her mother to leave Alainn Ros and take their chances in the next village, even though such a move was likely to ensure they fell further into hunger and despair.

But when Brigid spied Connell on the other side of the room, his eyes as grey and impenetrable as the manor walls, she felt a different kind fear. If he did ask her to marry him, could she say the words to accept him? In spite of everything, the idea of marriage still seemed like a wild and foreign country she was not yet ready to visit. Her feelings for Connell struggled against one another like two eels in a barrel. She both sought his gaze and hid from it, unsure of what either of them might do next.

Still, a feast night demanded enjoyment, and she urged her mother to eat her share of good things, although she herself could barely force a crust of bread past her lips. The plates of mutton and herring pie did not tempt her, but she piled her plate high anyway, lest she be thought more strange than she already was.

Finally, when the table had been relieved of all its delicacies, and no one could force another bite, the villagers drifted into the churchyard in search of the rest of the evening's merrymaking. Father Diarmaid stood at the church door urging the villagers to return to their cottages and say their prayers, but not even the most devout among them would forgo a night of music and dancing. They would have their pleasure even if it meant a visit from the devil himself.

The preferred spot of ground for playing music and dancing was in front of the alehouse. The squat two-room building was never empty. Far enough away from the church to be safe from Father Diarmaid's disapproving gaze, and not too close to the forest to make the villagers uneasy when they stumbled home in the dark after too much drink. But the dance for the Easter cake took place outside, where the hard, stiff ground of winter gave way to spring, softening the earth so that the rise and fall of the dancers' steps would be almost soundless. While the women, including Brigid and her mother, set to work helping the ale wife pull out wooden chairs and several tables from the alehouse, the men who played an instrument ran back to their cottages to fetch them. When all was ready, Brigid glanced over at her mother, who looked pale and tired in spite of her filling meal.

"Shall I walk you back to the cottage, Mother? You look ready for bed."

"I shall be well enough once the music starts."

Brigid knew why her mother stayed. She wanted to see if Connell would speak to her, for if it did not happen tonight it likely would not happen at all. But so far, Connell had only nodded briefly in her direction. Most of the villagers were lined up in front of the alehouse, but Connell and his mother stood apart from the rest, seemingly deep in conversation. The expression on his face made Brigid think her words gave him no pleasure.

Once the air came alive with the delicious sounds of harp and hornpipe, Brigid felt her anxiety drift up and out of her like a spirit. Her feet began to quiver and she wanted nothing more than to dance until her legs collapsed beneath her. Brigid considered staying at her mother's side to give Connell proof that she was not wild like the villagers claimed, but she could not stop herself from dancing any more than she could stop herself from breathing. She'd rather go without bread or ale than miss a dancing night. When her body filled up with music, she could not be sad about anything. Besides, there was a cake to be won and she would have it. And such a lovely cake it was, at least what Brigid could see of it. The pastry sat on a round board surrounded by meadow flowers and was advanced on a pike stuck in the ground about ten feet high. Brigid turned to her mother. "We shall take this cake home with us tonight."

"Brigid, love, perhaps you should . . ."

But Brigid had already taken her place amongst the other dancers in a large ring around the cake. They would dance around and around until only one of them was left standing, and she had no doubt it would be herself.

Brigid allowed the sweet music to seep into her veins and then she was away. Away from the disapproving eyes of the other villagers, away from her mother's fond but anxious expression, away from Connell and his undecided intentions. Once she was inside the music nothing else mattered. She felt as free and untouchable as the lord himself. As she advanced around the ring, her feet tapping lightly against the ground, she was dimly aware of the other dancers. Two had already left; their desire for more ale greater than their desire for the cake. Ahead of her, Isibeal, Tanner's daughter, stumbled and Brigid danced around her like the wind.

Brigid never got a cramp in her side or lost her footing. Once she started dancing her tiredness fell away from her like a heavy, velvet cloak. She could go round and round the ring until a new sun rose in the sky. But she would not have long to wait for her victory. One by one the other dancers began to tire. Fin, the Falconer's son, one of Brigid's long-ago playmates fell to the ground gasping for breath.

"No more," he said before struggling to his feet.

Mary, the Baker's daughter, and Isibeal also took their leave. Brigid could feel their jealous glances burning into her back after they rejoined their families who stood around the ring waiting to see who would falter next.

Now only Brigid and Deirdre Faolan were left. The two girls danced alone together on many such occasions. Deirdre did not possess Brigid's love of music, or her graceful footwork, but she was sturdy and strong from her work in the fields, and the desire to win radiated from her well-muscled limbs.

The dancers shared the same steps but their movements were as different from one another as the sun and the moon. Deirdre's brow glistened with sweat, two hectic spots of colour staining her ruddy cheeks, while Brigid felt as cool and weightless as a shadow. But if her feet held some magic, her shoes possessed none. Already worn through in several places, she felt the soles of her feet connect with the hard ground. Still she danced on, her pale face upturned to the sky, which was now well and truly dark. She wished she could dance her way up to the highest star and disappear into the sky's inky blackness.

"'Tis not natural the way you dance, Brigid O'Flynn," Deirdre said, clutching her sides as she left Brigid alone in the ring.

Brigid won the cake. She felt the familiar sense of loss when the music ended for it was the dance and not the prize that brought her out that night. Still, when the ale-wife rushed out of the tiny tavern and bent to the task of lowering the cake from the pole, Brigid felt a tiny surge of pride at her win. She may not be welcome in the village or a good cook, or handy with a needle and a thread, but she could dance until she felt her very soul coming out through her feet.

The ale-wife handed Brigid the pastry. "There ye be. 'Tis no contest when you're in the ring."

Brigid heard a ripple of unease underneath the ale-woman's simple words. Perhaps she should have let one of the other dancers win. It was foolish to invite more dislike where there was more than enough already.

Brigid returned to her mother's side. "For you, Mother," she said before gently placing the cake on the older woman's lap. "It will make a nice change from our lumpy bread."

Mary smiled when she touched the brightly coloured garland, but Brigid knew she wished she hadn't won. I am a burden to her, Brigid thought with a rush of sadness followed by a hot, fierce longing for her father. He would have made a story about her, the girl who danced as though she had wings on her feet.

"You dance like the wind," a voice behind her said. "But even the wind must rest now and then."

Brigid turned to see Connell holding out a mug of ale for her.

She took the drink and allowed Connell to lead her slightly away from the others.

"When I'm dancing, I forget that I'm made of flesh and bone, but when I stop," she added, rubbing the heel of her leather shoe, "I'm sorely reminded."

Connell's face relaxed into a smile and Brigid felt a sudden warmth towards him. If he smiled more often, I would not be so afraid of his seriousness, she thought. But the smile was quickly replaced by his usual grave expression.

"Brigid, I waited to speak to you because . . . because it seemed you needed time to get used to the idea. But I can wait no longer: Will you be my wife?"

Brigid breathed deeply, the pain in her feet forgotten. Was this how it was done? She'd not expected Connell's proposal to come so quickly.

"Why, Connell?" The words tumbled out of her mouth before she could stop them. "Why do you want to marry me when you could have any girl in the village?" Brigid glanced over at Deirdre, who seemed to have recovered from her exertions and was watching Connell with hungry eyes. Next to Connell, Deirdre's father had the largest parcel of land in the village, and the prosperous farmer made no secret of his desire for Connell to marry Deirdre.

If Connell was taken aback by her question, he did not show it. "It is true that you have no dowry, and will bring little to your marriage in the way of material things, but I have watched you these many years. You are a good daughter, a hard worker, and I believe you will be a good wife. I am not a man for tales. Whatever happened—if indeed anything ever did—is long past. I need a wife and it would go better for you in the village if you had a husband, and so"—Connell shrugged his broad shoulders—"I am prepared to overlook certain . . . shortcomings."

Brigid fought to hide her disappointment. If he'd called her a silly girl, or even a shrew, his words would have shown more passion than his tally of assets and 'shortcomings.' She might have been a calf he inspected, found wanting, and decided to buy anyway.

Her own true love would not have spoken so coldly. Could she spend the rest of her days with someone who only thought to protect her from further ruin? Surely true love was not just for knights and ladies? She would rather live alone with her mother forever than have it be so. And yet, tonight her head was filled with music and her belly with food. The morning would bring watery porridge and her mother's pale skin stretched too tightly over cheekbones that grew sharper every day. As much as she longed for her own true love, she would not sacrifice her mother's health to wait for it.

"Brigid, will you give me your answer?"

"Your mother doesn't like me."

Connell's love of honesty would not permit him to lie. "Whatever her feelings now, I know she will grow to love you like a daughter. She has many valuable things to teach you, and the learning of them will bring you closer."

Again, it was not the answer she hoped for, but Connell

could not be other than he was any more than she herself could. The difference was she must be the one to try.

"Thank you, Connell. I shall try to be a good wife to you."

Connell's face suffused with colour, and for a moment Brigid thought he was going to speak the pretty words she hoped to hear. But he just clasped her hands in his and said, "It is settled then. I will speak to the lord immediately. The banns can be published on Saturday."

It was done. If her true love came now, he would be too late.

Chapter 7

The day Connell was to speak to Lord Osin, Brigid could scarcely breathe for fear something would go wrong. Would the lord refuse Connell permission to marry her because he wanted her for himself? The lord's wanting was as shallow as the mill pond. He saw her as an appealing diversion between a good hunt and a hot dinner. Surely he would not take such trouble over a servant girl?

She did not have long to wait for an answer. The following Saturday Father Diarmaid published the banns. Connell Mackenna and Brigid O'Flynn would marry in mid-summer.

"Why wait so long?" her mother asked when Connell and Brigid told her of their plans. The three of them were sitting at the kitchen table where Mary was kneading dough made with finely milled flour, another gift from Connell.

"There is much to be done before the wedding," Connell explained. "I'm building an addition on the cottage so Brigid and I might be alone when we wish it"—Connell blushed when he spoke these words—"and Brigid shall have a proper sitting room like a lady." And then it was Brigid's turn to blush. Even as the miller's wife, she would never be a lady, but it was kind of Connell to make such a plan for her, especially when his mother thought the idea, "a foolish extravagance."

"And of course Brigid must have a wedding dress," Connell added.

Mary removed her hands from the dough. "Surely, your

mother could help with that? There's no one in the village more skilled with a needle and thread."

"She'll sew the dress, of course. It's the material Brigid will be wanting. There's nothing fine enough in Alainn Ros. The day after tomorrow I'm off to the Great Town to fetch a bolt of cloth and some other bits and pieces for Brigid's housekeeping."

A frown tugged at the corners of her mother's mouth that had been smiling since the night of Connell's proposal. "You're leaving so soon."

"I'll be back in less than a fortnight," Connell promised. "The mill can spare me no longer than that."

Her mother's frown deepened until the space between her brows resembled a knife slash. "Surely, you won't travel through the forest alone? Robbers and outlaws and . . . other things make their home there. You must take someone else with you for protection."

Connell laughed. "I shan't be alone. Miri will be with me," he said speaking of his packhorse. "Besides, I do not fear the forest. Robbers and outlaws are not known to frequent these parts."

Mary nodded, but Brigid knew Connell's words did nothing to calm her fears. It was not robbers her mother feared, but something much more powerful. The Faerie were not interested in stealing food or coins. They sought something much more precious to the owner. Most of those who'd lived to tell of their encounter with the Fair Folk did so with a mind that seemed to have blown apart by tempests.

After Connell left, her mother said, "You must fill his pockets with yarrow gathered at mid-day and sew St. John's Wort into the hem of his britches before he leaves."

"Yes, Mother."

The morning of his departure, Connell came to the cottage to say goodbye. Brigid wanted to give him something for the journey. He'd been so kind to her it seemed only right that she give him something in return. But when they stood facing one another she could think of nothing to give him, not even the words of love from a woman to her betrothed.

"Brigid, I should like to make you a present before I go. It's not a betrothal gift, but something you may have need of while I'm gone." Connell reached into the cloth pouch he kept tied at his waist and pulled out a new pair of soft leather shoes.

"Connell," Brigid breathed. "Where did you find them? I've never seen such a lovely pair."

"I've been saving them since I saw you dance at Michelmas. The soles of your shoes were nearly worn through. It's past time you had a new pair."

Once more Brigid felt shamed by Connell's kindness when she offered him so little in return.

"Thank you, Connell. You are too good."

Connell cleared his throat. "I'd best be getting off. I don't want to lose any more of the day."

Brigid nodded. "Connell."

"Yes?"

"I should like . . . I should like to wish you a safe journey."

A shadow of disappointment crossed Connell's face. "Thank you."

When he turned to go, Brigid thought to call after him, but did not. She stood in the doorway of the cottage clutching her new shoes against her chest.

It was not until the day's light faded that Brigid realized she'd forgotten both the yarrow and the St. John's Wort.

After Connell's departure, Brigid's days returned to their usual pattern. She helped her mother in the garden, gathered mushrooms at the forest's edge, and served at the manor when needed. She'd not seen Lord Osin since the banns were published. He was said to be visiting the king himself on some important business.

Just as her mother predicted, the other villagers seemed to soften towards her now that she was to be Connell's wife. She tried to share in her mother's pleasure, but beneath her breast a hard kernel of bitterness remained. She wanted to be liked for herself, not because she'd caught the miller's eye.

But Mary's joy was short-lived. As a fortnight lengthened into two, the villagers' newfound regard for Brigid crumbled like an old piece of thatch. The low whispers about Connell's long absence grew louder, until finally, they no longer took care to see that Brigid was out of sight when they discussed Connell's fate.

"The Fair Folk have taken him just like her father," Brigid overheard Baker say to his wife while Brigid waited for him to fetch the sweet almond tart she hoped would tempt her mother's appetite. She was in bed with the ague, and Brigid feared Connell's prolonged absence was causing her to sicken further.

Baker's wife crossed herself before replying, "She's an unlucky one, and to think he could have had his pick. Deirdre's father would have given him two cattle and a new lamb for her dowry."

Elsewhere in the village the talk was worse.

"'Tis a Faerie curse. She brings misfortune to everything she touches."

"Aye, 'tis surely a punishment for her wicked ways. She dances like a madwoman."

"Doesn't Father Diarmaid tell us that sin comes with drink and dancing? The girl and her mother should keep to themselves."

"She's putting us all in danger by keeping company with the Fair Folk. We must protect the children. It will be one of our own they come for next."

This last was from Deirdre, the words spoken to Deirdre's mother loudly enough so that Brigid could not help but overhear when she met the two women in front of the candlemaker's shop. She could feel the other girl's dislike slicing through the course material of her overgown and kirtle, tearing at her flesh like one of Cook's boning knives.

The candles forgotten, Brigid left the shop and ran all the way back to the cottage.

"Why doesn't he come home?" Brigid cried to her mother, who was stirring their supper over the fire. A pottage that was little more than greenish coloured water.

Her mother put down the wooden spoon but did not look at Brigid when she spoke.

"Did you do what I told you?"

"What do you mean?" Brigid asked, although she knew full well. She'd thought of nothing else for days.

"The herbs. Did you see that he was protected?"

Brigid could not bring herself to answer. She felt as alone and unwanted as the Willow Women. Her mother was the only person in the world who loved her.

Brigid's silence filled the space between them until finally her mother said quietly, "I don't want you outside after dark."

"Because of the Faerie?" Brigid whispered.

"No. Because of the villagers."

The stares and whispers that followed Brigid's every step grew longer and louder until Brigid stopped going to the village altogether. To avoid encountering anyone on her way to the manor, she walked through the muddy fields on the village outskirts so that by the time she arrived her feet were nearly soaked through, and the back of her skirts were speckled with mud.

It could not be said that the manor household gave her a warm welcome, but their indifference was far better than what she'd come to expect in the village. Brigid was allowed to divide her time between Lady Osin's chambers and the kitchen where her hands were constantly in motion, sweeping floors, chopping vegetables, and scrubbing endless piles of linen. It was the only way she could keep thoughts of Connell at bay. If she rested, even for a moment, her mind churned with questions. Was he hurt? Did he lie alone and injured on the forest floor? Or in some muddy ditch? And worst of all: Was he dead?

Brigid had not worn the shoes Connell gave her. She hid them in the cottage beneath a pile of straw. But sometimes, after her mother went to sleep, Brigid would take them out and press their soft leather soles against her cheek. They were her most beautiful possession, and yet it hurt her to look at them. If she'd taken care of Connell the way she ought to have done, perhaps she would have danced in the shoes at her wedding. Now she would dance for no one, ever again.

And then it was May Eve. Connell had been gone more than three fortnights. Brigid used to love May Eve best of all. The music and dancing on that day seemed sweeter and wilder than at any other time. But there would be no May Eve celebration for her this year. She could almost hear the insults the villagers would shout at her if she were to join them in the village square.

The weight of these darks thoughts slowed Brigid's steps as she made her way home after the evening meal in the great hall. To Brigid's great relief, Lady Osin still dined alone. The noblewoman did not speak to Brigid about Connell's disappearance, but when she gave Lady Osin her evening draught of hot wine, the other woman laid one of her smooth white hands on Brigid's own. Their gaze met only briefly, but the troubled expression in her Lady's eyes made Brigid wonder if Lord Osin had returned. Her suspicions were confirmed when one of the pages came to the kitchen asking for a light supper to be brought to Lord Osin's chamber.

"I'll see that he gets it," Cook said to Brigid. "You go out to the kennels and feed the dogs."

She'd escaped this night, but how long would it be until he renewed his demands of her? Now, more than ever, it seemed there was no place for her anywhere. An outcast in the village, she and her mother would soon be faced with a choice: Fall upon the lord's mercy at great cost to herself, or try their luck in another village and risk starvation, or worse.

Brigid was on her way home when she saw the lights coming towards her. She stopped, one foot on rich manor soil, the other mired in the greyish muck that marked the beginning of a strip of peasant land. For a moment, earth and sky spun crazily. Had the Faerie come back to claim her after all? But as the lights grew closer she saw that their source was not the unearthly glow of the Faerie, but lengths of rush dipped in bacon fat. More than a half dozen of the village men carried them in their hands, and when they drew close enough for her to see their faces, the expression in their eyes made her stumble backwards.

"What do you want?" she asked. "My mother's waiting for me."

Tanner stepped forward, and Brigid could smell the stink of animal hides on his skin.

"It would go better for your mother if she were relieved of the burden of caring for you."

"What do you mean? There's nowhere else for me to go."

"The forest would take you." This from the bailiff's son, who used to stare at her in church as though she were a haunch of venison drenched in gravy.

The air held the warmth of high spring, but a fierce coldness seized hold of Brigid's ribcage and left her trembling. The villagers drew close around her, their rushlights carving deep hollows under their eyes. Brigid looked from one face to another, hoping to see some sign of pity or indecision, but there was none. They had come to drive her out.

"Come now, Brigid. This can go easy or it can go hard."

Brigid tried to drain the fear from her voice before asking, "Why are you doing this? I've done no harm to any of you."

Declan Dow, a farm hand whom she'd never heard utter a word, looked at her as though she were mad. "Not harm us? If the harvest fails, you'll have killed us all."

Brigid struggled for the words to make them see she was the same as all of them, but all that came to her lips was, "Please."

"Now!" she heard a new voice say, and then everything went black.

They'd dropped a sack over her Brigid's head like a grown man's version of Hoodman Blind. Strong hands pushed her from behind so that she stumbled forward.

"Where are you taking me?" she asked, but her voice was too muffled for anyone to hear. It didn't matter anyway. Brigid knew where she was going. They were going to take her to the forest and leave her there.

They walked for what seemed like an eternity, but may only have been the better part of an hour. Just long enough to make sure I cannot find my way back, she thought. Although she knew her part of the forest well, the rest of it was as wild and strange to her as everyone else in the village.

Brigid listened carefully underneath the sack, hoping to overhear something that might help her, but except for the occasional curse or grunt when they tripped over an overgrown root, the villagers were silent.

Finally, they came to halt, and Brigid gave a tiny sigh of relief. Her legs ached, and a part of her still didn't believe they would make good on their threat. Surely they only meant to frighten her? When they let her go, she'd go home and tell her mother they must leave at once. Young and strong, Brigid would make sure neither of them starved.

"Our Father who art in Heaven, hallowed be Thy name."

The villagers were praying, their voices low and serious, like they were kneeling before Father Diarmaid in church instead of in the middle of the forest. The sound of their voices brought beads of sweat to Brigid's forehead, but when they fell silent she was more afraid.

"Wait," she called out from inside the sack. "I beg you, do not leave me here!"

"Forgive us, Brigid, but we cannot take the chance. Do not fear. The Fair Folk will come and claim you, and you shall sing and dance with them just as you were meant."

She didn't recognize the last voice that spoke to her after the others had gone, but when the sound of his retreating footsteps faded away she knew she was truly alone. The silence of the forest fell over her, so heavy and deep she felt like she was drowning. She lay down on the forest floor and wept until the sack was wet against her cheek. She wished the Faerie would come for her. She doubted they would show her more cruelty than her own people. Better to live as the Faerie Queen's servant than to die cold and alone in the forest.

Brigid sat up. She would not die. Her mother would not survive losing both husband and daughter. She must at least try to find her way out. Brigid rubbed the warmth back into her fingers and felt for the rope around her neck. It was tied only loosely, and she soon freed herself. Not that it made much difference. The forest was black as pitch. She could feel rather than see the thickness of the trees around her, their leafy overhang enveloping her like a shroud. She would have to wait until morning to find her bearings. Surely, she had not walked with the villagers more than a couple of miles? Along the way she felt her feet sinking into the ground in several places. Perhaps she'd be able to retrace her steps. And if she was able to find her way back? How long until they came for her again? Or worse, sought to take their anger out on her mother. I'll find a way, she vowed before exhaustion overtook her.

Brigid awoke to the sensation of leaves brushing softly over her face. For a moment she thought herself back in her cottage, but instead of thatch, she was looking up at blue sky. The events of the night before fell over her like a net. She started to shiver uncontrollably, her body suddenly aware that it had spent the night on the cold, hard ground. With no fire to warm her, Brigid picked up the sack she'd torn off the night before and wrapped it around her shoulders.

Move! She had to keep moving. But with every step, her stomach churned in protest, and her head felt as though it were filled with butterflies. She dearly regretted refusing the hunk of bread and cheese Cook had offered the night before. If only she'd thought to put it in the pocket of her gown!

Brigid looked at the wall of trees that surrounded her. Which way should she go? She was not strong enough to make a mistake. If she chose wrongly, she would never find her way out. Her mother would be alone in the cottage wondering why she didn't come home. Would the villagers go home to their families and tell them what they'd done? Or perhaps there would be no need. Except for her mother, everyone would be content to think she'd just disappeared, or was stolen by the Fair Folk for good.

This last thought pushed Brigid forward through skeletal-like branches whose long, bony fingers tore at her hair and scratched her face. She searched the ground for footprints, but the forest floor gave away none of its secrets. There was nothing to guide her or mark her path. Every step brought her deeper into the forest until she felt the trees close in around her like a leafy cage. What had the Faerie Queen told her that day?

"Listen to what is underneath the silence."

Brigid closed her eyes and stood as still as she could, but all she heard was her own heart pounding in her chest.

Suddenly, Brigid's eyes flew open. Something moved in the underbrush, a soft, crunching sound. "Who's there?" She held her breath and waited. The crunching grew louder. Whatever made the sound was drawing closer. The footsteps of an outlaw? Or a robber? She twisted herself around, searching in all directions. There was no one. Still, the silence had lost its fullness. "Who's there?" she called again, although this time it was barely a whisper. And then she saw him. Not a man but a hart, the great white hart of the forest.

The animal took several tentative steps towards her, his head held high. Brigid had never seen the hart before, but many times she'd overhead Lord Osin speaking of him to his huntsman. Once she brought them wine and cheese while they sat in the great hall examining a number of small brown pebbles with a magnifying glass. When Brigid asked Cook what fascinated them so, the older woman told her it was shit.

"Why should the lord care about that?" Brigid asked, bewildered.

"The droppings mark the place where the hart has been," Cook told her, "and the lord wants to capture the hart more than anything. Even more than he wants an heir."

And now Brigid found herself face-to-face with the Lord Osin's greatest desire. The hart stood tall and proud, his deep dark eyes showing no trace of fear. He might have been a fairy steed he was so beautiful, and yet when Brigid looked into his eyes she thought them more human than fey.

"Can you show me the way out of the forest?" Brigid asked.

The animal cocked his head to one side as though considering her question before lowering his mouth to the ground to graze at a bed of lichen. Brigid watched him wishing that she, too, could fill her empty belly with moss and leaves. Her stomach twisted painfully. "Is there anything I can eat? Mushrooms? Or maybe some berries?" The animal lifted his head and stared at her for a long moment. Brigid reached out her hand and touched one of his antlers. She feared he might startle and leave her, but he endured her touch for several moments before he lifted his white head and sniffed the air. She watched him go; her body straining with the desire to seize hold of his fur and hold him to her. Is that how Lord Osin and his huntsman felt when they tracked his steps through the forest? The comparison sickened her, so she turned away and pressed her face against the pale trunk of a birch tree, breathing in the scent of leaves and bitter sap. When she turned around again, she saw the hart staring at her with somber, unblinking eyes. He'd taken only a few steps, and Brigid understood he was waiting for her to follow him.

They moved quickly, the hart's step graceful and sure while Brigid ducked constantly to protect her eyes from protruding branches. Within moments, the hart brought them to a small clearing where Brigid spotted some rowan bushes heavy with red, ripe berries.

Brigid seized a handful of the berries and crammed them in her mouth. "Thank you, thank you," she said to the hart as juice ran down her chin. So intent on her meal, Brigid did not hear the approach of hooves until they were nearly upon her. The hart's ears must have been more sensitive because when she looked up he was gone. Brigid watched the unseen rider slash his way through the trees, severed branches crashing into the underbrush. When he finally entered the clearing, Brigid found she was face-to-face with Lord Osin.

Brigid's legs swayed beneath her, but she did not fall. It was not the rescue she hoped for but it was rescue nonetheless. If he wished it, Lord Osin could see her safely home.

The lord dismounted and led his horse into the clearing.

"Did you see him?" he demanded.

"See who? My lord."

"The hart. I've followed him since daybreak. I was close upon him. I felt his fear. Are you certain you have not seen nor heard anything?"

"I am certain, my lord."

Lord Osin stared at her a moment before the strangeness of finding her alone in the forest began to show itself on his face.

"They drove you out then, did they?" he finally asked.

"What do you mean?" Brigid asked, ashamed that anyone, even Lord Osin should know that the villagers hated her enough to leave her in the forest to die.

Lord Osin threw back his head and laughed, revealing a set of too large, yellowing teeth. "You amaze me, Brigid. Truly you do. What do I mean, you ask? As if it was not as plain as the branches on these trees. You should have taken my protection when I offered it to you. It was only a matter to time, you know. If it were not for your mother, they would have done it years ago."

"But I've done nothing. You are a great man. Surely you don't believe the things they say. If you take me back . . ."

"Take you back? Why should I trouble myself to help you when you have already shown me such ingratitude? I offered you the greatest honour a woman could hope for. I shall not make that mistake again."

The surge of hope she felt after meeting the hart deserted her. She fell to her knees, but she would not beg for Lord Osin's mercy. It would be better to die whole and strong than broken and humiliated.

Lord Osin urged the mount forward until he stood towering above her. "Get up! Your lord has changed his mind. I shall offer you a wager."

Brigid struggled to her feet. "A wager, my lord?"

Lord Osin grabbed hold of one of her arms and pulled her roughly towards him. "Today, you shall be my hart," he whispered in her ear. "And because you are so fine and beautiful, I shall unmake you just as carefully. Not a drop of you will go to waste."

Brigid tried to pull away, but he held her fast. She felt the softness of his silken tunic, the same colour as the rubies in Lady Osin's wedding ring. But no material, no matter how fine, could mask the scent of his skin. Foul sweat mixed with iron filled her throat and nostrils until she was gagging with the stench. Lord Osin smelled of blood.

Finally, he pushed her away from him. "Run."

"What?"

"I told you to run. I fancy a hunt and a hunt I shall have. If I catch you, I shall have my reward, and if I don't . . ."

Brigid stared at him, uncomprehending.

"If I don't catch you, then you shall be free to starve to death or have your insides ripped out by wolves, whichever comes first."

"Please, my lord."

"Your lord has commanded you to run."

She ran. Twigs and branches stuck out in every direction, and loose stones turned underneath her feet, but this time she neither stumbled nor received a single scratch. The forest seemed to open up to receive her into its murky depths. At first she heard the lord close behind her, his sword slashing through the trees that dared to impede his progress, but the sounds of his pursuit soon faded away, and Brigid allowed herself to slow her pace. And then she heard something else; the glorious sound of running water.

Just as she'd done all those years ago, Brigid followed the sound until she came upon a large stream that rushed through the forest as though it, too, were trying to outrun an enemy. She knelt at the water's edge and wept with relief, but when she lifted the cold clear water to her lips, she gasped. The reflection in the water showed the figure of a man standing behind her. He was taller than any man in the village, the long lines of his body both strong and graceful. He wore his fair hair loose so that it fell to his shoulders like a sheet of golden rain. And his clothes . . . Brigid had never seen their like. His tunic and braies were similar in style to Lord Osin's, but they made the latter's look like rags in comparison. The fabric seemed to be made of spun silver, and instead of buttons, he wore some kind of sparkling jewels down the front and at the sleeves. But strangest of all were his eyes. They glowed like twin embers in freshly fallen snow.

Brigid whirled around to confront the stranger, but the man behind her was not a stranger.

Chapter 8

"Don't be frightened, Brigid. It's really me."

She shook her head. Connell couldn't be there. "You're dead, and maybe I am as well. That's why I saw the vision."

"What vision?"

"The vision in the water. A man. No, not a man, but someone. Someone glorious."

Connell reached for her hand and gently pulled her towards him. "You are not dead, I promise you. Just overwrought from hunger and exhaustion. I am truly alive and well." Connell's face brushed her neck. "Feel my breath on your skin."

She closed her eyes. Connell's breath, soft and reassuring, seemed to restore her senses. Whatever she thought she saw in the water was merely a trick of her fevered imagination. She started to say this but all she managed was his name.

Connell drew her into a tight embrace. "Hush, my love. Now that I have come back all will be well."

My love. Connell had never spoken to her so, but the man who held her was unmistakably Connell, his hair, his face, the coarse material of his tunic. Everything was just the same.

"I can't go back," she said when he finally released her. "They hate me, all of them. Some of the men from the village brought me to the forest to die. They think I'm cursed, that it was I who caused your death."

Connell laughed, a light musical sound she'd never heard before. "You didn't cause my death because here I am.

The villagers will regret their wickedness. You may be sure of that."

"You don't know what it's been like since you've been gone. It's not only the villagers. Lord Osin, he tried to . . ."

"Brigid, do you trust me?"

Brigid looked at the familiar planes of Connell's face. She might have doubted her ability to love him but she always trusted him. "I do."

She leaned against Connell as they made their way through the forest, and when she could walk no longer he lifted her into his arms and carried her as though she were no more than an armful of primroses. The surrounding ash, oak, and hazel were as dense and impenetrable as ever, but Connell did not stumble or hesitate. Finally, the trees began to thin, and when they emerged from the forest Brigid saw they were on the path that led home.

When the roof of her cottage came into view, Connell restored Brigid to her feet and her mother ran outside greet them.

"Brigid! Where have you been? I thought you were . . . and Connell, good Lord, I almost didn't know you." She looked at him, the faded blue of her eyes suddenly bright with wonder. "Come inside the both of you and warm yourselves by the fire. You must tell me how this has come to pass. No, first you must eat, and then you will tell me your story."

Once Connell and Brigid were settled in front of the fire, given cups of hot tea sweetened with honey, and a hunk of bread and cheese each, Brigid began to recount the events of the night before. When she got to the part about the villagers leaving her alone in the forest, her mother turned as white as a snowdrop.

"It was they that left it then. To ease their guilt."

"Left what?" Brigid asked.

"The bread and cheese you're eating, and a fresh comb of honey. When I opened the door this morning there was a basket of food and a jug of milk. I couldn't think who'd done us such a good turn, but now I know the truth of it."

Brigid put down the cheese that seemed to have turned to ashes in her mouth. "They said it would go better for you if I was gone."

Her mother took both of Brigid's hands in her own and kissed them. "From the day you were born, you were my life. There is nothing for me in a world where you are not."

Brigid smiled. "And I am glad to be home with you, but I've not yet come to the worst part of my story." When Brigid finished telling her mother and Connell about Lord Osin, both were silent.

"We must leave Alainn Ros," her mother said finally. She looked around the cottage as though considering how much they would be able to take with them.

"No," Connell said. It was the first time he'd spoken inside the cottage. "You both must stay. Brigid and I will be together just as we planned. I give you my word that neither of you will come to any harm."

Brigid rose from her seat. "Connell, you must see that we cannot. The whole village thinks I'm cursed. They do not want me among them. And even if the villagers did not hate me, there is Lord Osin. You are a well-respected man, but even you must obey the lord."

At Brigid's words, Connell's spine seemed to lengthen. He sat up taller and straighter as though he, too, were a lord instead of a peasant. "Brigid, I swear on both of our lives that all will be well. Will you stay?"

She knew what Connell promised was impossible, and yet when he spoke she believed him completely. Brigid turned to her mother who was looking at Connell with a mixture of fear and hope, and something else that Brigid could not name. "I will."

Connell clapped his hands together like a delighted child. "It is settled then. Now we must plan a celebration."

"A celebration?" Brigid and her mother asked at once.

"Of course. Have we not much to celebrate? Brigid and I have come home unharmed, and soon we will be as one. Tonight we shall have good food, music, and dancing."

"Dancing?" Brigid asked, as though she'd forgotten what word meant.

Connell laughed. "I should like a night of dancing more than anything."

"Connell, what about your mother? You must go home at once and let her know that you're alive and well."

"My mother," Connell said slowly. "Yes, of course you are right. I must go home and tell her our good news, but when I return we shall have our celebration."

Brigid stared at the lines of Connell's face as if they might reveal some other meaning behind his words. How could any of what he said be possible? When he got up to leave, she realized she dreaded his going.

His gaze met hers. "You will wait for me to return?" The way Connell spoke it was not a question.

"Yes." And then catching some of his confidence, she added, "Perhaps I shall try on my new shoes. I was saving them for your return."

Connell put his hands around Brigid's waist, lifted her off her feet, and twirled her around the cottage. "Of course you must wear your new shoes. Nothing would give me greater pleasure than to see you dance in them, and as soon as I can manage it you shall have a new silk gown as well, the same shade of violet as your eyes."

Brigid laughed. "Connell, what would I do with a silk gown? A single day of washing dishes and scrubbing floors would ruin such finery."

Connell returned Brigid to her feet and smiled a slow, languorous smile. "You shall have a new gown and more besides," he said, placing his hands on either side of her face.

"Beauty is a gift that must be celebrated, not hidden away like a shameful secret. From this moment on, I shall devote myself to your beauty."

The unexpectedness of Connell's declaration made the heat rise in her cheeks, but when she opened her mouth to protest Connell silenced her with a kiss. "Goodbye, my love," he said when he finally pulled away.

Brigid watched Connell until he was out of sight, and when she turned around she was surprised to see her mother standing close behind her. She'd only been aware of Connell, the sound of his voice, the feeling of his hands on her body.

"Do you really think Connell can do what he says, Mother?"

"Yes, Brigid love, I do."

Chapter 9

Connell returned the next morning with a new loaf of bread, a slab of goat's cheese, and a pint of fresh milk.

"What did your mother say?" Brigid asked after she thanked him for the food.

A puzzled look came into Connell's eyes. "There were more tears than words, but after that she was pleasant enough."

Brigid laughed. She knew Connell to be a good, hardworking man, but she rarely saw him smile, let alone make a jest. "Tell me true. She must think your return a miracle. The whole village thought you were dead."

"Perhaps, but her joy in seeing me did not prevent her from speaking of all the work that needed doing. If she had her way, I'd be tied to the mill wheel instead of here with you."

"It must have been difficult for her to manage the mill on her own. People need their bread. She wouldn't be allowed a moment to grieve for her own child."

Connell put his hand against her cheek, and Brigid thought how different the gesture seemed from when Lord Osin had done it.

"The time for grieving is past. Now we shall be happy all the time."

Brigid covered Connell's hand with her own. "No one is happy all of the time." But she wanted Connell's words to be true. His promises reminded her of her father's stories. Lovers torn apart by grief and sadness brought together again in a joyous union of prosperity and happiness. But this was not a tale. She and Connell were peasants, and in real life, lords were never defeated by peasants.

Brigid removed Connell's hand from her face. "'Tis foolish for us to speak like this. You risk everything by trying to protect me. The mill, your mother's safety. Lord Osin is not a man to be merciful. He will never let us be.

"We shall see about that."

Brigid drew back from Connell, startled. In the dim light of the cottage, his eyes glowed like two stars in an onyx sky.

"Connell," she said, but the effect was gone. His eyes returned to their ordinary grey. "What will you do?"

"At present, nothing. We shall bide our time. Lord Osin's Falconer told me the lord is away from the manor on the king's business, and is unlikely to return until mid-summer. He has already given us permission to marry. By the time he returns it shall be done."

"And after that? Surely you do not think that will be the end of it."

Connell shrugged. "Trust me, Brigid. All will be well. I do not fear Lord Osin and nor should you. He is, after all, just a man."

Once again, Brigid wondered at the change in Connell. He spoke as though he, too, were not just a man, and a much lesser one than Lord Osin. "A man who could ruin you if he chose. Surely you would not risk . . ."

Connell pressed his fingers against her lips. "Lord Osin is gone and we are here together. Right now that is all I desire to think on."

Connell's nearness overwhelmed her. The scent of his skin, a combination of honey and wildflowers, made her think of long summer days under a deep blue sky. Not even the memory of Lord Osin telling her to 'run' could dim the bright feeling of pleasure she felt when Connell drew her close. She closed her eyes and let Connell's assurances seep into her skin. Of course it would be alright now that they were together. Together. The word sounded as shiny and promising as a new coin.

"Let us go into the village," Connell said abruptly.

"Now?"

Connell lifted her head from his shoulder and cupped it in both of his hands. "What should prevent us? I am the miller and you are my betrothed. No one who likes his bread shall dare to speak a word against you."

"I cannot. You weren't there when the villagers came for me. You didn't see their faces. They hate me," Brigid finished quietly.

"Why do they hate you? Because you saw the Faerie Queen and kept your wits to tell of it? That is a blessing and not a curse as any fool should know."

Brigid looked at Connell's face, struck by how anger transformed his features, giving him the appearance of a stranger. Every moment she spent with Connell made her realize how different he was from the man she imagined him to be.

Connell offered Brigid his arm. "Let us go. I shall buy you the biggest, stickiest current bun in Bain O'Donnell's Bakery.

Brigid took hold of Connell's arm and wished to never let it go.

Brigid entered the village, every muscle in her body straining with the effort to keep her spine and shoulders erect. Connell walked close beside her, but she let go of his hand so he would not feel her trembling. She didn't want him to know how the villagers' actions had wounded her.

Brigid had spent her whole life in Alainn Ros, and still she was struck by its sameness. After all that happened to her in the forest she hoped to see some mark of it in the village, some sign of the villagers' unease or regret, but she was disappointed. The cluster of squat, timber-framed cottages in various stages of disrepair, the tiny windows covered with oiled animal skins to keep out the flies, the modest, but well-kept gardens in front of the cottages brimming with spring herbs. Everything was just the same. Brigid eyed the ox-eye, meadowsweet, and honeysuckle that sprung up on either side of the road with something close to resentment.

Tanner was the first person to see them. He dropped the bundle of animal skins he carried, and stared at Connell with a mixture of surprise and confusion, but when he saw Brigid he took a step backwards and crossed himself, his hands stained yellow by the ointment he used to cure the animal skins. "It cannot be," he said, his voice trembling.

Connell released Brigid's arm and started towards Tanner who cowered against the mud-encrusted wall of his cottage. "She is not a ghost come back to haunt you, but a live woman to whom you shall beg forgiveness."

"I-I m-meant no harm," Tanner stammered. "I-I only wanted what was best for the village. We feared for the harvest."

"Please, Connell," Brigid said. "Let us go."

"Hear me, Niall O'Leary, for I shall not warn you again. If you harm this woman in any way, if you so much as look at her with shadows in your eyes neither you nor your four children will be able to afford so much as a handful of flour from my mill. Do you understand me?"

Tanner raised himself up and nodded in Brigid's direction, careful not to meet her eyes. "She has nothing to fear from me, I swear it."

Connell turned towards Brigid. "Now you shall have the sweet I promised you."

News of Connell and Brigid's miraculous return from the forest spread quickly. When they arrived at Baker's door, they were treated with careful politeness by Baker's wife, whose hands trembled in their eagerness to serve them.

"I've a lovely almond tart fresh from the oven," she said. "Or perhaps you'd enjoy a bit of my spice cake?"

Brigid shook her head, accepting only a small currant bun at Connell's insistence.

On their way out of the bakeshop, Connell was greeted by Ahern Bain, the Blacksmith, who gave Brigid a little bow before asking after Connell's mother.

"She's well enough," Connell said. "Her hands are overfull making plans for our wedding."

Ahern nodded his head so violently Brigid feared it might come off his neck. "And a fine wedding it will be. Please accept my best wishes on your betrothal."

"Thank you, Ahern."

The way Connell spoke to both Tanner and Blacksmith bore a startling resemblance to the way Lord Osin spoke to his servants. And yet there was something unmistakably different in Connell's manner. Nothing in his voice sounded false. He walked beside her with an easy, long-limbed grace that made him appear almost elegant in his plain wool tunic and linen braies. Despite his peasant birth, Connell suddenly struck Brigid as seeming nobler than Lord Osin himself. She shook her head to dispel the wrongful comparison. It was treacherous to have such thoughts.

Brigid watched Connell's face as they walked through the village. He looked carefully at every cottage, as though seeing the crooked shutters and dirty bundles of straw tied to the roofs for the first time. Although he spoke with passion to Tanner, who'd been one of her attackers, he regarded the other villagers who crossed their path with what she could only describe as amusement. Brigid, however, felt sick. She took a bite of the currant bun so as not to seem ungrateful, but its sweetness turned sour on her tongue.

In spite of everything, she still hoped the villagers would see their mistake, that she was not cursed or wicked, just a peasant, the same as they. But now she understood that would never happen. As Connell's wife she might command their respect, but underneath that veil of regard was the same fear and dislike she'd known most of her life.

"I'm very tired," she said to Connell after they'd taken a turn around the village square. "I think I must go home and rest a while."

Connell, whose arm she still held, drew her closer. "I shall take you home at once."

When they returned to the cottage, Brigid's mother was waiting at the door, her hands clasped tightly in front of her. "How was it? Did they turn you away?"

"Not a bit of it," Connell said. "Brigid is the finest woman in the village and from now on they will treat her as such."

Brigid forced a smile. "There is nothing for us to fear. It is just as Connell said."

Her mother gave a little sigh of relief, but Brigid saw that her eyes were still troubled and her skin was pale.

Brigid reached for her mother's hand. "Have you eaten?"

"Yes, love. I've had a fine supper of Connell's good bread and cheese. Now come inside and sit down. I fear you are not fully recovered from your night in the woods."

Brigid nodded. She longed to lie down and close her eyes.

Connell followed Brigid inside. "What about our celebration? I promised you dancing. You were going to wear your new shoes, and I've found a fine bolt of silk," he added, frowning at her grey, wool gown.

"Tomorrow is a new day," Brigid's mother said quietly. "If she rests now, she will soon be restored."

A dazzling smile lit Connell's face like a candle. "You are right, of course. What is one day when we have so many ahead of us?"

Brigid's eyes were already half closed when Connell's lips brushed her cheek, his touch as light as butterfly wings.

Despite her exhaustion, Brigid awoke several times during the night. Someone was calling her name. The voice seemed to come from a great distance, but even so she felt its urgency. Finally, when she could bear it no longer she rose from her pallet and ran to the cottage door, but just as she was about to fling it open her mother grabbed her hand.

"Brigid, stop! You're dreaming. Come back to bed."

"I'm not dreaming. Someone is calling for me. They will not rest until I answer."

"Hush, Brigid. No one calls for you. It is just the two of us here alone, together. Come back to bed and rest a little longer. Morning will come soon enough."

Brigid allowed herself to be led back to bed, but she lay awake until she heard her mother get up to light the fire. The sound of her mother's gentle movements, comforting and familiar, lulled her back to sleep, and when she awoke again the sun was streaming through the cottage windows.

Brigid jumped out of bed. "I've slept too long," she said to her mother, who was stirring their morning porridge over the fire. "Why didn't you wake me?"

"You tossed and turned the whole night through. I thought it best to leave you be."

Brigid reached for her kirtle. "I've been too long away from the manor. Lady Osin will be wondering what happened to me."

"Not on the Sabbath day she won't."

"Oh," Brigid said. "I've lost track of the days. After my night in the wood, everything seems so . . . changed."

Her mother looked at her sharply. "We must go to church."

"No. I don't think I can bear it."

"But you said all was well?

"As well as it can be."

"Then we must go to church. Connell's mother will be there giving thanks for her son's safe return, and so must you."

Too tired to argue, Brigid agreed, but when it was time to leave, her mother complained of a pain in her chest.

Brigid placed the palm of her hand on her mother's heart as though to draw the pain into herself. "You must rest easy until it passes. I shall stay with you."

"No," her mother said firmly. "Go to Connell and tell him you wish to accompany him and his mother to church. I will rest here until you return."

"I cannot leave you."

Her mother pushed her gently away. "You must. Connell is your protection now. Let the village and Father Diarmaid see you well and happy together. Once you are married, no one will dare to harm you for fear of offending the miller."

"I shall come home straight away."

"And I shall be waiting," her mother promised.

Brigid took her time walking to the mill. It was one of the first truly warm days of spring, and she stopped often to admire the cluster of milkwort, forget-me-nots, and foxglove that seemed to have sprung up overnight, transforming the ground with bursts of pink, blue, and yellow. Despite her promise, she was not eager to see Connell's mother, whom she doubted would greet her warmly. But when the stone walls of Connell's cottage came into view, she felt a slight lift in her chest at the thought of living there.

Four times the size of Brigid's cottage with a timber roof instead of thatch and windows with real glass, it was the finest building in the village, save for the church and the manor. The front garden was tidy and well kept, giving the cottage a cheerful, prosperous air.

Brigid stared at the door of the cottage wishing she'd thought to pick some wildflowers for Connell's mother. Maeve Mackenna would surely frown on a future daughter-in-law who came empty-handed on her first visit.

No help for it now, Brigid thought. She lifted her hand to knock on the door when strong arms grasped her from behind.

"I've been waiting for you," Connell whispered in her ear. "I thought you'd never come."

She laughed. "How did you know I was coming?"

"Because you couldn't stay away for long. I wouldn't let you. And now we will go."

"Go? But I've come to accompany you and your mother to church."

Connell raised his face towards the sun. "It is far too beautiful a morning to spend indoors. Besides, I don't think Father Diarmaid will miss us, do you?"

"But your mother . . . I doubt she's missed a service in all her life."

Connell grinned, the unfamiliar expression seeming to alter the contours of his face. "And she need not miss this one. I have other plans for us."

Brigid looked in the direction of Connell's cottage. If Maeve truly didn't mind . . . Surely her own mother wouldn't want her to deny Connell a morning's freedom after all he'd been through. "Where are we going?"

"To the forest for a picnic."

"But we haven't any food."

"I have it right here in this basket."

Brigid looked at Connell's hand, which was indeed carrying a large basket covered with cheesecloth.

"I'll race you," she said.

Every day she spent with Connell brought some fresh surprise. A clutch of blue flowers with silver veins she'd never seen before, a gold broach inlaid with tiny glowing pearls, a silk chemise that was greener than the darkest leaf in the forest, and a veil of such snowy whiteness it might have been made of dove feathers. When she asked him where he found such treasures, he replied she was meant to have them. Brigid received his gifts with pleasure, but when she took them away with her she felt uneasy. Except for the flowers, which she placed on the kitchen table in a clay pitcher, she wrapped up the rest in an old strip of linen and buried them beside the sacred well.

Alone with Connell, all of her worries slipped away. They stayed outdoors from morning until twilight, one luxuriant hour melting into the next. In the morning, they went on long rambles in the forest, chasing one another through the trees like children, and in the afternoon they slept in the shade of some great tree, her head resting on Connell's lap.

The night of the Easter feast Connell told her he didn't believe in Faerie superstitions, but it seemed their love had cast a spell over him. Once a slave to the mill wheel's constant turning, he now seemed content to spend his days lying in the shade, tracing the shapes of the clouds overhead with outstretched fingers. At first, Brigid thought to protest their carefree existence. Should Connell not go to the mill and she return to the manor to see if she was needed? But every time she spoke Connell would silence her with a kiss, or the promise of some new pleasure, until one day Brigid stopped protesting. She even stopped worrying about Lord Osin's return for it seemed impossible that even he could disrupt the mesmerizing routine of their days together. Eventually, the mill, the manor, and everything in the village seemed to drift away like a leaf on the wind.

It was on one of these lazy afternoons that Brigid saw Eanna again.

After a leisurely meal of fresh milk, honey, and feather-light teacakes, Connell and Brigid curled up at the base of an ancient oak tree whose deep hollow might have been carved to fit the shape of their bodies. Brigid's eyes grew heavy, and the sweet summon of sleep began to steal over her body when a shadow fell across her vision.

Eanna was standing over them, her faded blue eyes wild and confused.

Brigid sat up. "Eanna, what are you doing here?"

Connell pushed Brigid off his lap and leaped to his feet. "Get away from us! You are not welcome here."

"Connell, it's only Eanna. She means us no harm." Brigid turned to the older woman who was twisting her long, wispy hair around her fingers. "Eanna, why are you so far from home? Has something happened?"

Ignoring Brigid, Eanna took several tentative steps towards Connell. "Are you truly real?" she whispered hoarsely. "I have dreamed of you so often." She put out one skeletal hand as if to touch him. "Am I dreaming now?"

Connell backed up against the tree. "Don't touch me!"

Brigid felt herself recoil from the naked disgust in Connell's voice while tears flooded Eanna's eyes and spilled down her cheeks.

"Connell, there is nothing to fear. Eanna is only . . . confused." Brigid touched Eanna gently on the arm and was struck by the slightness of the other woman's body. A strong wind would be enough to snap the delicate wrist that protruded from the sleeve of her ragged gown.

"Please do not cry. You have only surprised us."

"I don't understand," Eanna said, her face still streaming with tears. "Why didn't you come back? I waited for so long . . ."

Connell seized Brigid's hand. "We must go. This woman is mad."

Eanna shook her head violently from side to side, and then began to sing in a surprisingly strong, clear voice:

> *Come away, maiden fair, to a place so lovely and green,*
> *Come away, maiden fair, stay a night and a day and forever live a dream.*

The song's sad, wistful beauty made Brigid want to weep but Connell remained unmoved.

"Let us go, now," he said to Brigid.

"Does my song not please you? You once told me that the sound of my voice was the only thing you desired. Shall I sing you another? I remember all that you taught me."

Connell turned away, fixing his gaze on the tops of the trees, and when he spoke, his voice was calm. "I'm sorry you are unwell, Eanna. I hope that our next meeting will be a better one." And then without a backward glance to either of them he strode off into the trees.

Eanna stumbled after him, but after only a few steps she was overcome with weakness, and Brigid had to support her with both arms to keep her from falling down.

"Please, Connell's right. You're not yourself. Let me take you home so you can rest."

"You have taken him from me," Eanna said, sounding even younger than Brigid.

"No," Brigid said gently. "You are mistaken. Connell is still your friend. He brings you food. Don't you remember?"

Eanna shook her head. "I've not tasted a crust of bread or a morsel of cheese for several fortnights."

Brigid felt a hot rush of shame thinking of the meal she and Connell had just eaten. Whatever else ailed Eanna, it was hunger that made her weak and delirious. How could Connell have forgotten her?

"I shall see that you have bread and cheese and salted meat to take home with you," Brigid promised. "Wait here while I fetch my shawl."

Brigid left her side for only a few moments, but when she turned around Eanna was gone.

Abandoned by both Connell and Eanna, Brigid felt lost and uncertain. Why had Connell behaved so strangely? It was he who had introduced her to Eanna. His kindness to the Willow Women was something she would never forget. So why did Eanna's appearance, unexpected as it was, disturb him so? The image of Connell's soft, generous mouth twisted in disgust would not leave her. Until now, Brigid wouldn't have thought it possible that he could look at anyone that way.

Brigid returned to her resting place in the tree's hollow and pulled her knees into her chest. Had Connell returned to the mill? It was the first time he'd parted from her willingly. All at once the day lost its brightness and Brigid shivered a little in the shade of the tree. She sat there for a long time until, finally, her eyes began to close a second time.

"Miss me?"

Soft hands covered Brigid's face so she couldn't see. When she removed them, Connell was kneeling beside her holding a delicate crown of yellow blossoms.

"For my Queen," he said. "The Queen of the Forest."

"You mustn't say such things. The Fair Folk . . ."

Connell threw his head back and laughed. "Do not fear, my love. I shall give the sacred well a special gift to make up for any offense my tribute to your beauty may have caused."

Brigid touched one of the blossoms on top of her head. "Where have you been?"

"You did miss me."

"Connell, I must speak to you about Eanna. How could you be so . . . ?" She was about to say cruel, but for a moment the sight of Connell's open, generous face made her wonder if she'd imagined the encounter with Eanna.

Connell pulled Brigid gently to her feet. "Forgive me, my love. I didn't mean to speak so harshly. She caught me unawares, and if I overreacted it was only out of concern for your safety. Eanna may seem a pathetic creature, but that doesn't mean she's not dangerous."

Brigid shook her head, remembering the frailness of the other woman's body. "Connell I've nothing to fear from Eanna. I'm sure of it."

Connell kissed her fingers. "I will make amends with Eanna, but first you must promise to stay away from her and the rest of the Willow Women."

"But why?"

Connell's face darkened. "Do you trust me, Brigid?"

"Of course," she said, afraid of saying anything to make him go away again. "I promise not to seek Eanna out if that is your wish."

Connell pulled her close against him. "Dance with me."

"But there's no music."

"You are right. We must have music. Meet me at the edge of the forest after your mother is asleep. I have a surprise for you."

"I don't know," Brigid said, even though she knew she would. She could not bear the thought of him being anywhere without her.

Chapter 10

Brigid sat at the kitchen table wishing the sun would speed its descent in the sky streaked with burnt shades of orange and pink. Nearly wild with her desire for darkness, she could only sip at her mother's pottage, now thick with vegetables from their garden. Seemingly overnight, the soil had turned dark and rich, and leeks, carrots, and turnips sprang up where before there were only weeds.

Brigid felt her mother's eyes on her while she ate. Although glad at first of Connell's nearly constant presence, her mother had since grown uneasy, and Brigid could not think how to reassure her. Instead, she sat silent and still, her hands clasped on her lap until her mother finally settled into her pallet and blew out the candle. Brigid waited until she heard her mother's soft, even breathing before opening the door to the cottage as silent as a shadow. She ran down the path to the forest, her silver hair flying out behind her. She no longer wore it covered, letting it fall freely so that the ends nearly swept the ground.

Connell was waiting for her when she arrived. He took her hand without speaking and led her into the forest. Once they were safely inside the trees' protection, Connell removed something from the heavy cloth sack he wore around his waist tied with a silken cord. It was a harp, the most beautiful instrument Brigid had ever seen. The tuning pegs looked to be made of gold and the strings of pure silver. When Connell touched them with his fingers, the music made her want to weep and sleep and laugh, all at the same time. She reached out to touch it, but Connell snatched her hand away.

"Forgive me, my love, but I cannot let you have it. As pretty as it is, it would burn your delicate fingers."

"Why should it burn me and not you?" She thought it would be worth the risk to run her hands along the deep U of the harp's neck.

"'Tis no ordinary harp. It will only endure the touch of its owner."

"How did you come to have it?"

Connell brushed his fingers gently across the strings. "It was given to me as a gift."

"By whom?" Brigid asked, bewildered. There was no one in the village save for the lord himself who could afford such an instrument.

Connell leaned towards her. "'Tis a secret."

"If I am to be your wife, there must be no secrets between us."

Connell seized Brigid's hands and pulled her towards him. "I am not myself," he whispered in her ear.

Brigid drew away, startled by the wildness in his eyes. "What do you mean?"

"I know you feel it. I see it in your eyes when you look at me."

Brigid nodded, scarcely daring to breathe for fear of interrupting Connell's unexpected flow of words.

"Forgive me, Brigid. I should have confessed all to you before, but I could not."

"Tell me. I think I can forgive you anything, but I must know the truth."

"If I tell you where I got the harp, you must promise not to tell anyone, not even your mother."

"You know my mother would never betray a secret."

"Promise me, Brigid," Connell said, his voice low and serious. "I will tell you the story of how this harp came into my possession, but first you must swear on your mother's life not to speak of it to anyone."

Never in her life had Brigid kept a secret from her mother, but Connell was her betrothed, and she couldn't refuse him. "I swear."

"The truth is that the harp is stolen."

Brigid gave a sharp intake of breath. Before tonight she wouldn't have believed that the serious, hardworking man she'd known since he was a child could take so much as a pea that did not belong to him.

"I didn't mean to take it," he said, "but it was so beautiful. I couldn't let it go."

Finally, Connell told her what happened after he left Alain Ros. He was making good progress through the wood when he heard the most beautiful music. The light had begun to fade, but he followed the sound deeper and deeper into the forest until he was hopelessly lost. The path disappeared and an impenetrable wall of trees surrounded him in every direction. But what happened next was stranger still. The ground gave way beneath his feet, and after falling what seemed a great distance he found himself alone in a dimly lit corridor outside the entrance to a great hall. When he finally gathered the courage to peer inside, he realized he'd stumbled across what seemed to be some kind of Faerie ball. Fey men and women danced across a marble floor in glittering garments of white and yellow gold, but what caught and held his attention was the musician standing on a raised dais at the back of the hall. He appeared older than the dancers and his tunic was plain and unadorned. Connell caressed the harp on his lap. "This belonged to him."

"I watched the musician from his hiding place, my eyes never leaving the instrument," he told her. "The strings seemed to breathe with a life of their own playing songs of such unimaginable beauty. Its long, white neck seemed to cry out for my touch. I longed to feel the weight of it in my hands, to caress its fine curves with my fingertips. I knew that if I were the harp's owner everything I'd ever longed for would be mine." Connell stopped speaking and looked at Brigid.

"And what is that?" Brigid asked gently.

"You. I knew that if I brought you the harp's music, you would love me."

"But I'd already accepted your proposal."

"Marriage does not always equal love."

"Connell . . ."

Connell placed his fingers gently against her lips. "It doesn't matter now because everything's changed."

Connell told her how he waited until the musician followed the dancers to the banquet tables before creeping towards the dais and stuffing the harp under his tunic. Bursting with triumph, he thought to escape with his new possession until a woman's voice called out, "Stop, thief!"

Brigid leaned in closer as Connell described the woman. "Tall and slender like a Willow," he said, his eyes half closed, "with eyes that flamed like leaves on a bonfire. I knew I should run but I could not. The terrible beauty of her face held me fast."

"The Faerie Queen," Brigid said.

Connell nodded. "When she spoke again, her voice was cold and empty like the winter sky. 'How dare you take what does not belong to you?'"

Connell begged for her forgiveness, but the Faerie Queen waved away his apology like a troublesome gnat. "You have stolen from me. If I choose, I might keep you here forever as my prisoner, or kill you where you stand." The Queen fell silent, and for a moment Connell thought he would not leave the ball alive, but then she said, "You are fortunate, Connell Mackenna, because I have decided to give you a chance to do me a small service. Do you agree?"

"Of course," Connell said quickly. "I shall do whatever you wish."

"On All Hallows' Eve you will return to the forest and bear witness to a ceremony. When it is over you shall return to your village with no memory of what took place."

"All Hallows' Eve!" Brigid interrupted. "It would be madness to return to Faerie on that night. Surely, you didn't agree to . . ."

"I gave my word," Connell said, as if that explained everything.

"But you can't! Everyone knows that All Hallows' Eve belongs to the Fair Folk. They are more powerful at that time than any other. The Faerie Queen will never allow you to return to Alain Ros."

"She promised me that I shall return from the ceremony unharmed."

Brigid scrambled to her feet. "No, Connell. I won't let you go. Have you forgotten my father's tales? The Faerie Queen's word means nothing!"

Connell stood up, the strength of his resolve emanating from every muscle in his body. "Do not speak to me of tales, Brigid. I stole from the Faerie Queen, and I must make amends for that mistake. I will return to Faerie on All Hallows' Eve, and then I shall return to you." Connell pressed his hand against his chest. "I swear it."

"If I cannot stop you from going, then you must take me with you."

Connell shook his head. "I will not have you risk your life for my sake."

"I shall go with you whether you like it or not, Connell Mackenna. You left me once already, and I won't have you do it again. I met the Faerie Queen once and returned unharmed. I shall do so again."

A hint of a smile disturbed the stubborn set of Connell's features and Brigid knew she'd won. "That's settled then."

She sat down again, tucking her skirts around her legs. Despite her mother's countless warnings not to speak of the Fair Folk, she couldn't stop herself from asking, "What was Faerie like? Cold and dark like my father's tales? Did you feel the weight of the earth pressing down on you?"

Connell's expression turned fierce. "No! It was nothing like that. I've never seen such beauty. Everything shimmered as if it had been dipped in sunlight. The dancing couples, the trees overhead, the grass underneath my feet. Even the air was different, sweet and perfumed, untouched by the slightest scent of foulness. There was no ugliness, no sign of age or decay, as if these things had been banished forever."

Brigid looked at Connell, his eyes shining with the memory. She'd known him all her life and never thought his appearance remarkable in any way. But now she wondered how she could have overlooked the beauty of his face. Her father often spoke of the transformative power of love. He compared it to a potter's wheel, the way it could shape something grey and ordinary into a thing of unmistakable beauty. When first she heard her father describe someone so transformed, she thought it some kind of magic trick, but now she knew it was real. Connell's familiar face contained every wish that had ever touched her lips. She could hardly bring herself to look away. "You make it sound like paradise," she murmured.

Connell traced the curve of her cheek with his finger. "All will be well, I promise you."

A sudden thought occurred to her. "All Hallows' Eve. How will we find the way back?"

"The harp. The Faerie Queen taught me a special ballad. When it is time, the music will take us there."

Brigid shivered. Despite her bold words, she couldn't help but think of Morded's wife, Orla Cooley's baby, and all the other missing women and children. Did the Faerie Queen make them promises as well?

"You are troubled," Connell said, reading her thoughts.

"No," she said, trying to smile.

Connell picked up the harp. "Let me play something for you."

Brigid watched Connell's hands. She never noticed how finely made they were. His fingers were long, the fingernails smooth and pink, and his palms seemed almost opalescent in the moonlight. A sudden vision of strong weather-beaten hands, the knuckles red and raw, lifting her out of the sheep dung flashed in front of her. Connell's fingers quickened, the lilting notes rearranging themselves into a new and puzzling rhythm, and the memory disappeared.

The music wrapped itself around Brigid like a fur-lined mantle. How beautiful it was. If only she could touch it, even for a moment. She opened her mouth to speak, but then closed it again. She didn't want the sound of her voice to interrupt the music. After a while, her eyes began to close, but she pinched herself awake again. The harp seemed to be telling her a story, a story about true love and loss and betrayal, and she feared falling asleep in case she missed the ending.

Finally the music stopped. Connell's fingers hovered over the strings, and Brigid pressed his fingers, urging him to continue.

Connell shook his head. "That is enough for tonight. You do not know it yet, but you are nearly too weary to walk home."

"But we have only been here a short while," Brigid protested.

"No," he said. "Look up."

Brigid obeyed, and sure enough the darkness had begun to lift; the first rosy glow of daylight glimmered above the trees.

Brigid scrambled to her feet and brushed the dirt from her gown. "I must get back before Mother finds me gone."

Connell watched her, a lazy smile pulling at the corners of his mouth.

"Hurry," she said. "We must be careful. Your mother . . ."

Connell yawned, stretching out his arms and legs, before resting his head in his hands.

"Make haste if you must. I will stay a little longer."

Brigid ran as fast as she could through the forest and up the hill to her cottage, praying that her mother had not awoken and discovered her absence.

Chapter 11

Her mother was still asleep when she crept inside the cottage. She collapsed in her own bed, her arms and legs feeling as though they, too, were made of straw. In the forest with Connell it seemed impossible that she'd been gone more than a couple of hours, but now she felt as though she'd been awake for days. She closed her eyes, but the sound of her mother moving restlessly beside her made sleep impossible.

"'Tis cold," her mother murmured, caught between sleep and wakefulness.

Brigid got out of bed. "Try to sleep. I will light the fire. It will soon be warm."

Brigid waited until her mother closed her eyes before moving to the hearth. They had only a few pieces of kindling left. Connell promised to fetch more, but he must have forgotten. Since his return, they spent so much time running through the woods, laughing, dancing, listening to music it was a wonder any grain was ground at all. Strange to think that only a short time ago she thought Connell indifferent to pleasure. His life in the village seemed a rough tapestry woven of only two threads: work and service. Now, the mill and the happenings in the village seemed like half-formed clouds that occasionally drifted into the blue sky of their days together.

Although she'd just left him, Brigid felt a deep, steady ache spread through her limbs. It was always so when they were apart. The pain would grow through the morning, and by mid-day it was unbearable. She would go to him, careless of the chores she left unfinished. She'd not thought it possible to feel this way. Not even the divided lovers in her father's tales seemed to know such suffering.

Brigid gently stoked the fire until the feeble flames grew strong and bright. For the first time in days, she thought of Lord Osin. It was nearly mid-summer and still he'd not returned. Connell's promise to the Faerie Queen would come to nothing if Lord Osin sought his revenge first. How much longer did she and Connell have? They'd made no plans for the wedding, but it was only when she was away from Connell that such thoughts troubled her. When they were together, it seemed their morning rambles in the forest and lazy sunlit afternoons would go on forever. And now the music . . . she would rather die than have the music stop.

"Brigid, come here beside me."

Brigid turned around. Her mother was fully awake and looking at her strangely. "How thin you are," she said. "As slender as a daisy stalk and we have been eating so well. Your cheeks have lost their bloom. How can you be so pale when you spend all of your days in the sun?"

Brigid raised her hand to her cheek as though to feel the pallor of her skin. "I do not know. It is not for want of exercise. Yesterday, Connell and I walked for hours."

Brigid's mother sat up straighter in her pallet. "Is that how Connell spends his days now? Tramping through the woods? Who takes care of the mill? The village's grain does not grind itself."

Brigid turned her gaze back to fire. "I do not know. He doesn't speak of it."

"Why do you not ask him? Are you not his betrothed? Why has he not wed you yet? The summer has already begun to wane and still you are unmarried!"

Her mother slumped backwards, leaning on too thin arms for support, and Brigid realized how much the speech had cost her.

"We mean to be married, I promise you. Connell has said many times that we shall be together always."

Brigid's mother seized her hand. "Surely you must see it."

Brigid tried to pull away, but her mother held her fast. "What do you mean?"

"Connell says! What does his word mean? He's not been the same since he returned from the forest. I've watched the two of you together. Something happened to him, Brigid. I hoped that I was mistaken, that his behaviour was only that of a man in love, but now . . . You must tell me the truth. After Connell disappeared, did he cross paths with the Fair Folk?"

Brigid turned away, afraid her eyes would betray her. "Connell is a good man, Mother. There is nothing to worry about, I promise."

"Brigid, speak truly," her mother persisted. "You've known Connell since he was a boy. Is he not greatly changed these last weeks?"

"Yes, he is different," Brigid said slowly. "But so am I. Love changes everyone it touches. How many times did Father tell me that?"

Her mother released her hand. "Listen to me, Brigid. Life is not a tale. No Faerie magic is strong enough to create the happy ending you desire. That you must do for yourself. You and Connell must marry before Lord Osin returns. A husband is a woman's only protection. Tell Connell to speak to Father Diarmaid right away. Give me your word that you will do as I ask."

"I give you my word."

But when Brigid met Connell on the edge of the forest the following evening, she forgot her promise. Connell had news of his own.

"Lord Osin has returned. I am summoned to manor court."

"When?" Brigid asked.

"Tomorrow."

"What shall we do?"

"Do? We shall enjoy our evening together just as we planned. I have thought of nothing all day but the pleasure of watching you dance. There is a song I wish to play for you."

"Connell, are you not afraid of what Lord Osin might do? He has the power to take away everything you've worked so hard for. Your land, the mill, your mother's security. It's a hard thing to be poor and friendless. I do not want that for either of us."

Connell laid his slender fingers at the base of her throat, and then removed them. Brigid stood motionless while he gently put his lips on the same spot. "Brigid, my love," he whispered softly. "Still you do not trust me. Did I not tell you not to be afraid?"

"Yes, but . . ."

"Perhaps you will believe me if I tell you another way."

Connell removed the harp from his sack and walked slowly away from her, leaving a trail of fluttering red, orange, and yellow leaves. When he disappeared inside the trees, Brigid followed him until they reached a small clearing inside a circle of young hawthornes. Connell stopped, and sunk gracefully into a soft pile of heather. Brigid sat down beside him, closed her eyes, and waited.

Connell began to play, and the pleasure Brigid felt was so exquisite her body seemed no longer her own. She had not thought it possible that any music could be as beautiful as what she heard the night before, but she was mistaken. The new song filled every corner of her mind and seeped into her veins. Her feet trembled beneath her long skirts until she could sit still no longer. She leaped to her feet and began to move, slowly at first, and then more quickly as the music lengthened and swelled, taking her with it. And then Connell was beside her, his long, graceful movements intersecting with hers. She felt his hands brush against her shoulders and run down the length of her arms. Brigid leaned into him until their shoulders were touching. He drew her to him so gently it was not like being pulled at all, but rather like falling into a warm spring. Connell's lips pressed against the delicate hollow of her throat and still the music played on.

Brigid opened her eyes, and the forest swirled around her. How did the music play when Connell's hands were in her hair, unwinding her plait? Was this part of the harp's magic? She opened her mouth to speak but instead of words she found Connell's lips. She had not known such a sensation existed. It was even better than dancing.

When Connell finally drew away, she pulled him back to her. She wanted to learn the steps to the new dance he'd begun to show her. He kissed her again and again, and once more she felt as though she were falling, but this time the forest floor rushed up to catch her in its earthy embrace and claimed her for its own.

Afterwards, she trembled a little, not from regret or shame, but surprise. She had not thought it possible to feel so transformed, and yet outwardly she was unchanged, aside from the leaves in her hair, and a tiny tear in her kirtle where it had gotten snagged on a rock.

She tried to tell Connell something of what she felt, but he only smiled.

"You are changed," he said. "You are mine now."

Brigid returned her lover's embrace, but his words sent a shiver of unease down her spine. What did it mean to belong to someone else? She did not know how to belong to anyone but herself.

"You are also changed," she said, echoing her mother's words. "Before these last few weeks, I would not have believed it possible for one to become so changed."

"If I am different, it is because of you," Connell said, tracing the outline of her collarbone with his fingertips. "You have made me a better man."

Brigid closed her eyes, savouring his words. Her father was right. Love did change everything, but nor could she forget her mother's warning. "Promise me, Connell, no more secrets."

Connell smiled and drew her close. "You have my word."

Brigid pressed her face against his chest, comforted by the steady beat of his heart. She believed him. Of course she did. Hadn't everything turned out just as he said it would?

"I shall go with you tomorrow," she said before they parted.

Connell grasped both of her hands and pressed them against his lips. "I will show you we have nothing to fear from Lord Osin, or any man."

She kissed him goodbye once more and allowed herself to be lulled by the reassurances he whispered in her hear. Connell misspoke when he told her he'd no talent for pretty words for he spoke many to her that night. Such sweet words she would not have hoped to hear if she were a lady in a tale. Words so beautiful they seemed to be made of music themselves, and yet . . . Connell still had not spoken of their wedding.

Chapter 12

"Why must you go with him?" her mother asked when Brigid told her she intended to accompany Connell to manor court.

"Because I must know what Lord Osin says against me. I'm not at fault for what happened in the wood, and I will tell the truth even if no one believes it."

"The truth will not matter! Brigid, please, you mustn't. Connell is your betrothed. Let him try to make it right."

"You said it yourself. My place is with Connell. I will not have him face Lord Osin alone."

Despite what Brigid told her mother, all her doubts returned when she met Connell on the village outskirts. What would Lord Osin care for their petty plans? Connell might be the most prosperous and well-respected man in the village, but he was still a peasant. Lord Osin had tried to murder her. He would not spare her now to appease Connell.

If Connell shared her fears, he did not show it. He took her arm in his as though escorting a lady to a feast and whistled a tune that made Brigid think of warmth and sunlight even though the sky was thick with clouds, and the air held the promise of rain.

"What is that song?" she asked. "I've never heard it before."

Connell shrugged. "My mother sang it to me when I was a child."

Brigid found it difficult to imagine Maeve's thin,

pursed lips opened in song, but perhaps she was not always so stern. Her own mother certainly used to smile more when her father was alive.

When the manor walls came into view, Brigid seized Connell's arm. "Perhaps there is another way. We could wait until he's gone. I will beg Lady Osin to take pity on us. She has always been kind to me and . . ."

Connell removed Brigid's hand. "No. Lord Osin has much to answer for and I shall see that he does. You may wait for me here if you wish."

Brigid shook her head. "I go where you go."

The porter opened the gate for them, and Brigid thought he cast her a pitying glance.

It will not go well for us, she thought. They were foolish to think otherwise. Lord Osin would never let her go, and he would ruin Connell for daring to challenge him.

Lord Osin's steward led them into the great hall without a word. His face showed an odd blankness, as though he'd never had a feeling strong enough to etch itself on his features. He has worked for Lord Osin too long, Brigid thought.

"Wait here," Steward said, and left them.

Something was wrong. In all her days at the manor, the great hall had never been so empty and quiet. Where were the other villagers who sought to bring their grievances before the lord? And why were there no pages scurrying back and forth with messages for the household?

Brigid turned around in a slow circle. Not a single servant lingered in any of the doorways. They were entirely alone.

Brigid shivered and reached for Connell's hand. "I'm afraid," she whispered.

Connell squeezed her fingers and smiled. "Do not fear. What happens next will go easier than you think."

Surely she misheard the eagerness in Connell's voice?

He sounded like a young boy waiting for some promised treat.

Brigid stared at the heavy wooden door that led to the upstairs chambers. Was he up there now? Would Lady Osin say anything on her behalf?

The door flew open and Lord Osin entered the room. As he came towards them, Brigid thought how much rounder he seemed. Everything about him gave the impression of ripeness. His face and neck were a mottled red colour and his chest seemed ready to burst from his velvet tunic. She could see the heavy outline of his legs in the blackberry-coloured hose.

Lord Osin cast an appraising glance at Connell before settling his gaze on Brigid. "I did not expect to lay eyes on you again. And yet here you are, rosy with good health."

"No thanks to you." Connell's voice was as sharp and strong as the hunting knife Lord Osin wore at his waist.

Brigid dug her fist into her mouth to stop herself from crying out. Connell was mad. He would kill them both.

"Do you dare speak to me, Miller?" Lord Osin's voice was barely above a whisper. "I will have you on your knees begging for mercy, and if your words please me you will leave here with the clothes on your back."

Brigid took a deep breath and fell to her knees. "Please, my lord. Connell is unwell. He does not know what he speaks . . ."

"Get up!" Connell commanded. The sound of his voice brought Brigid immediately to her feet. The words came from his lips, but they might have been spoken by the earth beneath their feet, or the sky overhead. It was a voice that would not be refused, not even if it meant that she be drowned in the mill pond for disobedience.

"You are past saving yourself," Lord Osin said finally, "but do you not seek to save your betrothed?"

"I grow weary of waiting," Connell said.

Lord Osin laughed incredulously. "I believe Brigid is right. You have lost your wits. Do not fear. The loss of them shan't trouble you for much longer."

Lord Osin raised one of his fleshy white hands. He is summoning the Steward to take us away, Brigid thought. She would never see her mother again.

But at the very moment Lord Osin raised his hand in the air, Connell leaped forward and seized Lord Osin by the shoulders. Brigid watched, transfixed, as Connell put his mouth against the lord's right ear and began to blow, softly at first, almost like a lover, and then harder. For a moment it seemed as though a violent gust of wind blew through the empty hall.

Lord Osin's hands fell to his sides, and Connell stepped away from him in one fluid motion.

Brigid stared at Lord Osin, who gave a strange high-pitched giggle.

"Shall I get us some tea?" he asked. "I should like a nice cup of tea and bread with drippings. Do you think Cook would give us some?"

Brigid reached out blindly for something to steady herself. Was Lord Osin trying to trick them?

Connell took hold of Brigid's outstretched hand and pulled her to his side. "Thank you for your hospitality, Lord Osin, but I'm afraid that Brigid and I must take our leave of you."

Lord Osin nodded happily, the jowls of his cheek jiggling with the movement. "Yes, yes, yes. Off you go." And then as though something delightful had just occurred to him. "I know a ballad," he said to Brigid. "It is as pretty as you are fair. Would you like to hear it?"

Brigid glanced at Connell before replying, "Of course, my lord."

Lord Osin cleared his throat, which prompted another fit of giggling. Finally, be began to sing in a surprisingly sweet, clear voice:

"Fair Lady Isabel sits in her bower sewing,
Aye as the gowans grow gay
There she heard an elf-knight blawing his horn.
The first morning in May

If I had yon horn that I hear blawing,
An yon elf-knight to sleep in my bosom.

This maiden had scarcely these words spoken,
Till in at her window the elf-knight has luppen

'It's a very strange matter, fair maiden,' said he, 'I canna blaw my horn but ye call on me.

'But will ye go to yon greenwood side?
If ye canna going, I will cause you to ride,'

He leapt on a horse and she on another,
And they rode on the greenwood together."

When he finished, Lord Osin clapped his hands together like a delighted child. "Did you like it?"

"It was very good indeed," Connell said in the same manner that a master would praise his dog for rolling over.

"Do you think Cook will give me a treat with my tea?" Lord Osin asked hopefully. "I should like an almond pudding, or a slice of marzipan."

"Steward," Connell called out. "Come here at once. Your lord has need of you."

Steward entered the room, his blank features twisted with dislike. "How dare you summon me? I serve Lord Osin, not you."

Connell shrugged. "As you wish. My only care is for Lord Osin's comfort. I think you will find he is hungry."

Steward bowed to Lord Osin. "How may I serve you, my lord? Shall I call for one of your attendants?"

"Tell Cook I'd like some bread and drippings, and a pudding."

"Of course, my lord."

Brigid gripped Connell's hand tighter. She wanted to be far away from whatever strange sickness had taken hold of Lord Osin.

"My lord," Connell said. "May we take our leave of you now? You are busy with more important things and we have no wish to detain you further."

"Of course, of course. You have my blessing, both of you. Come again soon. Cook shall bake us a cake in the shape of a rabbit, no, a lamb. That is what I should like . . . a soft furry lamb to hold in my hand."

Lord Osin walked away from them in the direction of the kitchen, leaving Steward with no choice but to let them go.

Brigid felt the man's eyes on her back, hard and accusing, as she and Connell left the great hall. It was not the first time she felt the weight of such a stare, but it was the first time she thought she might deserve it.

Brigid still held Connell's hand, but neither of them spoke as they made their way back through the village. A thousand questions fluttered in Brigid's throat, but she could not find her voice to ask a single one. Every few steps, Brigid paused to look over her shoulder, expecting to see Lord Osin's men pursuing them. She did not understand what happened at the manor, but it could only be a temporary reprieve. When Lord Osin came to his senses, his desire for revenge would be that much greater.

As if reading her thoughts, Connell said, "You have nothing to fear from Lord Osin. He shall not trouble you again."

"How can you be certain?"

Connell shrugged. "Because a thing once done cannot be undone."

What had been done? Brigid wanted Connell's answer above all things and yet she did not ask him.

When they came to the mill, Brigid released Connell's arm. She needed to be away from him. Even if she could not bear the separation for long, she had to be alone to try to make sense of what happened.

Connell looked at her in surprise. "Why must you leave? The best part of the day is still before us."

"I must go to my mother and tell her . . . tell her that we are both safe."

Connell seized her hand and kissed it. "Go if you must, but meet me in the wood tonight."

Brigid gently withdrew her hand. "I will do my best."

"Promise me," Connell said.

"I promise."

Chapter 13

"I don't understand," her mother said when Brigid finished telling her what happened. "'Tis a strange story and I fear that you have left something out in the telling."

Brigid looked away. It pained her to keep lying to her mother, but the truth would only make things worse. Besides, what was the truth? Already, the details of what happened in the great hall were beginning to blur and fade, like a dream in the clear light of day. Connell whispered something in Lord Osin's ear. Or had he? Perhaps that, too, was a dream. Brigid got up from the table and went to the window. The sun had begun its descent in the sky, and the desire for solitude fled from her like a frightened animal. The embrace of darkness couldn't come soon enough. She wanted nothing more than to be in Connell's arms, and to hear his music.

"Brigid, come away from the window. You've not touched your supper."

"I'm not hungry," Brigid said, still staring through the open shutter. Somewhere out there Connell was passing the day without her. Where did he go? Who did he see? The last time they met in the forest, she'd helped him fasten his braies, and felt a sudden burst of jealousy for the thin straps of material that spent so many hours against his skin. "I wish I were these straps," she whispered against his bare shoulders.

Connell pulled her close against his chest. "Do you?" Connell murmured into her hair. "Would you give up everything and come away with me?"

The seriousness in his voice startled her. "Why should we go away? Is it Lord Osin you fear? Or the Faerie Queen? I thought you said—"

"No one can harm us, I promise you, but there are many wondrous places beyond Alainn Ros. I should like to take you to every one . . ."

A sparrow lighted in a branch overhead and began to sing.

"'Tis nearly dawn," she said. "I must go."

Connell released her. "I will come to you later."

A sudden draft from the window roused Brigid from her thoughts. Her skin was covered in goose bumps, but she was too tired to kindle the fire that was barely an orange flicker in the hearth. She wanted to lie down on her pallet and sleep until the sun was swallowed up in the ebony sky and it was time to meet Connell in the wood.

"Brigid, did you hear me?"

Brigid turned around. The outlines of her mother's face seemed soft and indistinct—a stranger's face. Brigid pressed her palms tightly against her face until her eyelids hurt. When she removed them, her mother's anxious expression came sharply into focus. "I'm sorry. What did you say?"

"Claire's baby was stolen."

"Stolen?"

Her mother's usually soft voice was tinged with impatience. "She awoke this morning to find the cradle empty and the fire gone out. The Faerie have taken the baby away with them. Claire is so distraught I fear she will harm herself."

"Why didn't you tell me this before?"

"I've done nothing but tell you, and yet you stand at the window as still and silent as a ghost!"

Brigid reached for her cloak that lay in a heap on the floor. "I must go to Clare at once. She will need looking after and Aed . . ."

"Wait!"

"What is it?"

"Go to Connell first. Make him understand how important it is that Clare's baby be returned to her."

"Connell? He will be sorry for Clare I'm sure, but what can he do?"

Her mother hesitated. "He might help you look for the child."

"Where? If what you say is true and the Faerie have taken him, how would anyone know where to look?"

"Will you ask him, Brigid? For the sake of the child?"

Brigid looked at her mother's face, the lines and angles of which she knew better than her own, and for the first time she didn't recognize the expression written there. "I will go to him right away."

"At least have a bite of bread before you go."

Brigid shook her head and then started in surprise when her mother grabbed both of her hands. "Am I to lose you, too?" she asked.

Brigid squeezed her mother's hands reassuringly, but the gesture carried all the strength of a hummingbird. "It is Clare who has lost a child, not you." She let go of her mother and went to the basin to splash her face with water but discovered it was empty.

"I've not yet fetched the day's water."

How long had her mother been going to the well? It was a hard task, and one that Brigid had taken over since her mother's hands began to pain her, but she could not recall having fetched water the day before, or the day before that. Brigid looked slowly around the cottage. The floor was unswept, and cobwebs dangled from the ceiling. The hearth was empty of firewood, and a pile of unwashed linen lay on the floor.

Brigid pressed a thin hand to her forehead. "How could I have forgotten?" she murmured.

Her mother picked up a long broom made of twigs. "My hands feel better today. I will start on this floor and you can help me with the rest when you return. Right now it is Clare who needs you."

Brigid ran all the way to the mill determined to make up for her idleness. She did not understand herself. She and her mother had always been poor, but they kept a clean house and a good fire in the hearth. Since her mother's strength had begun to fail her, it fell to Brigid to do the heavy chores. How could she have left her mother without enough water to drink? I will make it up to her, Brigid vowed. Connell and I will search every corner of the woods until we find Clare's baby.

But when Brigid opened the door to the granary, Connell was nowhere to be found. The mill was deserted, except for the sacks of grain that lay on the floor, piled haphazardly on top of one another. Some of the sacks had come undone, spilling their contents onto the dirty floor. Brigid hovered uncertainly in the doorway. How had Connell let this happen? She took several tentative steps forward, but the sight of several rats scurrying across her path quickly drove her back out again. He was not outside either. The mill wheel stood silent and still, bits of grain caught in its gears.

Eager to put these signs of neglect behind her, Brigid went around to the front of the cottage. She knocked on the door, the sound unnaturally loud in the stillness that seemed to have settled over the mill like a thick blanket of dust.

Connell's mother opened the door. "I might have known it was you. If you've come to lure Connell into another day of idleness when he should be putting bread on the village's table, including his own, you're too late. I've naught seen him since breakfast."

Brigid took a step backwards. She knew Maeve Mackenna was not overly fond of her, but since Connell asked her to marry him the older woman had treated her well enough. Even when it seemed Connell was lost to them, she did not blame Brigid like the rest of the village was wont to do. But now Maeve's face, so much like Connell's, radiated fear and dislike.

"I'm sorry," Brigid said, cringing at how feeble her voice sounded. "I didn't mean to cause trouble. I only wanted to tell Connell that Clare Ryan's baby is missing. I thought . . . I thought he could help me look for him."

Maeve looked at her in surprise. "Do you really think that you can help Clare? It would serve you well to think on this before you do more harm to that poor woman."

Brigid felt her ribcage expand as the seed of resentment she carried inside her burst into flower. "I've done no harm to anyone in this village," she said in a voice she barely recognized. "I will find Connell myself, and together we will find Clare's baby and bring him back to her."

"Away with you then. I've work to get on with," Maeve said before slamming the door in Brigid's face.

Brigid left the mill, not knowing where she was going, only that she needed to get as far away as possible from Connell's mother and everyone else in the village who hated her. When she finally stopped to catch her breath, she saw that she'd come to the outskirts of the forest. A scarlet leaf drifted across her path and Brigid bent to pick it up. The veins of the leaf were bright gold, and she wondered what tree it had fallen from. She'd not come to the forest alone since the morning she went to the pool hoping for some sign about her future. She left the woods disappointed that day, but now the densely covered branches opened up in a welcoming embrace. Above her, the rustling leaves seemed to whisper, "We want you even if no one else does."

Within moments she was deep inside the forest, her feet gliding along a path that unfolded before her like a stream of green ribbon. With every step, thoughts of Connell, Clare, and her baby became more and more distant. When her legs began to tire, she thought to sit down and rest, but every time she slowed her pace it seemed a more beautiful and comfortable spot lay just ahead. The leaves on the trees grew thicker and darker, and she couldn't resist plucking one from a low hanging branch and rubbing it between her fingers. She marvelled at its velvety softness and lush green colour.

Brigid tucked the leaf inside her dress and continued on the path. The trees blocked out most of the light, but their branches emitted a soft golden glow to light the way ahead. Her step quickened. The musky smell of damp leaves and earth mingled with a new fragrance, so rich and sweet, she slowed her breath to drink it in. She was close now, so close her body trembled with anticipation. The anger and resentment that brought her to the forest faded like a child's dream. The path twisted and turned and straightened again, before bringing Brigid to an abrupt halt in front of a grove of alder, whose branches arched protectively over a patch of the most glorious yellow flowers. Her fingers itched with the need to yank the stems from the ground. She wanted the flowers more than her next breath. An armful of the bright petals would put everything right. She got down on her knees and—

"Don't touch those!"

Brigid turned around. Connell. He grabbed her by the shoulders and pulled her roughly to her feet.

"What are you doing here?" he demanded.

Brigid stared at him unable to speak. Why did she come to the forest? Flowers. She wanted the flowers and Connell had stopped her from having them. Disappointment, mingled with some stronger emotion, bubbled up inside her chest like one of Cook's spicy, hot stews. How dare he . . .?

Connell put his hands on both of her shoulders. "Answer me, Brigid. Why did you come to the forest alone?"

"I came to find you," Brigid managed at last, the morning's events flying back to her like an arrow. How could she have forgotten? "Clare Ryan's baby. The Faerie have stolen him."

"How do you know it was the Fair Folk who took the baby?" Connell asked, as though Brigid had told him that Clare had lost a bowl or a shoe.

Brigid looked at him in surprise. "What do you mean? Of course it was the Faerie. It's happened before, you know it has."

Connell shrugged. "If her baby is gone, she will soon make another."

"How can you speak so carelessly of Clare's suffering? Has the Faerie Queen's harp stolen your senses? Clare's baby belongs with her, not with the thieving Faerie!"

Connell cocked his head to one side, as though puzzled by her anger. "Perhaps the child will have a better life with the Fair Folk. Clare is a poor woman. Her husband is a farm labourer who has been known to cough blood into the sleeve of his tunic. A short time from now she's likely to find herself a widow. I told you how beautiful Faerie are, how prosperous. Would the child not be better off in a place where it will not want for anything? Where he will never feel the cold or the twist of hunger in his belly?"

A strong breeze rustled through the trees overhead gently showering her and Connell with leaves. Several caught in her hair and she tore them away. "He will want for his mother's love! I know what it is to be cold and hungry, and I would suffer those things a hundredfold rather than lose my mother. The Faerie cannot come into our village and take what does not belong to them."

Connell reached out for her, but she pushed him away.

She smelled the forest on his skin. No longer intoxicating, it gagged her with its cloying sweetness.

"I don't understand you," he said. "Why should you care for the village's suffering? When have the villagers ever cared for yours? Even Clare would not speak out on your behalf for fear of being known as your friend. Have you already forgotten how you were dragged into the forest like an animal and left there to die? Your village doesn't deserve the mercy of the Fair Folk."

"If you do not understand me, I understand you even less. You speak of Alainn Ros as thought it were not your village as well as mine. You've done more for the people in the village than anyone. And now, when a good woman needs your help you turn your back? I wonder if I know you at all, Connell Mackenna."

Connell cupped her face in his hands so she couldn't look away. "If what you say is true, then there is no help to be given. The Faerie will not return a child once they have claimed it for their own."

"How can you be certain? Did the Faerie Queen tell you so?"

Connell released her, letting his hands fall to his sides. "Yours is the only story I know where a child has encountered the Faerie and returned unharmed."

"Then I am proof that the Faerie can be merciful if they choose," Brigid said eagerly. "We could use the harp to summon the Faerie Queen . . ."

Connell shook his head. "It is impossible."

"If you won't help me, I shall do it myself!" Brigid turned on her heel and began to retrace her steps through the forest.

"What will you do?" Connell called after her.

"I will go to Clare and make her tell me all she knows about Aofie's disappearance, and then I will . . ." Brigid stopped to pick a stone out of her shoe, nearly falling over in the process. "I found the Faerie Queen before. Perhaps I can find her again."

"Wait," Connell said. "Perhaps there is another way."

Chapter 14

Clare and Aed's cottage was even smaller than the one Brigid shared with her mother. The poverty Connell spoke of showed in the roof that needed mending and in the shutters that hung from the windows like broken limbs. But if the outside of the cottage was wanting, the inside shone with Clare's care and attention. The floor was swept clean and fresh rushes scented with sweet-smelling herbs from her well-tended garden were strewn in the entryway. A stack of freshly washed linens lay neatly folded on the scarred wooden table. Brigid thought of the disarray in her own cottage and felt ashamed. Even in her despair, Clare would not neglect her family.

Brigid had seen even less of Clare since her pregnancy and wondered if the cooling of their friendship was because Clare had come to share the belief that Brigid was an unlucky presence in the village. What if Connell's mother was right? That her interference would do more harm than good? But when Clare opened the door, Brigid saw only gratitude in her friend's swollen, red-rimmed eyes, and surprise when she saw Connell standing behind her.

"Thank goodness you've come," Clare said, ushering them inside. "No one will speak to me since it happened. They leave food by the door but they won't come in. I feel as though I'm losing my mind. I'll do anything to get Aofie back, anything." Clare touched the sleeve of Brigid's gown. "You know something of Faerie ways, Brigid. Tell me what I should do. Help me find my son."

Brigid looked away from her friend's pale, freckled face, the skin stretched too tightly over prominent cheekbones. What made her think she could help Clare, or anyone for that matter? She did not understand why the Fair Folk, who lived like Kings and Queens, sought to steal the children of peasants. Her own encounter with the Faerie Queen had taught her nothing.

"Where was the child when he was taken?" Connell asked, the sound of his voice startling both women.

"There." Clare pointed to the tiny wooden cradle placed near the hearth for warmth. "Before Aed and I lay down, I wrapped him up nice and warm like always. And then I kissed him right here." Clare pressed her finger against the centre of her forehead and two fat tears rolled down her cheeks. "I slept only a little, but when I opened my eyes he was gone. Oh God, why didn't I keep him safe?" Clare turned her wet face towards Brigid. "Your mother gave me a length of crimson thread to tie around his wrists. She told me placing the thread against his skin would protect him, but he worried at it so that I cut it off."

Brigid put her hand on Clare's arm. "You must not blame yourself. No child could ask for a better mother."

Clare shook her head. "They will blame me. You know they will. They will say it's because . . . Even Aed looks at me with shadows in his eyes."

Brigid tightened her grip on her friend, but she could not find the words to reassure her. She knew better than anyone how cruel the villagers could be.

Clare took one long, shuddering breath. "They pity me now, but soon they will begin to whisper that I did something to anger the Fair Folk.

"That is nonsense," Connell said abruptly. "The Faerie take what they want because they want it. If they took him, it was for no other reason than because he was fine and fair."

Both women stared at Connell. No one spoke with such calm certainty about the Fair Folk. One might tell tales around the fire about Faerie manners, but no one knew what Faeries thought or felt, or even if they were capable of such things. Brigid longed to ask Connell what else he'd learned the night of the Faerie ball, but she couldn't speak in front of Clare.

Clare sank onto the wooden stool she'd placed beside the empty cradle. "If I've done nothing to offend the Fair Folk, then how do I get my son back?"

Connell looked at Clare as though she were some exotic forest animal he was encountering for the first time. "Are you certain you want your child returned to you? What if he is . . . changed?"

Seized by a fresh outburst of hard, wracking sobs that seemed to come from the centre of her being, Clare could barely manage enough breath to respond.

"Of course I want him! He's mine! I would sooner die than let anyone take him from me."

"Then listen carefully to what I tell you. For if you do not succeed, your son is lost to you forever."

Clare wiped the tears from her face and stood up so that she was facing Connell. "Tell me what I must do."

"How do you know this?" Clare whispered when Connell was finished.

They were seated at Clare's table, three mugs of ale untouched in front of them.

Connell traced a scar in the wood with his fingers. "The Willow Women cannot afford my services, so on occasion I have accepted a story in lieu of payment."

"I don't understand," Clare said. "What kind of stories?"

"The Willow Women like nothing better than to tell how they were lured away by their Faerie lovers. They tell their story to anyone who will listen in the hope of finding someone who can tell them the way back."

Clare's face fell. "The Willow Women are mad. Everyone knows that."

"Perhaps, but they have travelled to the same place your son is now, and they returned to tell of it."

"But not for years and years," Brigid said. "Why didn't they come back sooner if they knew the way?"

Connell looked at her for a long moment. "They did not want to come back."

Connell turned to Clare. "I do not promise you will succeed, but if you hope to challenge the Faerie's claim on the child, I know of no other way."

Clare reached for Brigid's hand. "Will you pray with me?"

"Of course I will."

Brigid got down on her knees beside Clare, and when she looked up, Connell was gone.

Brigid stayed with Clare until it was nearly twilight. Although she was reluctant to leave her friend on her own, Connell's instructions were clear; Clare must go to the sacred well to make her offering, the metal band she wore on her middle finger and three drops of her own blood.

Brigid did not say so to Clare, but she doubted the Fair Folk would be satisfied with such an offering. When she closed her eyes, she could still see the Faerie Queen as she'd appeared that day in the forest, the twisted white gold circlet around her head, the cluster of diamonds and pearls gleaming at her throat and wrists. Why should the possessor of such finery want Clare's simple metal band? Connell's instructions to place rowan boughs across the cottage threshold were common enough. The bush was known for its ability to ward off the Fair Folk, but if the Faerie could be satisfied with Clare's offering, then why would they try to take him back? Brigid wanted to ask Connell these questions, but when she left Clare's cottage Connell was nowhere in sight. Why did he not wait for her?

Brigid arrived home to find her mother sitting at the table crushing leeks into a stone pestle. "Did you find him?" her mother asked, rising from her seat.

Brigid shook her head. "But Connell believes there is a way . . . He told Clare to throw her wedding ring into the sacred well."

Mary fingered her own wedding ring that she wore around her neck and frowned. "How will that bring back her child?"

"Because the ring is her most valuable possession. Connell says the Fair Folk only accept offerings that are dear to the giver. If the Faerie are pleased with Clare's sacrifice, they will return Aoife."

"And if they are not pleased?"

"What else is she to do?"

Brigid's mother was silent for a moment. "We must hope that Connell is right."

"I could not bear it," Brigid said. "I could not live in the world knowing that someone had taken my child and meant to keep him away from me. I would rather die barren and alone than to know such grief."

"Hush, Love. Once spoken, such words take on a power of their own. You have done enough this day. Sit down and rest yourself."

Brigid removed her overgown and lay down on her pallet. She wanted to be lying inside Connell's arms underneath the moonless sky, but she did not think her legs would carry her to the forest. She squeezed her eyes shut, but the longed for oblivion of sleep did not come. Caught between half-formed dreams and wakefulness, she embraced neither. An image of Clare's face, the soft skin around her eyes lined with worry, hovered behind her closed lids.

Brigid opened her eyes and sat up. The walls of the cottage began to dissolve and the outline of her mother's body blurred and softened until she seemed no more than a shadow. Brigid called out to her, but her voice made no sound. The light in the room continued to fade until Brigid couldn't see anything at all. Was she awake or dreaming? As her eyes began to adjust to the dark, she realized she was no longer inside the cottage. Instead of straw beneath her hand, she felt the smoothness of silk and soft fur. Disoriented, she stood up, her feet sinking into a carpet of such velvety softness it would silence a cavalcade of horses.

The walls gave off a faintly golden glow, and were hung with silk tapestries depicting some kind of royal procession. The figures were so beautiful and lifelike Brigid felt compelled to admire them up close. But when she stood in front of the tapestry, the images lost their crispness. Hues of emerald green, scarlet, and lemon-yellow bled together in a dazzling blur. She stared at the wall, confused, until she realized that the figures in the tapestry were moving. Beautiful men and woman on horseback moved through the forest, their golden hair mingling with leaves, and the reflected light of the sun shining through the trees. Brigid watched until she felt so dizzy she was forced to turn away.

In the centre of the room grew a silver tree with unnaturally elongated branches that glittered strangely. Brigid moved towards the tree, but a faint sob followed by a sharp cry made her freeze in mid-step. The sounds were coming from *inside* the branches. Brigid ran towards the tree, which was farther away then it seemed. By the time she reached it, her legs ached and she was gasping for breath. The sobbing grew steadily stronger until it was nearly unbearable. She tore at the silver leaves with her fingers, trying to pry apart the rough, heavy branches that seemed to fight against her touch. Finally, the tree gave way and she saw him, Clare's baby. He was still wrapped in his swaddling clothes, cradled in the upper branches of the tree. She reached out to pick him up. Her fingertips brushed against his linen wrappings, but before she could place her hands around his tiny body, strong arms grasped her from behind and yanked her away. Brigid whirled around and cried out. The beautiful man with the burning eyes she saw beside the stream was standing in front of her.

Brigid awoke, her shift drenched in sweat. Her skin was hot to the touch, but she shivered with cold. "Mother," she called out weakly.

"I'm here," her mother said, coming to her side.

"I dreamed of him," Brigid whispered.

Her mother placed a cool hand on Brigid's cheek. "You have a fever," she said, and Brigid heard the fear in her voice.

"I must go to Clare and tell her what I saw. I must know if . . . Aoife has come home."

Her mother shook her head, and Brigid could see the hard set line of her mouth in the darkness. "It is late and you are unwell. I will go to Clare in the morning."

"Go now, please. I must know if the child is alive and well."

"I cannot leave you. Once the fever has broken . . ."

"No! You must go now. I saw someone . . . I shall not be able to rest until I know the child is returned to his mother."

Brigid's eyes ached painfully, but her gaze didn't leave her mother's face until, finally, the older woman reached for her cloak.

"I will be fine," she assured her mother who gave her a final worried glance before closing the door behind her.

Brigid waited in the cottage until she was sure her mother was safely away. Then she threw off the wool blanket and put on her cloak. She must find Connell. Her legs trembled beneath her, but she forced her feet into her shoes and stumbled towards the door. How did Connell know what to offer the sacred well? Her last encounter with Eanna was proof of the woman's addled wits. If the Willow Women knew anything of Faerie ways, they'd long since forgotten. And where did Connell go after he left Clare's cottage? She must make Connell tell her everything. If they were to be married, there could be no secrets between them.

Brigid ran down the path towards the forest. Connell was waiting for her. She could feel his presence as she moved through the trees towards their meeting place. The aching of her limbs seemed to ease with every step, and when she approached the clearing, her brow felt cool and smooth. A sudden feeling of lightness came over her body, and her toes tingled inside of their worn leather shoes. She would ask Connell to dance with her.

When she entered the clearing, it was empty. "Connell?" No reply save for the whispering of the trees. Brigid turned around slowly. She was so sure of seeing him. For a moment the forest seemed to shimmer around her, and Brigid grabbed hold of an alder branch to steady herself. A piece of bark came away in her hands, and when she looked at it, she saw that it was silver. Brigid dropped the bark. Was she still dreaming? And then she saw him, just as she remembered that morning beside the stream, and again in her dream. Tall and fair with wide, slanted eyes, the irises darker than her own, except for the strange flicker of light at their centres.

"Brigid, what are you doing here alone?"

"Who are you?" she asked. "How do you know my name?"

"Why do you jest? You know who I am. Who else but your own true love?"

Brigid shook her head wildly. "Connell Mackenna is my betrothed. I do not know you, although I have seen you twice before."

"Brigid, I fear you are unwell. I am your betrothed. Why do you not see me?"

"I see you." But even as she spoke, the man in front of her began to change. At first she thought it was a trick of the moonlight falling through the trees, but no earthly light could make a man of flesh and blood appear as though he were fashioned of air and shadows. Brigid did not remove her eyes from the man's body through which she could see the foliage, silver-green in the moonlight, behind him. Under Brigid's steady gaze, the shifting play of light and shadow over tree and earth ceased, and the air in front of her grew thick and opaque. Brigid's eyes began to tear. She wiped them with the sleeve of her gown, and when she took her hand away, it was Connell who stood before her.

Sweat broke out on Brigid's forehead and her legs trembled like a new foal's. Her fever came rushing back like a star falling from the sky.

Connell reached out his arm to steady her, but Brigid pulled away. Too weak to stand, she wrapped her arms around the alder. "You are not Connell," she whispered.

"My love, tell me what's wrong. What has brought on this foolishness?"

"I saw you. Tell me about Clare's child. Where have you taken him?"

Despite his skill at transformation, the man who was not Connell couldn't hide the startled look in his eyes. Brigid realized he didn't know she'd seen his true form.

"The child of which you speak is safe and well in his mother's arms," he said finally.

"You're lying, just as you lied about the harp, and everything else . . ."

"It's the truth. I swear it!"

"Why should I believe anything you say? I don't even know who you are."

"I am your own true love."

She wrapped herself more tightly around the tree, as though to absorb some of its strength. "Who are you?"

The man, if he could be called so, held out his arms to her, and Brigid watched the beauty emerge from the regular lines and angles of Connell's features like a butterfly coming out of its chrysalis. The radiance of his face was so dazzling she buried her face against the rough bark of the tree.

"Please, come near to me and I shall tell you."

Brigid let go of the tree and ran as fast as she could, faster even than she'd run from Lord Osin when he hunted her like an animal. She ran despite the deep ache that returned to her limbs and the heaviness in her chest, afraid that if she slowed her pace she might turn around and run back to him. Brigid listened for the sound of his pursuit, but there was only her own harsh, ragged breath coming in uneven gasps.

She emerged from the forest, her gown torn and her face caked with dirt and dried sweat. She'd escaped something, and yet she did not feel free. The forest still beckoned with its swirling red-gold leaves that made the trees look as though they were on fire. It took all of her remaining strength to drag herself along the path home. What would she tell her mother? How long would it be before everyone in the village discovered how she betrayed Connell? They would never believe she didn't know the truth. How could they when she herself wasn't certain what that truth was? But most important of all: What had happened to Connell?

When Brigid finally reached the cottage she stopped in front of the door, caught between forwards and backwards. There was no choice to be made, she told herself. She could never go back. Everything he told her was a lie and yet . . .

The cottage door opened and Brigid's mother came out, her face twisted with worry. "Brigid, thank God. Where have you been? We've been so worried." The door swung all the way open, and there, behind her mother, stood Connell.

Chapter 15

Brigid fell to the ground, her head thudding into the soft earth before either Connell or her mother could break her fall. She relished the new pain because it was real and true, not some strange illusion that would evaporate when she opened her eyes. And then she felt Connell's strong arms around her, and she could smell the scent of his skin, not honey and wildflowers, but sweat and tallow soap.

"I don't understand," she said as he lifted her from the ground and swung her into his arms. "You were gone, and now you're here, alive. Is it really you this time?"

"She's delirious," Brigid heard her mother say.

"I am here with you now, and I shall never leave you again."

"Let's get her inside," her mother said. "I need cool cloths to place on her skin. She's as hot as a flame."

Brigid listened to her mother and Connell speaking softly to one another in hushed voices, but could not make out the words. They seemed somehow apart from her and she did not know how to reach them. Her throat ached with the need to speak, but she was afraid of what she might say. Finally, she managed, "Clare's baby?"

Her mother kneeled beside her and placed a damp strip of linen her forehead. "Aoife is safe and well in his mother's arms." She turned towards Connell. "I don't know how you came by such knowledge, but you were right. Clare will spend the rest of her days looking for ways to thank you, both of you," she said, touching Brigid's cheek.

Brigid saw the confusion in Connell's steady grey eyes but he did not speak.

Why has he not told her? she wondered. Why does he not say that a lie has stolen his life these last weeks?

Unable to bear the concern in Connell's eyes, she closed her own. Her mother held some warm liquid against her lips. She drank it, although she felt no thirst.

"Now you will rest," her mother said.

And indeed, the walls of the cottage began to fade, but not before she saw Connell's tired, serious face that bore new lines around his eyes and forehead standing over her.

"I'm sorry," she whispered before everything went dark.

Chapter 16

"Come away with me." The voice was as gentle as summer rain, but Brigid responded as though it were a command. She got out of bed and searched for the shoes her mother had removed from her feet while she slept.

"Leave everything behind. Where we are going you will want for nothing."

She moved towards the door, but the sound of her mother turning over in her pallet stopped her before she reached it. "I cannot go with you. My mother will . . ."

"She will not awaken until you are safely home again. Come away with me. It is a dancing night."

Brigid looked at her mother, who was indeed sleeping soundly.

"Hurry," the lovely voice whispered. "The music has already started."

She opened the door and went out into the moonlight. He was waiting for her just beyond the garden, even more beautiful than the day before when she was too shocked and frightened to really look at him. His snow-white tunic had been replaced by one of shining silver, and around his waist he wore a belt encrusted with diamonds.

He held out his hand to her. "I've been waiting for you."

Brigid hesitated only a moment before taking his hand. Once his slender fingers covered her own, the ground beneath their feet seemed to give way and she felt herself falling. She could hear the faint sound of the harp and some other instrument she didn't recognize. The music grew louder as the darkness closed above her. She raised her arms over her head to speed her descent, and when her feet touched the earth they made no sound. There was only the awareness of being somewhere else, and the strange thrilling presence of her lover beside her. Her lover. She had not called him so before, but she had no other name for him.

She looked around. They appeared to be standing in some kind of dark tunnel, but just ahead Brigid saw an open meadow of shining stars, and the music was all around them, much stronger than before. Her lover took her hand and together they ran into the starry meadow. The sudden, dazzling brightness made her dizzy and she gripped his hand more tightly. They waded through stars, some of which clung to Brigid's feet and ankles, making them tingle pleasantly until they came to the edge of a vast forest. Brigid recognized the familiar shape of oak, ash, hawthorne, and alder, but their leaves were burnished silver like the tree whose bark she'd torn away in the clearing. The low hanging branches parted at their approach to reveal a winding gilded path.

Brigid put a restraining hand on her lover's arm. "Wait. Tell me your name. Your real name."

"My name is Midir." And then he kissed her.

Their feet seemed to have barely touched the path when they entered a clearing, or what should have been a clearing, but was in fact an enormous glittering ballroom with no walls or ceiling to contain it. Although she'd never been anywhere near a ballroom, she recognized her surroundings from her father's stories. Lords and ladies glided across the dance floor dressed in garments that shone so brightly it hurt to look at them for long. Brigid immediately felt ashamed of her own worn, patched gown, but when she looked down she saw that her bodice was silk instead of wool, and her skirts were shot through with glittering threads of silver, green and gold, and when she reached a hand to her hair she felt a delicate net of crystals covering the silver-white strands like dewdrops.

"Dance with me," Midir said.

Brigid placed her hands in Midir's and did not resist when he pulled her close. The music moved in and around them, every note bringing them closer and closer together until their bodies formed a single shining line of pearly white flesh. If she pulled away now, she wouldn't be able to stand on her own.

Inside Midir's embrace, Brigid was only dimly aware of the other dancers. The men and women were all so beautiful there was little to distinguish them except for the colour of their finery in varying shades of russet, emerald, rose-gold, and silvery white. Most of the women had long golden hair, the colour of new corn that delicately swept the floor. The men were equally fair, and moved with a grace and lightness that Brigid would not have thought possible in men so tall and long-limbed.

Occasionally, one of the other couples would turn to look at them, but no one seemed unduly concerned by her presence. She was less strange here than in her own village surrounded by people who'd known her all her life. This thought was followed by one even more unsettling. If she were to stay in Faerie (for where else could this be?) she wouldn't have to fear the villagers' scorn and disapproval ever again.

She closed her eyes. It was easier to follow the music when she pictured it in her mind. The unfamiliar melody seemed to lead here and there without every quite arriving. She tried to seize hold of every tenuous note and store it carefully in her mind so she could recall it later, but as soon as they reached her ears every one of them melted like snowflakes.

A sweet lassitude came over her body, making her limbs so heavy she longed to lie down on the ballroom floor. But just as she felt her head begin to slide down Midir's chest, a tiny pinprick of pain shot through her foot. Instantly alert, Brigid pulled away from Midir and bent to pull off her leather slipper, the same slipper Connell had given her she realized with a start. It was the one thing that remained unchanged when she crossed into Faerie. Except for her leather-clad feet, she resembled the rest of the Fair Folk.

"I have a stone in my slipper," she said to Midir, who looked at her in askance.

The shoe felt strangely heavy in her hand. She removed the tiny, sharp stone that had found its way into the heel and placed the shoe back on her foot.

The music enticed her as much as ever, but once the heaviness in her limbs disappeared she wanted to explore the unnatural splendour of her surroundings. They seemed to be in the middle of a great forest except there was no night sky overhead, and the ground beneath their feet was made of gilded leaves. Beyond the clearing, she could see the outline of the gold and silver trees, their branches heavy with unfamiliar shiny, round fruit. "Where are we?" she asked Midir. "I know we are in Faerie, but where is that exactly?"

"We have many names for our land. The one easiest for you to remember is Liradon."

She repeated the name softly. "You told me it was beautiful, that night in the forest. Why did you wish to leave it?"

Midir led her slightly away from the other dancers before he said, "Because I wanted you."

"I don't understand. How did you find me?"

"There are times, such as tonight, when the barrier between my world and yours is as unsubstantial as morning mist. I have been close to you many times although you did not know it."

"No, sometimes I felt you, when I was alone in the forest."

Midir nodded thoughtfully. "I wore the guise of your betrothed, and yet you saw me in my true form. I don't understand . . . it has never happened before."

"Before? You've known other women in the village?"

Midir seized Brigid around the waist and lifted her easily off her feet. "There is no one in the world for me but you," he whispered in her ear.

Brigid smiled. She had dreamed of hearing such words since she was a little girl. Once you found your true love, you would never be lonely or frightened again. Her father's stories taught her this.

Once Midir returned her to her feet, she noticed a dark-haired woman standing alone on the edge of the dance floor. She seemed to be looking for her partner, but when her gaze fell on Brigid and Midir it caught and held. The look in her leaf-green eyes, indifferent at first, hardened into an unmistakable mask of dislike.

"Who is that woman?" Brigid asked Midir.

"Where?" Midir returned, his eyes never leaving Brigid's face.

"Over there, near the trees. She is staring at me, at the two of us together."

Midir put his arms around Brigid's shoulders and led her quickly away. "She is no one. If she stares at you, it is only because she admires your beauty."

"I don't think she admires me at all. She looked at me the way one looks at maggots in spoiled meat."

A look of repulsion creased Midir's flawless face. "No one could look at you in such a way. You are perfect, beautiful. As beautiful as the Faerie Queen herself." Midir smiled widely as if pleased by the comparison.

He should not speak so. Brigid heard her mother's voice whisper inside of her head. But her mother was far away. Farther even than if Brigid had crossed the sea. Would her mother be able to understand any of this? And Connell, what of him? She told him she was sorry for betraying him, and yet she was here listening to words of love from another man. But these unsettling thoughts were easily brushed away when Midir seized her hand.

"Come with me. Now that you are here I must see that you receive a proper reception."

Brigid allowed Midir to lead her across the ballroom where the other dancers stopped their graceful twirling to let them pass. Brigid looked for the woman with the dark hair but she seemed to have vanished.

Brigid returned her attention to Midir. "Where are we going?"

"To the high table. The Faerie Queen and her consort await us."

Midir's announcement roused Brigid from her bemused state. From the moment they arrived in Liradon Brigid felt herself being seduced a second time, but now Midir had more than words. The sights and sounds of Faerie embraced her at every turn. Midir had deceived her once already. She mustn't allow him to do it again. "The story you told me about the Faerie Queen, that was a lie, wasn't it? She never gave you the harp?"

Midir gave her a distracted look. "The harp? Ah, yes. Now I remember. The harp was indeed a gift from the Faerie Queen. That much is true."

"What about the ceremony on All Hallows' Eve? The one she made you promise to attend?"

Midir pressed his hand against her cheek. "I confess I don't recall all I said that night. You needed a tale so I gave you one. Now come. The Queen will turn us away if we're late."

Once they left the dance floor, their surroundings changed again. They still seemed to be in the middle of as vast wood, but instead of walking on gilded leaves Brigid felt soft grass beneath her feet, and the surrounding trees changed from gold and silver to green. But it was not the green of Alainn Ros. Each leaf was perfectly formed without a single tear or tinge of brown, as though untouched by wind, or heat, or rain.

As before, the trees parted in front of them, but this time when they passed through they emerged at the entrance of what resembled a great hall although it was nothing like the great hall at the manor. There was no smell of smoke from the fire, or the sweat of labouring servants. And not a single scrap of food marred the floor's gleaming marble surface. The only similarity was the elevated position of the high table. Like Lord Osin, the Queen sat on a raised dais that allowed her to survey the entire room while seated. Above the table was an enormous glittering chandelier made of rainbow-coloured glass. Brigid stared at the chandelier until her eyes blurred, but she could not see how it was suspended in the air. Like the ballroom, the great hall appeared to have no ceiling. The table itself was piled high with a variety of dishes, some of which Brigid recognized from Cook's kitchen, but others were strange. Despite the abundance of heavy sauces and rich gravies, the snowy white tablecloth showed not a single spilled drop. The only drink was an enormous crystal flask of amber-coloured liquid that had been placed in the centre of the table.

More impressive than all of this was the Faerie Queen herself. She sat at the head of the table, and beside her was a young man who resembled Midir a good deal, except for his eyes, the colour of fresh heather.

"Good evening, Midir."

Brigid immediately recognized the Faerie Queen's slow, languorous way of speaking. The sound of her voice ran down Brigid's spine like the honey Cook let drip from her wooden spoon to sweeten the sauce.

Midir bowed his head, a slight, almost imperceptible movement that made Brigid wonder if he made the gesture with some reluctance. "I have brought someone to meet you, just as I promised."

Except for the slight arch of one delicate eyebrow, the Queen seemed unsurprised by Brigid's presence.

"Welcome to my court, Brigid O'Flynn. I had a feeling we might meet again someday. Tell me, what do you think of our dancing night?"

"It's wonderful," Brigid said. "I've never heard such music. If I could choose, I would listen to nothing else for the rest of my life."

The Faerie Queen laughed. A surprisingly deep, harsh sound from such a finely shaped mouth. "Not an unusual request, I'm afraid, but one that is rarely granted." The Queen placed a slim white hand around the neck of the crystal flask. "May I offer you some wine?"

Before Brigid could respond, a whisper thin goblet filled with the amber-coloured liquid appeared in her hand. Suddenly aware of an overwhelming thirst, Brigid raised the glass to her lips, but Midir yanked it away from her before she could take a single sip.

"Brigid may have all the food and drink she wishes, but first she must say her goodbyes."

"Goodbyes?" Brigid questioned softly, but neither the Faerie Queen nor Midir seemed to hear her.

"What is the use of a goodbye when she is already gone?" The Faerie Queen's voice was low and sweet.

"Her mother would wish it," Midir said, and for the first time Brigid thought he sounded unsure of himself.

The Faerie Queen shrugged her white shoulders that rose from the top of her dress like sea foam. "You profess to understand human attachments?" she asked Midir.

Brigid stood close enough to Midir to feel his body stiffen beside her. "I have learned something of their ways."

"Then you have been away from us too long." The languor slipped from the Faerie Queen's voice like an overripe berry from the vine revealing the dry stalk beneath. "I care nothing for their ways and neither must you. If you want her, take her."

Brigid listened to Midir's exchange with the Faerie Queen as though she was in a dream, but the mention of her mother awakened something inside of her. "I go where I choose to go."

The Faerie Queen looked at Brigid as though she'd forgotten she was there. "For those such as you there is little choice in the matter. A truth you will soon come to understand."

The Faerie Queen's words seeped into her veins, making her shiver. Lady Osin had spoken nearly the same words to her only a short time ago. But despite the differences in their stations, Lady Osin shared Brigid's sense of duty and obligation. She understood what it meant to be bound to something more powerful than herself. Brigid doubted the Faerie Queen was bound to anything but her own desire. If there was a choice to be made, it would be she who did the choosing.

"We shall take our leave of you now," Midir said.

The Faerie Queen smiled pleasantly, and gave an elegant wave of her hand. "Farewell, Midir. I expect to see you again soon. There is a matter of some importance I should like to discuss with you."

Midir frowned. "Of course." But the Faerie Queen had already turned her back towards them and was whispering something in her companion's ear that made him smile.

Midir led Brigid out of the great hall, and once more they found themselves alone in the forest. Midir was silent beside her and Brigid sensed their audience with the Faerie Queen did not go as well as he hoped.

"What does the Faerie Queen want to speak to you about?" she asked.

"She granted me a favour, and in exchange she wants me to help her with something, a matter of great importance for our people."

"The favour she granted you. It was the return of Clare's child, wasn't it?"

Midir looked at her a moment before nodding.

"I dreamt of you and Clare's child," she said, "but I didn't understand what it meant until now."

Midir shrugged. "It was important to you."

"Thank you, Midir. Clare would be so grateful if she knew . . ."

Midir raised his hand as though to stop her words. "Do not thank me. The debt I owe to the queen shall soon be repaid."

The Faerie Queen had not invited them to join her at the high table, and Brigid longed to sit down and rest. She took Midir's hand and pulled him down beside her on the forest floor that was surprisingly cold. "So many things are different here, and yet in some ways they are just the same. Everyone seeks the favour of the queen, the same way the peasants in the village seek the favour of the lord."

Midir leaned towards her, his face alight with a mixture of horror and surprise. "You seek to compare my world to yours? My people belong to the most noble race the world has ever known. We are not peasants, who spend our days sweating in the lord's fields, and contenting ourselves with scraps from his table. We do not live in filthy cottages or share our food and drink with animals. We know nothing of the despair and ugliness of your world. Do not think to compare my duty to the queen to your people's slavery to that witless swine of a man."

Brigid felt her face grow hot. She bore no love for Lord Osin and had spent most of her life isolated from the villagers, but she still felt the unfairness of Midir's words. Hard work was nothing to be ashamed of, and despite Alainn

Ros' ignorance and superstition when it came to the Fair Folk, they looked out for one another. Besides, it seemed to her that service was service, whether it was to a beautiful woman or a red-faced lord. "I must go home," she said. "My mother will be looking for me."

Midir caught one of her hands in his own. "I have offended you and that was not my intention. I brought you here to show you what might be yours, what will be yours if you stay with me. I love you, Brigid. Stay with me and be young and free and happy forever."

Brigid's anger faded. The lilting sound of Midir's voice held all of the beauty and power of the music in the ballroom. "If I were to stay with you, I could never return to Alainn Ros?"

A single leaf fluttered onto Midir's lap. "No."

"I would never be able to see my mother again?"

Midir took both of Brigid's hands and raised them to his lips. "I shall make up for everything you think you've lost. We will be everything to one another. Every day we spend together will be more glorious than the last, I promise you."

The lilt in Midir's voice was stronger now, and Brigid felt how easy it would be to allow herself to be swept away by the beauty of his words, the promise of her own happy ending, like one of her father's tales. But when she closed her eyes, she saw her mother's sad, worried face.

"I cannot leave my mother. She needs me."

"Your mother will not suffer for your loss. For the rest of her days she will have soft bread to eat and sweet milk to drink. The herbs in her garden will grow fragrant and plentiful, and every patch of soil that she touches will grow the best vegetables. This I promise you. It is our way. We never fail to show our generosity to those we have taken from."

A vision of Aoife, Clare's rosy-cheeked baby, swam before Brigid's eyes. "What would you have given to Clare to make up for the loss of her child? A fat pig? A cow? Humans are not so easily replaced."

Midir's eyes burned into her own. "Many a woman's grief has been satisfied for less. I once knew a woman who begged me to take her child in exchange for the Fair Folks' favour. Fear and hunger drive your people to dark deeds. You know I speak truly."

Brigid turned away from him. "My mother is not like the woman you speak of."

Midir took hold of her shoulders and turned her around so that their faces were only a breath apart. "Listen to me, Brigid. Your mother is old and unwell. Why should you throw away your own happiness for what few years of comfort you might give to one who will soon leave you?"

Brigid pushed his hands away, afraid of his touch, of how light it made her feel, as though she were not bound to anyone or anything. "She is not so old, and if God wills our time together be short it is all the more precious for that. I would give anything to have my father back, even if it were only for a single day."

Midir examined her face as though she were a difficult lock for which he must find the key. "I don't understand you," he said finally. "How can you not see that such attachments are a burden? Soon, perhaps very soon, your body will weaken and twist from carrying their weight. I wonder if you truly understand what I am offering you: A life of perfect freedom without worry or care of anyone. There will be no lord to rule over you, no villagers to scorn you, and no labour to steal your strength. We shall dance and laugh and sing. Day and night. No grief or work shall interrupt our pleasure. Would you give up all of this to return to Alainn Ros where you have nothing to comfort you but the love of an ailing woman?"

Brigid shook her head from side to side to dislodge the image of her future conjured by Midir's words. "I cannot make you see what you refuse to understand. What bonds one person to another matters more than anything. It is all there is in the world."

Midir touched her cheek with his hand, and let his fingers slide down the length of her face. "I could have taken you whether you were willing or no, but I gave you a choice, and you have not chosen well."

"Perhaps you are right, but I cannot be other than I am."

"So you will leave me?"

An intense longing to stay seized hold of her. She had spoken truly before, but she was also afraid. If she left Midir now, would she come to regret it? When her mother died, she would be left alone, except for Connell. Would his friendship and protection be enough to sustain her in the lonely days ahead?

"If I had not seen you in your true form, would you have told me the truth?" she asked.

"I can hold human form for one year. After that, the glamour of my disguise would begin to fade, and I would have asked what I am asking now."

"And Connell? Did you cause him to lose his way in the forest so you could take his place?"

Midir shrugged. "Does it matter? He came to no harm."

Brigid shivered inside of her flimsy gown. "I think it would matter to him."

Midir unfastened the gold broach at the neck of his white wool cape and placed the garment around Brigid's shoulders.

"You are not used to our land. The air is different here."

"I think I will not have the chance to become used to it."

"You will change your mind," he warned. "When time

has stolen your youth and strength, you will realize your mistake, but it will be too late."

Brigid lowered her head, not wanting him to see how much she feared the truth of his words.

"Very well." Midir stood up and helped Brigid to her feet so that they faced one another. "Will you kiss me farewell?"

The fierceness of Midir's embrace when he pressed his lips against hers seemed to hold all that she was leaving behind: love, freedom, safety, and the music that seemed as much a part of her as the breath in her body.

When she finally pulled away, Midir held out his hand and pointed to a grove of oak trees bursting with crimson boughs of holly. "You must enter the grove and continue walking without once looking back. When you hear the sound of running water, you'll know that you are home.

"Thank you for letting me choose. It is a gift not many men would bestow."

"Do not thank me," he said to her for the second time that evening. "I would have shown you greater kindness if I made you my prisoner."

Brigid held her breath as she walked towards the grove. Once inside, she heard the whisper of leaf and bough as the branches closed behind her, a sign perhaps that Liradon was lost to her forever. She felt a slight tingling in her hands and feet, and when she emerged on other side of the grove she was wearing her old wool gown and the net of crystals was gone from her hair that now lay in a long tangle down her back. She quickened her step, pushing herself across the forest floor that seemed unnaturally rough and steep. She walked until her breath came hard and fast, and then she heard it, the sound of running water. All at once the darkness lifted like the cover of a well, and Brigid raised her hands to her eyes to shield them from the pale light of dawn, as dazzling as a thousand mid-day suns.

Chapter 17

Brigid awoke to the sensation of her mother's lips pressed against her forehead. "The fever is broken."

Brigid sat up and stretched her arms over her head. "I feel much better."

"You're as pale as a winter sky," Mary said, the twin slashes of worry between her brows deepening further.

"I'm well now, I promise." Brigid swung her legs out of bed and stood up. "The first thing I'm going to do is to put this cottage in order. The spiders' work has been left undisturbed for too long."

Mary took her hand and led her to the kitchen table. "Sit down. The cobwebs can wait until you're fully recovered. You must be healthy and strong for your wedding day."

"Wedding?" Brigid asked.

Mary sat down beside her. "Connell and I spoke of it last night. I told him that it's high time the two of you were married. Haven't you spent the entire summer courting?"

"And what did he say?" Her voice was as thin and fragile as the cobwebs she brushed away with her fingers.

A shadow crossed her mother's face. "He agreed of course, but . . ."

"The thought was not a happy one," Brigid finished.

"Not happy? How can you speak so of a man who has neglected his mother, his home, and his livelihood for the love of you? No, I fear he's come to realize what his behaviour this summer has cost him. The entire village speaks of being poorly treated by the miller. Many have had grain sitting at the mill since May Day. Between the mill and the goings on at the manor . . ."

"What about the manor? Is Lord Osin . . . unwell?"

"I don't know. No one has seen him. Lady Osin has taken over his duties. It is she, no doubt, who will hear the villagers' complaints of Connell when they come to manor court."

"Did Connell tell you all of this?" Brigid asked.

"When he came here looking for you, he'd just come from the mill. Maeve must have been very angry with him, and rightly so, but her words have finally found their mark. I've never seen a man look so troubled."

"And when he found me gone?"

"He feared for you. We both did. Although when I told him about Clare's baby . . . he seemed to have forgotten all about it." Her mother looked at her closely. "If Connell lived in a Faerie dream these last weeks, it seems he's finally awoken. I hope you will do the same."

Brigid stood up. "I must see him."

"Brigid, love, sit down and break your fast. No matter how great his troubles, Connell will not stay away long. If you'd seen his face last night, the way he watched you while you slept. It made me forgive him all the rest."

Brigid knelt beside her mother and took one of her rough, reddened hands in her own. "I promise you, from now on things will be better for us. I will work hard. Perhaps Lady Osin will let me return to the manor, but I . . . I do not know if Connell and I will marry."

"Do not speak such foolishness. You and Connell are betrothed. A man like Connell would never break his promise."

Brigid released her mother's hand and stood up. "I don't want him to marry me because he thinks it his duty."

Mary rose stiffly to her feet, and Brigid nearly cried out at the expression of pain that broke across her face. *She is unwell and may not live long.* Midir's words swam through her mind like brightly coloured fish.

"I will not hear another word of this, Brigid O'Flynn! If you place no honour on Connell's promise, then what of your own? Have I raised you to treat the vows between a man and a woman so lightly?" Her mother bowed her head and covered her face with her hands. "You are so changed, Brigid. I fear I do not know you at all."

Brigid pulled her mother's hands away from her face and kissed them. "Forgive me, Mother. I can bear anyone's disapproval but yours. I will try to make things right with Connell, but I fear he will be angry with me."

"Why should he be angry with you?"

Brigid shook her head. "I must speak to Connell. If we are to marry, there are many things we must settle between us."

Brigid was sorry for the confusion in her mother's eyes, but she would say no more until she spoke to Connell. She had given herself to another man. If he did not guess all that happened while he was away, he soon would. Could either of them forget such a betrayal?

Brigid shivered slightly although the room was unusually warm. A large fire blazed in the hearth and there was a fresh pile of wood stacked beside it.

"Connell brought it last night," her mother explained following Brigid's glance. "He was so tired I feared the axe might slip from his hand, but he insisted."

Brigid stared at the fire. If she'd stayed with Midir there would be no need to explain or ask forgiveness. No need to face Connell's disappointment or to calm her mother's fears. It would have been so easy . . . "I must go to Connell at once."

"Go then, but do not stay too long. The clouds in your eyes say you are not fully recovered."

If there were clouds in her eyes, they were in her mind as well. Brigid's thoughts still swirled with the strangeness of the night she spent with Midir. She told him she'd made her choice, but what did that mean for her and Connell? How could she explain what had happened between her and Midir when she didn't understand it herself? The weeks they spent together were like some kind of dream, but her feelings for him were real enough. Her lips were still sore from his kiss. It felt wrong to go from the arms of one man to another, the kind of wanton action the villagers were so eager to accuse her of.

Besides, would Connell even want her when he learned the truth? Surely not even Connell could fail to be angry that his betrothed willingly accepted another in his place. Another who was not even human.

Chapter 18

Connell's mother opened the door when Brigid arrived, breathless, at the mill.

"I see you are recovered," Maeve said stiffly. "I expected as much. No illness could keep you long from my door. Connell is breaking his fast, and I ask that you do not interrupt his meal. He's not had so much as a sip of ale since he left you. My son has finally come to his senses. He spent the night at the grindstone."

"I've not come to cause trouble, but I must speak to him as soon as possible."

For a moment, Brigid thought Maeve might shut the door against her, but then Connell called out from the other room, "Mother, why do you delay in inviting Brigid inside?"

Maeve stepped reluctantly aside and Brigid entered the cottage. Immediately struck by the room's brightness, she marvelled at the windows made of real glass that chased away the shadows. It usually took her eyes several moments to adjust to the darkness of her own cottage, but Connell's home fairly sparkled in the daylight. The sun filtering through the windows even warmed the cottage floor that she noticed was covered with a large woven rug instead of straw rushes. Connell sat at a sturdy oak table at the far end of the room, a plate of cold meat and a trencher of bread untouched before him. When he saw Brigid, he rose from the table and beckoned for her to sit down.

"I am glad to see you looking so well. Will you break your fast with me?" Connell's voice was at once strange and familiar. Midir might have matched Connell in appearance, but he never captured the gravity of Connell's manners or the deliberateness of his words.

"Thank you, but I'm not hungry," Brigid said, uncomfortably aware of Maeve Mackenna's eyes upon her. "I only wanted to speak to you."

Connell turned to his mother. "Thank you for the food, but now I would speak to Brigid alone."

Maeve Mackenna bowed her head at her son's request, but Brigid did not miss the mingled fear and dislike in the other woman's eyes.

"I thank you not to distract my son from his work too long," she said before leaving the room.

"Please sit down," Connell said, before resuming his own seat. "You must forgive my mother. She's had a difficult time of late. The mill, the animals, our land in the lord's fields. Everything is in disarray." Connell ran his hands down his face that was pale with exhaustion. "I do not know if I will be able to put it to rights."

"I'm so sorry, Connell. If there's anything I can do . . ."

"Tell me, Brigid. Tell me what happened these last weeks. I know my mother was cruelly deceived by one who took my place . . . But what I must know is if you were deceived as well?"

Brigid clasped the sides of her chair. How could she explain all that had happened? "We thought you were dead," she said finally. "So when you, when he . . . found me in the forest that day it seemed like a miracle. I was so relieved and grateful . . ."

"So you believed this creature was me, that he was your betrothed returned from some misadventure in the wood."

Brigid nodded. "I know it's hard to believe, but he resembled you in every way."

"In every way?" Connell spoke slowly, as though it pained him to part with his words.

She hesitated before answering him. "No. He played the harp. His music, it was so beautiful, the most beautiful I'd ever heard."

"I play no instrument, Brigid," Connell said softly.

Brigid couldn't bring herself to tell Connell the story Midir told her about the harp. She would make no excuses for herself. "I know."

"Mother said nothing about a harp, only that I have shamed her in word and deed since the day I returned from the forest."

"I don't understand. Why haven't you told her the truth? That one of the Fair Folk took your place? If the village knew you were not to blame, you would be forgiven everything."

Connell tore a piece of bread in half with his fingers. "The villagers might forgive me, but they would not forgive you. If they knew the truth of what happened in my absence, I fear my protection would not be enough." He pushed the bread away and placed his palms flat against the table. Brigid stared at his hands. They were brown and rough from days spent in the sun and hard work, the fingers blunted by thick, red knuckles. Brigid thought of Midir's smooth moon-white hands, his long tapered fingers caressing the silver harp strings. Hands that had touched her face, her hair, the soft fingertips running down the length of her body making her skin tingle with pleasure. Why did she not wonder at the beauty of those hands? Were her words to Connell a lie? Did she know the truth all along, but refuse to admit it?

Brigid raised her face to Connell's. "No one can protect me from the village's hatred. They've proven that already."

"What do you mean?"

She told him how she came to spend the night alone in the forest, of Lord Osin's pursuit, and how she believed he'd come back and rescued her. Brigid did not tell him of the white hart or the vision she saw in the water. She could tell by the strange, closed look on his face that she had given him enough to consider.

"The village already sees me as a threat to their peace and happiness. You must think of yourself, and your mother."

Connell held her gaze briefly, before turning away. "Nothing has changed. You and I will marry, and no one will know the truth of these last weeks."

"Can you bear the weight of such a lie?"

"It is the right thing to do."

"For me?"

"Yes."

Brigid's chest squeezed. She'd held her breath waiting for his answer, but when it came she felt no relief. "I am grateful to you for my mother's sake. She has done nothing to deserve . . . And of course I am grateful for myself," she finished quickly.

Connell nodded stiffly. "We must make plans for the wedding. The ceremony should take place as quickly as possible."

Brigid placed her elbows on the table and leaned towards Connell so her words would not be overheard. "You've not yet told me what happened to you when Midir took your place. Where have you been all of this time?"

"Midir," Connell whispered softly. "That is his name?"

Brigid felt her cheeks suffuse with colour, a reaction she could not hope to hide given her extreme pallor. "Yes."

"When did you learn the truth?"

"In the wood. I was looking for you, for him, and I saw him in his true form. He had no choice but to confess the truth."

The lines on Connell's forehead deepened. "He showed himself to you?"

Brigid shook her head. "He did not mean for me to see him. I just . . . did."

"And then what did you do?" Connell spoke calmly, but the skin on his knuckles turned taut and white, as though there were not enough of it to cover his hands.

"I ran away. Then I saw you."

"You will not see him again?"

"No." Brigid's chest eased a little. At least this much was true.

Connell stood up from the table, and she could feel his eagerness for her to be gone. "Forgive me, but I must return to the mill. There is much to be done before nightfall."

Brigid rose unsteadily from the table. "I shall leave you then."

"Please give my best wishes to your mother."

"I shall. Goodbye, Connell."

Brigid left Connell's cottage more confused than ever. She expected him to feel betrayed and angry, but somehow his concern for her safety seemed worse than either of those things. Connell pitied her. He would marry her, not out of love, but to keep Brigid and her mother safe from those who might harm her if they knew the truth. "You should be grateful," Brigid whispered to the dark clouds overhead. But she did not feel grateful, she felt ill. An unpleasant saltiness filled her mouth, and she stopped to retch into the bushes. There was so little in her stomach she wondered what could have caused the sudden bout of sickness. *Mother is right. I must learn to take better care of myself.*

A cool breeze rustled through the trees and caressed Brigid lightly on the cheek. I should make a visit to Clare and her baby, she thought. A longing to witness a happy ending, even if it was not her own, gave her a sudden burst of energy. Brigid turned in the direction of Clare's cottage, but she had not taken more than a few steps when the sound of hoof steps, as loud as thunder, filled her ears. And in the space of a breath, a great dark horse that seemed to be made of night itself reared up in front of her, casting the surrounding trees in its enormous shadow. Brigid strained her neck as far as it would reach. The largest horse at the manor did not stand even half as high.

The horse's rider was stranger still, his expression as dark and impenetrable as the blue-black flank of the animal beneath him. Brigid turned to run, but like a rabbit caught in a hunter's snare, the ground held her fast.

"What do you want?" she whispered hoarsely.

The man did not answer. He merely stared at her as though there was neither a sky above her nor a ground below. He sat motionless in his saddle, his back as sharp and straight as a blade until, finally, he lifted one arm covered in chainmail as black as soot, and beckoned Brigid to climb up behind him.

Every muscle in Brigid's body urged her forward. If she made the slightest movement towards him, she knew she wouldn't turn back. The rider seemed to sense this for he gave no sign of impatience. He simply waited, as though it were inevitable that she would go wherever it was he wished to take her.

Brigid's feet were still firmly rooted to the ground, but her legs trembled with the effort to keep them there. If I go with him, she thought, Connell will be free of his obligation to me. She lifted one foot off the ground when a voice behind her shrieked, "Stop!"

Brigid whirled around to see Eanna Mare standing a few feet behind, her wispy grey hair floating around her head like a cloud of smoke.

"Stay where you are, Brigid O'Flynn. If you ride with the Dark Man, you will never return."

Brigid turned back to the Dark Rider, whose stony gaze remained fixed on her face. Unmoved by Eanna's appearance, he lifted his arm again in silent entreaty.

"Get away from her!" Eanna shouted. "If it's a woman you want, take me."

Eanna spoke this last with such intense longing Brigid didn't know whether she sought to help her, or simply take her place. Her confusion increased when a moment later Eanna hurled her pitiful, wizened body against the horse's legs and began weeping violently.

Finally, the rider shifted his gaze to the woman below him, his expressionless face suddenly creased with disgust. He picked up his reins, and horse and rider disappeared as quickly as they'd come, leaving behind a short trail of tiny blue flame, the only sign they'd been there at all.

Eanna picked herself up with surprising agility and turned towards Brigid. "I saved you from a terrible fate, and a glorious one."

"Who was that man? Where did he want to take me?"

"To a place you've already been, but this time there would be no return, or at least not until they'd sucked every last drop of youth and beauty from your body."

"If that's true, then why did you wish to go with him yourself?"

The older woman fixed her faded green eyes on Brigid and cocked her head curiously to one side. "Ahh, you do not feel it yet, but perhaps one day you will. Only then will you understand."

"You said I'd been there before. How do you know that?"

Eanna laughed, and Brigid was struck by the strangeness of such a girlish sound coming from the grey, withered lips. "It takes one to know one. The silver light of Faerie still shines in your eyes." She raised her hand to her face. "Once, my eyes used to make the Fair Folk weep with their beauty."

Eanna's words disturbed and touched Brigid at the same time. Whatever the truth of her story, the suffering of two lifetimes etched the deep hollows under her eyes and the creases on her brow. Brigid saw in her face the sorrow of a woman who had loved too well.

Eanna held out a trembling hand to Brigid, who took it in her own, and was startled by its coldness.

"You must be careful," Eanna said. "All Hallows' Eve will soon be upon us. If they want you, that is when they will take you."

"Let me escort you home," Brigid said gently.

"Will you heed my warning?"

"I promise to be careful."

Eanna seized the sleeve of Brigid's gown. "On All Hallows' Eve you must remain inside your cottage, and not leave for anything. Do you have a bit of cold iron to keep about you?"

Brigid nodded. "My mother shares your desire for protection. Now let me take you home. Your companions will be worried about you."

Eanna shook her head. "They are gone."

"Gone?"

"Dead. It is a hard thing to live with the memories of what you have lost. Of what will never be again. Most cannot endure it for long." Eanna leaned heavily against Brigid, as though her words had robbed her body of its remaining strength. Brigid could feel the older woman's bones poking through her woollen cloak.

"I think you are a good girl," Eanna whispered against Brigid's shoulder. "But the Fair Folk do not care about that. It is only beauty that they crave. And of that, I have none."

"Hush, we need speak no more of this. When did you last eat?"

"This morning. I thought he'd forgotten us these last weeks, but he came at first light with new bread and a fresh pot of honey."

Connell. No matter that he'd worked day and night since his return, he did not forget those in his care. Is that what I am to him? she wondered. Another abandoned, defenceless woman in need of his protection?

"Connell is a good man," Brigid said.

"*And I so fair and full of flesh, I fear it will be myself,*" Eanna trilled.

"Did the Fair Folk teach you that song?"

"No. It is not a song to sing in the presence of the Faerie Queen." Eanna lowered her voice to a whisper. "Some things must not be spoken out loud."

"Their music is so beautiful," Brigid said, her words followed by a sharp pang of regret that made her gasp out loud. If she'd gone with the Dark Man, she could have danced to that music forever.

Eanna sighed. "Do not speak of it. The rest goes easier if you do not speak of it."

But Brigid longed to speak of it. Eanna was perhaps the only person in the world who would understand about Liradon. She had so many questions: How did Eanna find her way into Faerie? Did she dance underneath an open sky? Where did she live, and with whom? But the sadness in Eanna's eyes stopped her from asking. If the other Willow Women died because they couldn't live with the memory of what they'd lost, then Eanna was right. It was better not to speak of it.

When they reached Eanna's cottage, Brigid saw that some repairs had been made since her last visit. The roof was newly thatched and the door no longer hung from its hinges. She did not need to ask who'd done the work.

"I must be getting home. Is there anything you need? Fresh water? Firewood?"

Eanna shook her head, but when Brigid turned to go, she seized her hand. "What is love?"

"Love?" Brigid repeated.

"Describe it to me."

To anyone else it might have seemed an odd request, but it reminded Brigid of the nights when men and women from the village would come to the cottage and beg her father to tell them story; a story of love that would lift their spirits and make them forget the chill in their limbs and the hunger in their belly.

"Love is like listening to the most beautiful music all the time. It makes you want to dance and sing, and cry out for joy. Love is wanting to be near someone so much you fear you will die of it."

Eanna dropped Brigid's hand and turned away, seemingly disappointed by her answer. "You have given me a tale."

Brigid looked at her, confused. "Tales are full of love. It's why people clamour to hear them."

"Goodbye, Brigid. Guard yourself well."

Brigid watched Eanna enter the cottage and close the door behind her. She remained motionless outside the cottage for several moments before finally making her way home.

Chapter 19

"Have you been with Connell all this time?" her mother asked once Brigid was settled in front the fire. Despite the warmth of the evening, she couldn't stop shivering. She wanted to wrap the orange flames around her like a blanket.

Brigid shook her head. "I left him to his work. I would have returned sooner, but I met Eanna Mare on the path. She was unwell so I took her home. The other Willow Women have died. She is all alone now."

Mary frowned. "It was good of you to help the poor woman, but if anyone from the village saw the two of you together . . ."

Brigid leaped from her chair. "I don't care what they think of me! Is there not wickedness enough in Alainn Ros? If it were not for Connell, the Willow Women would have died years ago."

"What you say is true, but there is goodness in the village as well. It's fear that makes them shun Eanna. They think only to protect themselves and those they love."

Brigid thrust another piece of kindling on the fire and watched the flames devour it. "I am sick of the village. Let them hate me if they will."

Her mother touched her gently on the arm. "The day has exhausted you. Everything will look better on the morrow, I promise. We must start planning for your wedding. There's no cloth for a dress, but I've gathered enough bits of lace for a lovely veil. Shall I show them to you?"

"Tomorrow, perhaps. I am very tired."

"Of course. You must rest. Will you take a cup of tea before bed?"

Brigid sat down on her pallet. She had no desire for tea or anything else. She wanted only to sleep and forget all that happened that day, but when her mother placed the cup of steaming liquid in her hand she accepted it gratefully. It would feel good to have something warm inside of her. But after one sip she put the cup down. "I miss a bit of sugar," she said in answer to her mother's puzzled expression.

"I put in sugar, a generous amount. I thought you had need of it."

Brigid tried to smile reassuringly. "It's the after effects of the fever. I shall soon be right again."

Her mother opened her mouth to speak, but was interrupted by a knock at the door. Brigid rose to answer it. "Who can it be so late?"

Connell stood in the doorway, his powerful frame bent from exhaustion.

"I did not say all I wished to this morning," he said.

"Please, come inside."

Connell gave an embarrassed nod to Brigid's mother. "Good evening, Mary."

"Good evening, Connell. Will you have some tea? It's freshly made."

Connell nodded gratefully, and sank into the chair Brigid held out for him.

After she gave Connell his tea, Brigid's mother left them by the fire and settled into the far corner of the cottage where she busied herself sorting pieces of lace.

"I did not answer you this morning," Connell said. "You asked me where I've been and I did not tell you."

"Will you tell me now?"

"'Tis a strange story, but I think it will seem less so to you."

Brigid curled her legs underneath her like did when she was a child, eager for her father to begin one of his tales.

Connell gave her a long look before rubbing his hands over his eyes as if to summon a vision of what he meant to say. "The journey began like any other," Connell told her, his voice hesitant and uncertain, the voice of someone unused to telling tales. "I'm not certain when I began to notice that something was . . . different. Was it the forest's sudden stillness? The velvety softness of the forest floor that smothered the sound of every footstep? Or the leaves on the trees that seemed unnaturally lush and green?"

Brigid nodded silently. She knew the place he spoke of well. She hugged her arms close to her chest and listened as his tale unravelled.

By nightfall everything had gone wrong for Connell and Miri. Despite the evenness of the ground, the horse began to weave and stumble until she would go no further. Connell had no choice but to make camp for the night. He'd just closed his eyes when Miri began to whine. That's when he saw the lights. At first he thought it was a band of robbers or outlaws carrying torches. But there was no sound of footsteps, no sound at all, just the strange glowing lights above them. They hung from the trees like stars, and the more he looked at them, the more he felt as though they were trying to tell him something. And then they disappeared, leaving Miri and Connell alone in the darkness. "I felt sick with grief," Connell said, "as though something precious and beautiful had been taken from me." So when the lights reappeared a few moments later in the trees ahead, Connell followed them, leaving Miri behind. Every time he drew close, the lights would disappear, only to reappear a few moments later. When the lights finally stopped moving, Connell found himself in a clearing with a large flat stone at its centre. "Is this what you wanted to show me?" Connell spoke to the lights as if they were alive, for that's how they'd seemed to him then.

The clearing was silent as death when Connell entered it, but suddenly the sound of hoof beats crashed through the bracken, and a party of men and women on horseback seemed to fly through the surrounding trees. He didn't know from where they came, or how. The bodies of their milk-white steeds were so slender he wondered at their ability to carry a rider at all. And yet, somehow they forged a path through what seemed the very heart of the forest.

Unsure if he was awake or dreaming, Connell didn't think to hide from the cavalcade. "They sensed my presence immediately," he told her. One of the women, tall and fair-haired with marble-white skin, crinkled her nose when she drew near to him, as though scenting an animal. At first Connell expected the Faerie to unleash some kind of fury at finding him in their meeting place, but they welcomed him instead, offering food, wine, and silken cushions. Not wanting to offend them, he accepted their company but refused both food and drink for fear that he would never find his way out of the clearing again. One of the women led him to a divan of russet-coloured silk and urged him to sit down. She raised one arm over her head in what must have been a gesture of command, because a small group of women went to work transforming the clearing into a drawing room fit for a king. Connell watched the women carefully, but he couldn't follow their movements, so graceful and quick their forms seemed to blur into a tangle of shining limbs and flowing hair.

All of the men and women were tall and beautiful, most with shining white-gold hair and wide, slanted eyes, but Connell thought there was an inequality among them. The women who spread the ground with silk coverlets and poured goblets of sweet smelling amber-coloured liquid from a crystal flask appeared to be servants. They waited on the Faerie masters, who lay sprawled on cushions, their long elegant legs crossed at the ankles.

It must have been close to midnight, Connell told her, but when all was ready, the forest glowed with light. When he looked up, he saw a sparkling chandelier the size of the mill wheel. It hung above the clearing as though it were suspended from the sky itself. As if to signal the commencement of the night's festivities, the Faerie masters clapped their hands. The woman who'd given Connell his seat sat down beside him and whispered in his ear, "Now we shall perform a play for you, our special guest this night."

The Faerie woman's voice was low and sweet, but her words made Connell uneasy. Why should the Fair Folk take pains to entertain a mere peasant? Surely such efforts deserved a more noble audience. Connell tried to tell her this, but something in the unnatural brightness of her eyes silenced him.

The Faerie woman placed her hands on Connell's chest and eased him back onto the divan's soft cushions. Some of the Fair Folk took their place on the smooth, flat stone in the centre of the clearing that had become a makeshift stage. None of the Faerie players altered their dress for the performance. The women all wore shining white shifts made of such light material the slightest breeze might have freed them from the wearer. The men's clothing was equally fine, white wool tunics and braies with silver-coloured hose.

The audience laughed and whispered softly to one another until suddenly, a deep hush fell over the clearing, and all eyes fixed hungrily on the stage. "How can I describe what I saw that night?" Connell asked. "It was like one of your father's tales come to life except that it did not seem to have a beginning, middle, or ending. And there was music. Strange, beautiful music that made you want to laugh, sleep, and weep in turns."

"What did it mean?" Brigid interrupted him.

"I cannot say. The last thing I remember of that night is the burst of applause after the actors took their bows. The sound descended over the clearing like a storm, and then I must have fallen asleep for when I awoke I was alone in the clearing."

"They left nothing behind?"

Connell shook his head. "I thought it some kind of fevered dream until I tried to retrace my steps back to Miri. But every severed trunk, shrub, and branch looked the same. I wandered aimlessly through the forest. The sun set and rose again before I finally collapsed from thirst and exhaustion. The forest held me fast. The Fair Folk did not need to blind me or steal my wits to make sure I never found my way home again.

"What did you do?"

"I walked. Sometimes it seemed as though I was walking in circles, but I knew if I didn't keep looking I would die there. I found water, and eventually some food. I lived on hazel nuts and berries, and mushrooms when I could find them. I dreaded the fading of the light. The nights were so dark and cold I almost wished Death himself might come for me, but then I thought of . . ."

"What did you think of?" Brigid asked tentatively.

"I thought of you. If I died alone in the forest, I would never see you dance in your new shoes at our wedding."

Always with Connell, Brigid could not seem to find the words she wanted to say, so she just smiled and hoped that for now it was enough.

Connell cleared his throat. "I might have died there anyway if had not been for the hart."

"The white hart?" Brigid asked.

Connell nodded, his eyes shining with the memory of the animal's beauty.

"The last night was the worst. The trees pressed in on me, crushing the breath from my body. The sky was so cold and black it seemed that nothing could live there. Not a single star glimmered overhead. When at last I felt the morning sun on my face, I did not think I could face another day of wandering. He was there when I awoke, standing over me. For a moment I thought he belonged to them he was so beautiful. But when I looked into his eyes, I knew he belonged to this world. For all the burning beauty of the Fair Folk's eyes there's no warmth in them. The hart looked at me like . . . I cannot explain it, except to say that I felt hope for the first time since I awoke alone in the clearing."

"I know. I saw him, too," Brigid whispered. "The morning after the villagers left me in the forest."

"I was so weak from hunger I could barely stand. The hart led me to a rowan bush brimming with fruit. After I ate my fill, the hart nuzzled my hand, and I understood he wanted me to follow him. We walked through the forest like companions, and it was not long before the surrounding trees lost some of their strangeness. I recognized the oak coppice, and the stream where Miri had stopped to drink. The hart must have known I was no longer lost, for when I turned around he was gone."

Connell paused. "The rest you know. I arrived home, but I did not receive the welcome I expected. Mother was furious at my absence, but it was for an afternoon's missed work, not for the better part of the summer I knew I'd been gone."

"When did you know?" Brigid asked. "That someone had . . . taken your place?"

"I guessed it soon enough. Mother was so full of stories of my selfishness, I had no chance to speak. She berated me for my neglect of the mill, and of course she spoke of you . . ."

"How she must hate me."

Connell placed his hands over hers, and Brigid started at the sensation of his rough palms. She had become so used to Midir's soft, white ones. It is the first time Connell has touched me since we were children, she thought.

"My mother will grow to love you, and in time it will be as though this summer never was. I hope you will come to believe this. I came here to tell you my story, but I also have a question I must know the answer to: Do you love him?"

When Connell spoke of his time in the forest, she was dimly aware her mother's movements, the steady swish of the broom against the floor, the clinking of wooden bowls. But now all was still. The air seemed to have frozen around them. Connell leaned stiffly towards her, and Brigid felt a sudden chill at the base of her spine. He waited for her to say the words that would thaw the distance between them and make it summer again.

Brigid felt a tearing in her chest. Did she love Midir? If she closed her eyes, she could recall the sound of his harp when he played for her in the forest. The image of their bodies intertwined on the forest floor floated before her eyes, and she felt her face grow hot with shame. That night, the feeling inside of her was so big she thought she might burst from it. She remembered Eanna's question: "What is love?" And her own reply, "Like wanting to dance and sing all the time." Was that not how Midir made her feel?

Brigid could say none of this to Connell. She'd betrayed him enough already. "I told him we couldn't be together. That my place is here."

Connell's shoulders sagged, and he suddenly looked far older than his one and twenty years. The days and nights spent alone in the forest had etched themselves on his face. His once smooth and untroubled brow creased with disappointment.

"But you would go to him if you could?" he asked wearily.

She shook her head. "It is not possible. I could never leave Mother . . ."

"That is no answer."

"I do not know what other answer to give."

Connell stood up and brushed invisible dirt from his tunic. He did not look at her when he said, "We need not speak of this again. What is past is past, and we must think to our future."

"Connell, wait. There is more for us to . . ."

"I have stayed too long already, and there is work to be done. My replacement did not give the same care to the mill that he gave to my betrothed."

Her stomach twisted. Until this moment, she'd never heard a word of bitterness cross Connell's lips.

He moved towards the door, but her mother stepped forward and placed a staying hand on his arm. "You have suffered greatly, but I must know: Will there be a wedding?"

"I shall not break my promise," Connell said.

Brigid could not see his face, but she imagined he wore the same expression as he did when he pulled her out of the muck, or when he was patching Eanna's roof. Connell would do the right thing no matter what it cost him.

"Good night, Mary, Brigid." And then he was gone.

"Now you know the truth of it," Brigid said to her mother.

Her mother sighed and sank into the chair that Connell had just abandoned. "I saw he was changed from the moment he brought you home, but I did not want to think too deeply on what it meant. It was not until I began to fear for you . . ."

Brigid didn't want her mother to say any more. They had accepted Midir into their lives because of what he offered them. For her mother it was the promise of security and protection, and for Brigid . . . the excitement of being with someone who desired nothing but her company. It was easy to be with Midir, as easy as waking up in the morning.

"What shall I do?"

"If you are wise, you will marry Connell and be a good wife to him, and one day the rest will be forgotten."

"And if I am not wise?" she whispered.

Her mother shifted her gaze to the dying fire. "No, Brigid. I will not think of that."

Chapter 20

The next morning Brigid was pulling weeds from the garden when she saw Connell trudging towards the cottage. She could not help but notice that he moved with none of Midir's grace or lightness, and yet she took comfort in the sound of his footsteps, steady and sure.

"'Tis a fine morning," Connell said.

She brushed her dirty hands against her apron and tried to smile. "I can scarcely believe the summer is at its end."

Connell looked at the ground as if he'd suddenly run out of words.

"Will you have a cup of ale?" she asked helplessly.

"Yes. I should like a drink."

Connell followed Brigid inside the cottage where her mother sat at the kitchen table scraping the remains of the morning's porridge from the bottom of a pot. Mary's face lightened when she saw Connell, reminding Brigid once more how important he was to both of them. Brigid poured the ale, unwilling to meet Connell's eyes that seemed to regard her with a mixture of confusion and disappointment. When she did look into their grey depths, she wondered how she could have been deceived by Midir. His transformation, however compelling, never quite concealed the dark flame that burned in the centre of his eyes.

She and Connell joined her mother at the table and drank their ale in silence. Finally, Connell put down his cup. "I came to ask if you would come home with me. Mother has found a bolt of cloth for your wedding dress and she wants to do a proper fitting. Afterwards, I thought you might help me in the mill. I could hire an extra hand, but you could perform the tasks well enough, and it would save me wages I can ill afford."

The morning's brightness seemed to dim. She should be grateful for Connell's forgiveness, but could not smother the feeling of resentment beneath her breast, its unyielding hardness pressing against her like a cold, hard stone. The thought of facing Connell's mother was bad enough, but Connell's desire to put her to work seemed further proof of his true feelings towards her. He made no claim on her heart. Unlike Midir, Connell had not spoken a single word of love to her. He was fond of her perhaps, but what he really wanted was a help-mate, someone to see to his dinner and the running of his household.

Connell tapped his fingers against the table while her mother smiled encouragingly in Brigid's direction.

"Of course I will come," she said. "I must thank your mother for her trouble."

Connell's shoulders lifted, and he looked pleased, if not quite happy. "It's settled then. I will fetch Mary more water while you make yourself ready."

"Thank you, Connell," her mother said gratefully.

After Connell had gone, Brigid carefully plaited her hair so that it fell in a silver coil down her back, and scrubbed at the dirt on her hands until her skin was pink and shining. She did not want to give Connell's mother another reason to disapprove of her. There was little she could do about the tiny holes that had formed on the hem of her gown, but she rubbed at the worst of the stains with a piece of cloth.

Connell returned with the water and a handful of wild mushrooms. "To thicken your pottage," he said.

Brigid kissed her mother, who placed a round clay pot in her hands. "Some of my rowan berry jelly. Please give it to Maeve with my good wishes."

Connell thanked her, but Brigid doubted a pot of jelly would be enough to sweeten the bitterness Maeve must feel, knowing her son was to marry a girl she thought lazy as well as cursed.

Silence settled between Connell and Brigid on their way to the mill. Would it always be so between them? Could she learn to live with a man who had no thought for anything but the next day's work? Would he never tell her his true thoughts, or ask to know hers? Although she had feared Connell's anger, she realized she would have preferred it to his quiet stoicism. She cast a sidelong glance at Connell's mouth, set in a thin hard line. Only a few nights before that same mouth had sung the sweetest ballad to her. But of course it wasn't the same, she reminded herself.

When they arrived at the cottage, Connell's mother was waiting for them. She greeted her son warmly, and nodded briefly in Brigid's direction.

"I shall leave you now," Connell said to Brigid, the first time he'd spoken to her since they left the cottage.

Maeve handed him a large flask of ale. "Take this with you."

Connell accepted the flask and Brigid thought she saw some kind of meaningful glance pass between mother and son. Had Connell warned his mother to be kind to her?

"Come inside then," Maeve said. "I will show you the cloth for your dress, and you can tell me if it is to your liking."

Brigid followed Connell's mother inside the cottage and, despite her misgivings, she could not help but be cheered by her surroundings. If Maeve Mackenna's manners lacked warmth, her housekeeping did not. No effort had been spared in making the cottage comfortable and welcoming. Brigid's last visit had been so strained, she failed to notice the curtains that hung from the windows in a froth of cream lace, or the pale blue glass pitcher on the kitchen table filled with wildflowers. Maeve's skill at weaving and dying cloth was evident in the brightly coloured tablecloth, and in the chair cushions that bore an unusual floral design.

"Your home is lovely."

Ignoring the compliment, Maeve said, "You'll need to take off your gown so I can see you properly."

Brigid removed her outer garments and stood shivering in her shift. The air had not yet turned cold, but Brigid could not seem to stay warm. A chill had seeped into her skin that even a blazing fire could not seem to chase away.

"'Tis no wonder you are cold with no flesh on your bones to warm you." Maeve's voice was as sharp as the pin she held in her fist. "I needn't have worried about having enough cloth. With the size of you, there's enough for two dresses."

Brigid forced herself to remain silent as Maeve placed her large, capable hands around Brigid's waist, and across her shoulders. When she brought out the cloth, a long length of cream-coloured wool embroidered with tiny gold butterflies, Brigid gasped. "I've never seen cloth so fine. Where did you find it?"

"I've been saving it for Connell's bride," she said, as though it were not Brigid she spoke of, but some mysterious girl who had yet to make herself known. "The embroidery was done by own hand," she added with a hint of pride.

"It's fine work," Brigid said admiringly. "Not even Lady Osin has such skill with a needle and thread."

"A woman's skills are a sign of her worth. A good wife brings comfort and order to her husband's household. That is what my son needs, not a woman who spends her days running wild and neglecting her responsibilities."

Maeve's words stung like nettles, but she could not deny the truth in them. Connell's mother had good reason to be angry with her. She'd brought Connell nothing but ill luck since the night of their betrothal. If she weren't so selfish and afraid, she'd make Connell see that he need not keep his promise to her. No doubt both he and his mother would be happier if he were marrying Deirdre with her large dowry and sturdy hips.

"I may not possess many skills, but I am a quick learner, and I hope to be a good wife to Connell."

"Your mother should have taught you better. If I had a daughter–"

Brigid pushed the beautiful cloth away. "Do not speak of my mother. She is the best of women. Whatever my shortcomings, they have nothing to do with her."

Maeve stepped back and the hard straight line of her mouth turned into a round 'O' of surprise. "I am finished with you. Put on your gown and join Connell in the mill. Lord knows he has need of some help."

Brigid lifted the gown over her head. "I'm sorry for speaking sharp. I shouldn't have . . ."

"'Tis not a bad thing for a girl to be loyal to her mother," Maeve said, her back towards Brigid. "Now get off with you. I have other work to do before it's time to start the supper."

Brigid found Connell outside cleaning grain out of the mill wheel. He must have been at it for some time because the various gears, teeth, and axel fairly sparkled in the sun.

"I've come to help," Brigid said when he did not look up from his work.

Connell nodded at her briefly.

Did the man never speak? She resisted the urge to stamp her feet like a spoiled child. "What would you have me do first?"

Connell wiped his brow with his sleeve. "I'd be grateful if you could help me carry these sacks of flour inside. Unless you think they're too heavy?"

"I can manage." Brigid picked up one of the sacks, which was heavier than it looked, but she wasn't going to tell Connell that.

Brigid followed Connell inside the granary, trying not to let her burden drag on the floor. The building was utterly transformed from the last time she saw it. The floor had been swept clean. Not a single blade of straw marred its surface. The bags of grain were neatly stacked in the corner of the room, and Brigid saw there were not half as many as there'd been before. No wonder Connell looked exhausted. He must have been running the mill wheel non-stop since his return.

Brigid let her sack down for a moment to rest her arm, but when she picked it up again a rough piece of twine caught her finger, making her cry out.

"What is it?" Connell asked.

Brigid popped her injured finger in her mouth. "It's nothing."

Connell came towards her. "Let me see the wound. Is it bleeding?"

Brigid pushed him away, a sudden burst of fury making the movement more forceful than she intended.

Connell fell backwards before regaining his footing. "What's wrong with you? Why won't you let me help you?"

"I don't want your help! I am not some poor, injured creature you must rescue. I am not Eanna!"

Connell stared at her, his calm regular features twisted into an expression that was nearly as wild as her own. It was as though someone had hurled a heavy rock into a still pond, shattering its smooth surface. "That is not how I see you," he said finally.

"Well that's what it feels like to me, Connell Mackenna! If I were not in need of your protection, I wonder if you would care for me at all."

Connell's voice rose to match her own. "You attract trouble, Brigid O'Flynn. It has always been so."

"And you think that is my fault?"

"I did not say you were to blame. You have been ill used by the people in this village. That is why I . . ."

"That is why you wish to marry me," Brigid finished. "So you can protect me if the crop fails and the villagers once more decide to punish me for their loss."

"I would not let you be harmed, but you are wrong if you think that is why I wish to marry you."

"Then why?"

Connell turned away from her. "My reasons are the same as any man's."

"That is all you wish to say?"

"You ask a great deal for a woman who told her betrothed that she loves another."

"Those were not my words," Brigid said softly. "I told you . . . my life is here in Alainn Ross."

"I know that, Brigid, but I wonder if you believe it yourself."

The last of Brigid's anger faded at Connell's words, but as soon as it was gone she wished it back again. She preferred the warmth of her anger to the cooling numbness that seemed to have invaded her senses, turning everything into a confusing jumble. Once more, she and Connell had disappointed each other, but neither one of them possessed the words to make it better between them.

Connell removed a pair of soft leather gloves from the pouch he wore at his belt and handed them to her. "These will save your tender fingers."

Brigid accepted the gloves and went back to the sack of flour. She and Connell worked side-by-side until the shadows on the wall grew long and thin, and the outline of the mill wheel began to fade with the dying of the light. Finally, Connell brought in the last sack of flour, and wiped his brow with the sleeve of his tunic. "I thank you, Brigid. I should not have accomplished nearly so much without your help. Will you stay and have your supper with us?"

Brigid shook her head. "I must go home and see to my mother."

The reason for her refusal was only partly true. She knew her mother would gladly give up her company if it would please Maeve Mackenna, but Brigid did not think she could sit through a meal with Connell's silence on one side and his mother's disapproval on the other. If she were to marry Connell, there would be a lifetime of such suppers ahead of her. *If she were to marry Connell.* The angry words they'd spoken earlier were better than silence, but so much remained unsettled between them. A fine dress and a comfortable cottage had not given her the certainty she wanted, the kind of certainty that only true love could bring.

"Then I shall see you safely home." Connell's voice was as thin and brittle as the fresh straw Brigid scattered on the floor.

"I must say goodbye to your mother. Thank her for my . . . wedding dress."

"Very well."

As if anticipating their arrival, Maeve Mackenna met them at the cottage door, her face flushed from standing over the fire.

She does not want me inside any more than I want to come in, Brigid thought as Maeve's sturdy frame filled the doorway, blocking her entrance.

"I wanted to bid you good night, and to thank you for my lovely dress."

Connell's mother frowned slightly. "It is my duty to see you properly dressed. I won't be embarrassed at the church with my son's betrothed dressed in rags."

"Good night then." Brigid turned on her heel and ran down the lane as swiftly as if she'd been transformed into a hart. She wanted to be far away from Connell, his mother, and their quiet comfortable cottage. She was nearly halfway home before she heard Connell breathing hard and fast behind her.

"Brigid, wait. Please," he said when she continued walking. "You are not safe alone in the dark."

She stopped, but did not turn around. "It is not the darkness I fear, Connell."

"Mother should not have spoken so harshly. If you'd given me a chance, you would have heard me tell her so."

"I do not want to be the cause of more trouble between you and your mother, and I meant what I said. I'm not afraid of the dark."

Connell put his hand on her shoulder and turned her towards him. "You say that you want me to speak, and yet when I try you run away from me."

"I'm not running away."

"We've known each other since we were children, but as a man and a woman we are strangers to one another. I had hoped . . . I had hoped that before we married this would change."

"I wanted that too, and I thought . . ."

"You thought you were getting to know me, perhaps even love me. Except now we both know . . ."

Brigid was suddenly aware of the forest's nearness. She could feel the strength of the trees, the thickness of their knotted trunks, their long elegant branches reaching up to trace the night sky. If she were to stray only a few steps from the path, she would find herself enveloped in their leafy embrace. She looked at Connell and saw the hurt hidden in the shadowy outlines of his face. Only a short distance from where they stood, she'd kissed his throat that was not his throat, felt his lips that were not his lips, in her hair and on her neck . . .

"I want to make things right between us, Connell."

Connell placed his hands on her shoulders so gently she barely felt his touch, but his voice was fierce. "Give me a chance, Brigid. Let me show you there's a life for us in Alainn Ross worth having, and that you belong here with me, not in the shadow land of Faerie."

Brigid smiled. "I thought you did not speak pretty words, Connell Mackenna."

Connell surprised her by smiling in return. "Perhaps I have not had need of them until now."

Brigid took hold of Connell's outstretched arm. They spoke little the rest of the way to Brigid's cottage, but this time the silence between them brimmed with the promise of all they might soon say to one another. The forest receded into the background once more, and when Connell held her close and whispered, "Sleep well," her thoughts were with him and nowhere else.

"Goodnight, Connell."

Chapter 21

Brigid awoke the next morning feeling more rested than she had in weeks. She'd slept deeply, untroubled by strange dreams and the echo of Midir's sad, sweet melodies. She still missed the sound of his harp, but the aching feeling of longing inside her chest had begun to ease a little. Still, when she put on her shoes, she wondered when she might dance again. Faerie music might be the most beautiful, but she could dance to anything. She closed her eyes and imagined herself dancing in Connell's arms. She turned the image over slowly in her mind, aware of its fragility. It was the first time she'd allowed herself to picture her wedding to Connell, and although still new, the thought no longer filled her with fear and uncertainty. Perhaps Connell was right, that in time it would seem like this summer never happened at all.

"You are awake and dressed," her mother said, entering the cottage, her arms filled with turnips and onions.

Brigid slid a comb through her unplaited hair. "I promised you things would be different. No more lying about in bed and staring at the fire. I mean to put this cottage to rights before supper."

Her mother placed the vegetables on the kitchen table. "So all is well between you and Connell?" She spoke lightly, but Brigid heard the concern in her voice.

"If things are not wholly right between us," she said carefully, "I think they soon will be."

Her mother sat down at the scarred wooden table and beckoned Brigid to join her. "Come and break your fast and tell me all that happened. Was Maeve kind to you? Was the dress to your liking?"

Brigid sat down at the table and picked up the slice of bread her mother had cut for her. She was hungry, having eaten only a little the day before, but as soon as the crust passed her lips, the juices in her mouth turned salty and her stomach heaved in protest. Her mother fetched the chamber pot, and she retched until her entire body trembled with the effort. When it was over, she sat up feeling better, and more ravenous than before. "Is there any bacon? 'Tis odd, but whatever sickness seized hold of me seems to have passed."

Her mother looked at her strangely. "Is this the first time you've been ill?"

"Yes. No," Brigid said, remembering she'd felt unwell before meeting the Dark Rider on the road.

"When was the last time?" her mother persisted.

Brigid told her mother about the sudden wave of nausea and the saltiness in her mouth, but she was careful to leave out any mention of the Dark Rider.

"And now you're quite well again?"

"Yes," she said between mouthfuls of bread. "I feel fine. It is not another fever," she assured her mother. "My skin is not warm and there is not the slightest ache in my limbs."

Her mother stood up from the table. "I must finish sewing the lace on your veil. I will rest easier knowing that everything has been made ready for your wedding day."

She brushed the crumbs from her lap. "My dress will be lovely. Not so fine as the one Midir gave me . . ." Brigid froze in place. How could she have been so careless? After all she'd done to ease her mother's fears, to give herself away over a dress! Brigid waited for her mother to question her, but the older woman gave no sign of having heard anything amiss. Brigid could almost believe she'd not spoken out loud if it were not for the unnatural stillness of her mother's posture. The fixedness of her gaze on the needlework in her hands gave her away. Still, Brigid was relieved not to have to tell her mother about the night she spent in Liradon.

"I will go down to the well," Brigid said.

"When you get back, I should like you to try this on. I want to see how the lace looks against your hair."

Once outside, Brigid drank greedily of the fresh air. She promised to clean the cottage, but would have preferred to spend the day outside in the bright sunshine. The approach of her wedding day meant that summer was nearly at its end. After All Hallows' passed, there would not be many more days like this one. The air would tighten with the promise of cold, and night would fall more quickly, shutting everyone indoors. The lightness she felt upon waking faded at the thought of the long, lonely months ahead. Brigid and her mother had endured many winters, but now most of her time would be spent with Connell and his mother at the mill. Her mother would be nearby, but it would not be the same. As Connell's wife, she would be expected to make a home, and to care for the children when they came . . .

She raised her face to the sky to let the sun warm her skin. The brightness of the day reminded her of the afternoons she spent outside with Midir when the duties of marriage and motherhood seemed a far off dream.

Brigid opened her eyes. She was meant to be fetching water. The cottage wanted a good cleaning, her mother's store of herbs needed replenishing, and the clothes wanted washing. There was no time for her to stand dreaming in the sun.

Brigid might have fetched water in her sleep, so familiar was the well-worn path that veered off the village's main road. She approached the tall stone cross that surmounted the copious spring in a kind of trance, and once more her thoughts strayed to Midir. He'd promised her a life free from grief and care, a life where she belonged to no one but herself and would be free to do whatever she chose. She'd told Midir she could not imagine such a place. Was that because Connell was right? That in spite of everything she belonged here in Alainn Ross? Or did she simply lack the courage to embrace Midir's vision of their life in Liradon? If it were not for Eanna's intervention, would she have gone with the Dark Rider?

"Do not think on it anymore," Brigid said out loud.

"Do not think on what?" a sharp voice asked. "Perhaps you do not wish to dwell on the reason why a man like Connell Mackenna should wish to marry a nobody like you."

The sound of well water flowing into the stone trough had drowned out the sound of Deirdre's footsteps behind her. The other girl carried two empty pails in her well-shaped hands, and her ruddy face was shadowed with dislike.

"I doubt you care to hear my thoughts any more than I care to hear yours," Brigid said.

"You are wrong, Brigid O'Flynn. I wonder at your lack of care for anyone but yourself. You made the village go hungry once already, and now you have nearly cost Connell his life. What is to prevent you from causing further harm to those unlucky enough to cross your path?"

Something fierce and proud rose up inside her, and when she turned to face Deirdre she had the sense of towering over the other girl, although they were nearly the same height. "You know nothing about me. And if you truly believe that I command the wind and the rain, and the seeds in the soil, then I guess I should thank you for giving me so much power. Connell has nothing to fear from me. I have saved him from a far worse fate of marrying a sour-faced shrew like you!"

Deirdre's face broke out in caterpillar-shaped blotches, but it was Brigid who was shaking. Why could she not be silent and proud like Connell? Her angry words only made her feel worse, and did nothing to take away the heaviness beneath her breast.

"We shall see who is right, Brigid. You are cursed. I can see it in your black devil's eyes. Mark my words, Connell Mackenna will regret the day he married you. That is, if he does not first sicken and die from your Faerie ways!"

Brigid wanted to run from Deirdre's ugly words, but she couldn't return without water, so she waited while Deirdre filled her pails, and forced herself to endure Deirdre's final triumphant smile before she turned back towards the village. After she'd gone, Brigid fetched her own water with trembling hands. She knew Deirdre was jealous of her marrying Connell, but what if she was right? Connell himself said that she attracted trouble. Even if he did not blame her for what happened with Midir, would he be so forgiving if more ill luck were to befall them?

The idea that Connell should come to see her as a burden his honour forced him to carry burrowed inside her skin like a thorn. She arrived home drained of all her earlier energy and when she opened the door, Connell and her mother were seated at the kitchen table. The light in both their eyes faded when they saw her.

Her mother rose from the table. "Are you unwell again?"

Brigid wanted to tell her mother about her encounter with Deirdre, and hear her words of comfort, but she could not speak of it in front of Connell.

"No, Mother, I am quite well."

Connell stood up. "Again? Have you been ill, Brigid?"

She smiled widely, hoping to force some colour into her cheeks. Now that there was finally some understanding between them she didn't want Connell to revert to his role of protector. "Nothing that regular meals won't put to rights."

"Well then, my offer to take you on a picnic should be welcome."

"A picnic?" Brigid asked as though she'd never heard the word before.

"I was up with the sun so I might have a few hours of leisure this afternoon. That is, if you will join me," he added shyly.

"A picnic sounds lovely," her mother said when she did not respond.

"You must join us then," Connell said, still looking at Brigid.

Her mother shook her head. "Thank you, but I will not. I have much to occupy my time this afternoon."

"Brigid?" Connell asked.

"I promised to clean the cottage, but if Mother thinks I might put off my work for a little while I should be glad of a picnic."

"Of course you must go," her mother said. "It is a fine day, and there won't be many more like it."

Connell smiled, and the expression lent his features a beauty Brigid had not seen in his face before. "Mother was good enough to pack us a basket of her best honey cakes and some salted meat. If you're ready, we might leave now."

Brigid's stomach churned with an unease she hoped did not show on her face. The promise of an afternoon alone with Connell without the watchful eyes of Connell's mother upon them should have been welcome, but Deirdre's words had tainted her pleasure. The other girl's vow that Connell would regret his decision to marry her hung about her neck like an amulet of stone.

"I'm ready," she said.

Her mother gave her a quick embrace. "Don't go into the forest." The familiar warning made Brigid's insides churn even more violently.

Connell kissed the older woman. "We shall not, I promise you. I've no wish to return to the woods."

After they left the cottage, Brigid reflected on Connell's words. He, too, had been permitted a glimpse of Faerie, but unlike her the experience seemed to have no hold over him.

He walked beside her, each footstep connecting soundly with the ground, while her own tread was so light and unsubstantial the soles of her shoes left no mark upon the earth. Her arms and legs felt almost weightless, and she had to fight the sensation that her body was flowing upwards. If it were not for Connell's sturdy presence beside her, she feared she might drift away.

As if reading her thoughts, Connell took her arm and Brigid leaned lightly against him. Ever solicitous, Connell said, "I know a place not far from here. You shall soon be able to rest."

Brigid shook herself free of Connell's grasp. "I am not at all tired."

Connell frowned. "You look as frail as a butterfly."

Brigid leaped ahead of Connell, lengthening her strides until she was running ahead of him. "Your mother said much the same thing yesterday," she called back, "but size can be deceiving."

Her limbs protesting at the sudden burst of exertion, Brigid pushed herself forward. She would not be compared to a butterfly, so fragile and delicate a strong wind might mean its destruction. She refused to turn around, but could hear Connell breathing heavily behind her, and when the edges of her vision turned dark and fuzzy, Connell was close enough to reach out and break her fall.

Her eyes fluttered open. She and Connell were half lying on the ground, their limbs askew. When her vision cleared, she saw that the blue had leaked from the sky and the new clouds seemed to swim menacingly towards her.

She sat up, conscious of Connell's arms around her. "I must have lost my balance."

Connell released her. "You are with child." His voice was as dark and hollow as the sacred well in the forest.

She stared at him astonished. "No! It cannot be so."

"My mother told me of your swollen belly and I would not believe it. But now I know I've been a fool. You are made ill and dizzy because of the child inside of you, his child," he added meaningfully.

Brigid never imagined she might be with child, yet as soon as Connell spoke she knew it was true. It had been true the day the Dark Rider commanded her to go with him. Had Midir somehow guessed her condition? Was it he who had bid the Dark Rider to come for her? But if he truly wanted her, then why hadn't he come for her himself?

The feeling of weightlessness returned to her body, as though she had in fact been transformed into a butterfly, but the sadness in Connell's voice bound her to the earth.

"So it is true. You do not deny it."

Brigid shook her head, not trusting herself to speak. It seemed that every word she had ever spoken to Connell had done him harm.

Connell put his face in his hands, and for a moment she thought he might weep, but he quickly removed them, and when he raised his head she saw that his eyes were dry and clear. "It shall not be the first child born early to a newly married couple."

"Everything is changed now. I cannot ask you to . . ."

"We will not speak of this again. Tomorrow we shall go to church. All of the village will see us receive Father Diarmaid's blessing, and the day after we shall be married."

"Connell, you do not need to give your life for . . ."

"Another man's child? What would you have me do, Brigid? Let you and your child starve? Or worse, see you stoned in the village square."

Instinctively, she placed her hand over her stomach. Seeing the gesture, Connell turned away, revealing the hard-set line of his jaw.

"It is the right thing. The only thing," Connell said flatly. "Do not fight me in this."

She nodded, knowing that nothing she said could dissuade him. Connell was like the mill wheel he operated, sturdy and strong, never altering its course.

Connell righted the picnic basket, the contents of which were overturned by her fall.

"You must eat something. They say the first part is the most difficult. You will need your strength."

Brigid reached into the basket and pulled out a large linen bundle. Inside were teacakes, still warm from Maeve's oven, and a fresh comb of honey. Brigid offered Connell one of the teacakes, but he pushed it away.

"I'm not hungry."

Brigid felt little appetite herself, but when she swallowed a piece of teacake, it felt warm and comforting inside her. From now on I will take regular meals, she vowed silently. If she were to be a mother, she would have to give up her careless ways.

Connell sat close enough for her to feel his breath on her cheek, but he seemed farther away than ever. She heard his disappointment in every exhalation. The silence grew thicker and stronger, forming an invisible wall between them. She wished he would speak to her. Even if his words were hard or unpleasant, they would be better than nothing. Brigid thought wistfully of the night before when it seemed . . . but now that was lost forever. Marrying her was a duty he must perform, an obligation that his sense of honour would not allow him to abandon no matter how he might wish it. Brigid told Deirdre that she had saved Connell from marrying the likes of her, but in truth, Deirdre would have made a better wife. Whatever her faults, Deirdre was loyal and her feet were firmly connected to the earth. She would never have betrayed Connell with one of the Fair Folk.

"If you're finished, I will take you home," Connell said.

Brigid brushed the crumbs from her lap and rose to her feet. "We have not been gone long."

Connell stared at the ground in front of him as though he'd lost something valuable there. "I'd best be getting back to the mill."

Brigid held her breath. "Will you tell your mother?"

"I shall not speak of it to anyone. Nor should you," he added, a warning note in his voice.

"I will not."

The return journey was made quicker by Connell's long, steady strides. He's eager to be away from me, she thought, surprised by the unexpected stab of misery the knowledge gave her.

"I shall come and fetch you and your mother for church tomorrow," Connell said when they stood in front of Brigid's cottage.

"Our presence in church will change nothing. Father Diarmaid's blessing will not alter the village's dislike of me or our marriage. My mother hears things from the women she attends. Some whisper that I am responsible for Lord Osin losing his mind. It might be better for you if I stayed away."

"No. You will not hide yourself for imagined wrongdoings. I belong to this village and so do you, Brigid O'Flynn. Alainn Ros must not live in ignorance forever. We will go to church as is our Christian duty, and together we will receive Father Diarmaid's blessing."

It suddenly occurred to her that in some ways Connell and Midir were not so different. The words of both men carried a strength and conviction that were not easily disobeyed. Connell possessed none of Midir's Faerie gifts, but when he spoke of their life together, his certainty wove a spell of its own.

Connell was already walking away from her when she called after him.

He turned around. "What is it, Brigid?"

"I know I am not . . . I know I have disappointed you, and I am sorry for that. Truly."

Connell looked at her, the expression in his eyes unreadable. "What is done is done. What matters now is that each of us does what is right. I hope that . . . I hope that in time you will come to understand this as I do."

Brigid stood in the doorway of the cottage and watched Connell walk away from her. For a moment she thought to run after him, but what would she say? If he was Midir, she might have kissed him, and there would be no need for explanations. But Connell was not Midir. He would want more from her than that.

Chapter 22

Brigid entered the church on Connell's arm, her mother standing close beside her. Maeve walked stiffly behind Connell like a proud, diminutive shadow.

She anticipated her arrival would be greeted by heavy frowns and furtive whispered exchanges. Years of living in the village without truly participating in its daily life had accustomed Brigid to such behaviour. But she was not prepared for the looks of open hostility that followed her every movement, nor for the strength of her own reaction. She'd come to accept her lack of welcome in the village, but the thought of the child inside of her receiving the same treatment nearly brought her to her knees. The strange contrast between the Virgin Mary smiling serenely from the church's stained-glass windows and the villagers' faces twisted with dislike made it impossible for her to take another step inside the church. But then she felt Connell's strong arm encircle her waist, gently urging her forward.

On the few occasions Brigid and her mother came to church, they took their seats at the back so as to attract as little attention to themselves as possible. But today Connell led them right to the front. Brigid was so close to Father Diarmaid she could have touched the hem of his robe.

Connell helped the older women into their seats, sat down next to Brigid, and whispered softly in her ear, "Pay them no heed. This is God's house, not theirs, and he does not judge you so harshly."

A smile tugged at her face, but she took little comfort from his words. Why should she be the one to feel shame?

Surely, the villagers' crimes were greater than hers. If Midir had not found her that day in the forest, many of the men seated around them would be murderers.

Brigid leaned towards Connell, thinking to give voice to her bitter thoughts, but the solemn look on his face made her think better of it. Connell wouldn't understand, not really. He was kind to her and to the Willow Women, but he didn't know what it was like to be an outcast—to have to rely on the mercy of others in order to survive.

Swiftly aware that he must compete for the villagers' attention, Father Diarmaid cleared his throat and raised one arm in front of him. "Welcome, God's children. Let us begin this day's sermon."

Father Diarmaid was not an imposing figure, but what he lacked in height and robustness he made up for with his gift of clear and thoughtful speech. His words sometimes frightened Brigid for their ability to resonate in her head, even when she did not agree with them. She felt some of this fear now when Father Diarmaid's eyes came to rest on her after surveying the rows of hard wooden benches to see which men and women had come to pray forgiveness for their sins. His gaze shifted from her to Connell, and Brigid thought the corners of his mouth turned slightly upward. He thinks that church will make me a good woman, Brigid thought resentfully. The men who'd kidnapped her were regular churchgoers, and Father Diarmaid's sermons seemed to have had no affect on their goodness.

Unable to focus on the priest's warning about the dangers of pagan superstitions, Brigid turned her attentions to the church itself. It was lovely to be near the front, close enough to see the intricate detail in the skilfully woven silk tapestries that hung from the walls. Brigid thought them finer than the ones that hung in Lady Osin's chamber, but not nearly as strange and wonderful as the moving tapestries she'd seen in her dream. The delicately etched stained-glass figures in the windows reminded her a little of Faerie men and women. The sun shone through the glass, bringing the Virgin and her celestial cohorts to life. The rose-coloured panel depicting the Virgin Mary seated alone, her arms crossed against her chest, was Brigid's favourite. If it were not for her shy posture and her demure downward gaze, the Virgin's delicate beauty would have resembled the Faerie Queen. And of course the clothes were different. Mary's voluminous blue robes looked heavy enough to drag on the ground while Faerie women favoured gowns so thin and light they might have been spun from stars and spider webs.

The sound of Father Diarmaid clearing his throat a second time roused Brigid from her thoughts of the Fair Folk.

"Take into your hearts the knowledge that only God can answer our prayers to heal the sick and to make the earth yield plenty when it is cold and barren. Only God can forgive us for our sins and our weakness in the light of temptation. Only God in his infinite wisdom and mercy is worthy of our devotion. Without our Heavenly Father, we are alone and lonely in the world. It is his wrath you should fear, and no other."

Father Diarmaid glanced at the window as if mindful of God's ever-watchful gaze, before returning his attention to the villagers. "Now let us speak of more joyful things. Connell Mackenna and Brigid O'Flynn will marry on the morning of All Hallows' Eve. I hope you will join Connell and Brigid on their wedding day to share in their celebration."

A sudden gust seemed to blow through the stale air of the church, loosening the villagers' tongues, until the room was filled with whispers like the sound of rustling leaves.

Father Diarmaid frowned. "This morning's service has not yet ended and I would ask that you respect this sacred space. If someone has something to say, I invite them to speak now."

"I'm sorry, Father Diarmaid, but is it not strange to hold a wedding on All Hallows' Eve?"

Brigid recognized the voice as belonging to Deirdre. "Everyone knows that night belongs to the Fair Folk, and to the dead." Deirdre lowered her voice to a whisper.

The murmurings inside the church intensified. Deirdre was not the only one who believed the Faerie walked on All Hallows' Eve. Every year the villagers hung their doors with holly and mistletoe. Some even left small gifts of food they could ill afford to part with to gain the Fair Folk's favour, and most important of all: No one left their cottage until morning when the danger had safely passed.

Father Diarmaid raised his hand for silence and when he spoke, Brigid heard the weariness in his voice.

"I have long been aware of the dangerous superstitions of this village, and I fear that I have been tolerant for too long. I tell you it is time to be the true sons and daughters of God and cast off these pagan ways. All Hallows' Eve does not belong to the 'Fair Folk,' as you call them, because such people do not exist. Nor have you anything to fear from the dead. They do not walk among us on All Hallows' Eve, nor at any other time. Their souls are at rest with our God. There is nothing for you to fear but your own foolishness, and against this, there is no bush, flower, or charm to protect you."

Father Diarmaid's voice rang with truth and conviction, and Brigid sensed he'd been longing to make this speech since he came to the village. The villagers sat in respectful silence, but Brigid doubted anything the Priest said could undo Alainn Ross's 'pagan ways.' They had felt the Fair Folk's presence for too long to be swayed by Father Diarmaid's talk of God's protection. After all, where had God been when husbands lost their wives and mothers their newborn babies?

"Would anyone else care to speak?" Father Diarmaid challenged.

Brigid saw Baker and his wife shaking their heads out of the corner of her eye. No one would challenge Father Diarmaid. There was no need. The villagers would simply carry on as they'd always done with their Faerie charms and protections.

Father Diarmaid sighed, and for a moment Brigid felt almost sorry for him. He might have nice food to eat and more land than anyone else in the village, save for Lord Osin, but his life would be a lonely one. The villagers might come to him for a bit of cheer and comfort when their spirits were low, and celebrate the Holy Days that gave them a feast, but they would not abandon their true faith. Father Diarmaid was just another teller of tales, and though he might have a fine voice, his stories of Moses and Abraham, and Christian duty could not compete with the glittering, ruthless beauty of Faerie.

But as Connell helped Brigid to her feet, she almost wished that Father Diarmaid were right. If there were no Fair Folk, then perhaps her father would not have died and Brigid would not have been blamed for his death. She would have been an ordinary girl getting ready to marry a good man, instead of a strange and lonely outcast who did not seem to belong anywhere. She pressed her hands against her belly. Would her child bear some mark of the Faerie? Something that would betray his or her true identity? Brigid shivered inside the too-warm church. She could not bear for her child to suffer even the slightest injury.

"It would be better for you to give him up," someone whispered close to her ear.

Brigid whirled around, but there was no one. Eager to return home for their mid-day meal, most of the villagers had already left the church. Only Brigid, Connell, and Father Diarmaid remained.

"Where is my mother?" Brigid asked Connell.

"She and my mother are waiting for us outside. I wanted to have a word with Father Diarmaid."

The priest stepped towards them, smiling broadly. "Pay no heed to your neighbours. It will be a fine wedding. They will soon see the error of their ways."

"Thank you, Father Diarmaid," Connell said gravely. "Brigid has suffered greatly under the weight of the villagers' superstitions."

"I offer only the word of our Lord for those who will hear it. You are a fine example to the rest of the village, Connell. I hope that in time . . . more will come to follow you."

Connell lowered his head, and Brigid wondered if he was thinking of the time he spent with the Faerie. She smiled to think of what Father Diarmaid would say if he knew the truth of their strange courtship.

The two men clasped hands, Father Diarmaid's looking impossibly soft and pink against Connell's sun-browned ones.

"I shall see both you on the morrow," the priest said.

Once outside, Brigid breathed deeply of the fresh, cold air. As much as she admired the church's beautiful interior she preferred to be underneath the open sky, and feel the breeze against her skin. Unwinding the cloth that covered her hair, Brigid raised her face to the sun until bright spots of colour appeared beneath her closed lids. Surely she'd imagined the voice in the church? She must have, for only she and Connell knew the truth.

Suddenly aware of Connell's eyes on her, Brigid turned towards him.

"Mother and I would like for you and Mary to join us for supper," he said.

Connell's mother nodded stiffly beside him as though unable to voice the invitation herself.

"We should be glad to join you," her mother answered quickly. "It will be a fine way to spend the last evening before your wedding."

"I've made a fine eel pie," Maeve managed finally.

The thought of eel pie made Brigid's stomach turn over, but she gave Connell's mother what she hoped was a grateful smile.

Connell offered Brigid his arm when a woman's voice rang out behind them.

"Sweet lady, won't you buy one of my silk ribbons? Such a lovely one I have to show you. 'Tis the very colour of your eyes."

Brigid turned around to see a slight hooded figure standing on the edge of the churchyard. The woman beckoned Brigid towards her, one slender hand emerging from the depths of a heavy green cloak that hid the rest of her body.

"Come away," Maeve said. "The woman's naught but a beggar. She promises silk, but 'tis more likely torn strips of dirty linen she carries with her."

But Brigid was already halfway across the churchyard. Something about the woman's voice was strangely familiar, like a half-remembered ballad. She felt herself pulled towards her, heedless of Connell and her mother's pleas that she remain. When Brigid drew close enough to see her face, the woman bowed her head so that the hood of her cloak fell forward.

"Fine lady, will you take pity on an old woman and buy one of her poor wares?"

Brigid ran a hand down the length of her plain wool gown. "I am not a lady as you can plainly see. And you do not stand like an old woman. Do I know you?"

"Clever girl." The woman threw back her slender shoulders and shook her head free of the hood.

Brigid gasped and made the sign of the cross over her breast. It was the dark-haired woman who had watched her so closely on the dancing night. Brigid recognized the leaf-green eyes that looked searchingly into her own. Midir said she was merely jealous, but Brigid did not believe him, and now the woman's gaze was more curious than resentful.

"I'd not decided whether to show myself to you, but even so, you sensed my presence. Midir spoke truly. You are different from the others."

"I've been told so all of my life. The words bring me no comfort."

The dark-haired woman nodded thoughtfully. "Neither here nor there nor anywhere. Still, there is a place you could be happy if you choose it."

"I've already chosen," Brigid said. "Did Midir ask you to–"

The dark-haired woman drew herself up to her full height, and Brigid realized her slightness had been no more than a Faerie trick.

"No man, not even Midir, commands me to do anything."

The power in the dark-haired woman's voice was unmistakable. "I'm sorry," Brigid said. "I thought . . ."

"Of course you did. That is how all human women think. They devote their lives to heeding men's desires and ignoring their own."

"That's not true," Brigid said, louder than she intended. "I would do as I wished if it were not for . . ."

"What prevents you from doing as you wish? Your mother? Or the man who long ago claimed you for his own? Who watches you even now?"

Brigid shook her head, confused. "Nothing holds me back. I told you, I've made my choice."

"It is not too late to choose more wisely. All Hallows' Eve will soon be upon us. For a short time the barrier between your world and mine will be lifted. Come to me tomorrow eve. I shall wait for you in the forest by the sacred well."

"I cannot," Brigid said. "I am to be married."

"Don't be a fool," the dark-haired woman hissed, but then her voice softened. "Do you think to be happy here? Truly? What happens when the harvest fails, or another child goes missing? You can be sure it is to your door they will come carrying torches in their hands and hatred in their heart. They will seek to punish you for things over which you have no more control than they. Even if you would choose this for yourself, surely you would not choose it for the child you carry inside of you?"

Brigid clasped her hands over her belly as if to protect him or her from the dark-haired woman's words. "Does Midir know?" she whispered.

"All Hallows' Eve. Come to the forest. I promise you have nothing to fear from me. I can show you how to leave the grief and cares of this world behind you. There is a way for you to be happy, happier even, than you were before your father died."

Brigid stepped backwards into something warm and solid. Connell.

"Come away, Brigid, and let this good woman try her luck elsewhere."

"I was just coming."

The dark-haired woman replaced her hood, but Brigid could feel the burning intensity of her gaze through the heavy material. Brigid turned around so that her face was pressed against Connell's chest. They stood there a moment before Connell released her and led her quickly through the churchyard.

"Wait, sweet lady! You forgot your ribbon."

Connell put a restraining hand on her arm, but Brigid pushed him away and ran back towards the dark-haired woman whose slender white hand stretched out towards her.

"Take it," she said, opening her palm to reveal a length of shining silver-white ribbon. "It belongs to you."

"I will not come to the forest. My place is here."

"Then accept it as a token of my good wishes for your wedding."

Brigid hesitated. Why would the Faerie woman give her a gift for refusing her offer? But her hand itched with the need to feel the softness of the ribbon against her skin. "Thank you."

The woman shook her head inside of the hood. "Our kind does not like to be thanked. Remember that," she said, a note of amusement in her haughty voice.

And then she was gone.

To Brigid's surprise, Connell did not ask her about the dark-haired woman. Both Connell's mother and her own remarked on the beauty of the ribbon she held in her had, but by the time they sat down to supper everyone except Brigid seemed to have forgotten her encounter with the faerie woman.

She feared the meal would be silent and awkward, but her mother had a gift for speaking of simple things, her praise for Maeve's good ale, the lightness of the pie crust, and the sweetness of the herbs she used to season the meat were graciously received by Connell's mother.

Brigid contributed little to the conversation, but at least she did not say anything to earn anyone's further disapproval. Maeve even complimented Brigid on her hair, fastened in a secure knot at the base of her neck. Brigid knew she should be grateful, but Maeve's newfound tolerance seemed further proof of the damage she'd wrought. Connell was the most honest man she knew, and yet he'd lied for her twice already. If they married, he would have to live with a lie forever: The greatest lie that could exist between a husband and wife.

Brigid watched Connell while he ate, searching his face for some sign of resentment or regret. The candlelight cast shadows on his face, but when his eyes met hers they were bright and clear. Like her, he spoke little, but she saw that he took pleasure in their mothers' easy talk. When he smiled at her, his face held all of the warmth of a blazing hearth. Brigid felt herself smiling in return, until she recalled the dark-haired woman's words.

Even if you would choose such a life for yourself, surely you would not choose it for the child you carry inside of you.

Brigid heard her mother ask Connell about his wedding gift, and Connell's teasing reply. The rhythm of their words was as familiar to her as the sound of her own breathing, and yet it was the dark-haired woman's voice that echoed in her head as though she were sitting there beside her instead of them. It will not be so for my child, she vowed. Connell will protect us both. But could he? She looked at her mother across the table. Before her father died, her mother had been known as a gifted healer, a wise woman whose advice was frequently sought by the rest of the village. All it had taken was a few whispered exchanges after Brigid's encounter with the Faerie Queen to make them outcasts. The dark-haired woman was right. If the village turned on her, there was little Connell could do to help, especially if Lord Osin refused to take her part. As her husband, Connell would suffer along with her, as would her child.

There is still a chance to choose more wisely.

Brigid found it increasingly difficult to distinguish the dark-haired woman's words from her own thoughts. She made the right choice, didn't she? The dark-haired woman spoke of Midir, but she did not answer Brigid's question. Did he know about the child? Would it make any difference to her if he did?

Her head ached. The light inside the cottage had only begun to fade, but she longed to lay her head down on the table and close her eyes. Yet, despite her exhaustion she did not want the day to end. Once darkness fell, she would have only one more night alone in her bed, and when she awoke it would be her wedding day, and then, All Hallows' Eve. After tomorrow there would be no going back. She shivered, and Connell got up from the table.

"I'll fetch you a blanket," he said.

Chapter 23

Brigid's wedding day dawned dark and cold. Winter had crept over the village in the night like a silver-haired crone, leaving the ground tinged with frost. The strange magic protecting the forest from the season's ravages had lost its hold. The green seemed to have leaked from the grass until it was stiff and brown, and the trees emerged from their protective coat of leaves like corpses whose flesh had fallen from the bone. When Brigid went to fetch the water, she stopped to gather some of the fallen red-gold leaves whose soft edges were just beginning to curl and darken. She couldn't help but think of the gold and silver leaves of Faerie, whose branches were never stripped of her beauty. They would remain lush and full forever, unmarked by winter's frost and harsh winds.

Fetching water from the well was the only chore Brigid was allowed to do that day. As soon as she returned to the cottage, her mother sat her down in one of the wooden chairs and began to brush the tangles from her hair.

"I have long looked forward to this day," her mother said. "You will be a lovely bride," she added, and Brigid heard a note of defiance in her voice.

Brigid wondered if anyone from the village would come to her wedding. When she thought of the hard, closed faces in church the day before, she could not imagine any of the villagers standing outside the church door showering her with seeds and grains of wheat, the village's custom for wishing a new couple a large family. Clare would come if she was able, but Aed was a superstitious man, and Brigid did want to be the cause of trouble between them after all they'd suffered. Nor did she expect to see anyone from the manor. Since Lord Osin had taken ill, the manor had drawn into itself. News of its noble inhabitants rarely found its way out of the high stone walls. At last night's supper, Maeve told them that Lady Osin continued to run the household, but no one knew how Lord Osin fared. Some said that he'd taken to his rooms with some strange malady, while others insisted he'd gone away on the king's business.

After hearing this news, Brigid found she couldn't look at Connell. Lord Osin was a cruel man, and she felt none of the loyalty a peasant was supposed to feel for the manor lord, but when she thought of what Midir did, she felt sick. She would not have wished such a fate on anyone. Far better to die of a plague or a fever than to lose one's mind.

"Why do you frown so?" Her mother smoothed Brigid's brow with the tip of her finger. "Today is a day for smiles and laughter. Connell is a good man. The two you will be happy together."

Brigid curved her lips into a smile while her mother removed her wedding dress from its linen wrappings.

"I have never made anything so fine," Maeve told Brigid when she handed her the carefully wrapped package. To Brigid's mother she said, "Make sure she has something blue about her for protection."

"I won't forget," her mother assured the other woman.

The something blue was a length of ribbon. It was slightly frayed at the edges, but when she fastened it around Brigid's waist it added a vivid touch of colour to the soft cream wool.

"Where did you find it?" Brigid asked.

"Your father bought it for me at the Great Town Fair to wear on our wedding day. My best gown was only slightly better than what I wore for every day, and your father wanted me to have something special." Her mother gently touched the bow at Brigid's waist. "It was the most beautiful thing anyone ever gave me."

"It's beautiful still. I'm glad to wear something Father gave you."

Her mother stood back to admire her. "It is a lovely dress," she said with a sigh, "but not as beautiful as the girl wearing it. Truly, Brigid, you have come back to yourself these last few days. For a while I feared . . . but there is no need to speak of that now. You are well and happy and soon to be a wife."

Brigid wished she had her mother's faith that a wedding would make things right, but since she awoke, the dark-haired woman's words rained down on her in a ceaseless torrent, drowning out everything else. How could she and Connell ever be happy with so much against them?

"I have the flowers for your hair," her mother said. "I finished them last night after you went to bed."

She watched her mother remove a delicate crown of fresh and dried blossoms from its hiding place underneath her pallet. The base of the crown was fastened with the dark-haired woman's shining white ribbon. The construction of flowers and silk shone unnaturally bright in the dimly lit cottage, and Brigid was reminded of the Faerie Queen who'd worn something similar on the night of the Faerie ball.

"They are protective flowers," her mother said, reading her thoughts. "The apple blossoms, primroses, and rosemary are dried, of course, but the yarrow is fresh. I collected it only this morning. And the ribbon . . . it was so pretty I thought it a shame not to put it to use."

"Thank you, Mother. I've never seen anything so fine and delicate."

"Shall I fasten it in your hair?"

Brigid nodded, knowing her mother's eagerness had more to do with invoking the crown's protective powers than with her appearance.

Brigid forced another smile as her mother placed the shining object on top of her head.

Her mother clapped her hands together, a rose-coloured glow lighting up her soft features. "It's perfect," she said. "I cannot wait for Connell to see you."

What was Connell thinking at this very moment? Did he regret his promise to raise Midir's child as his own? Could he really live each day with her knowing she'd born the child of another? A child that was only half human?

The small cottage was at once unbearably hot and the walls too close together. She felt the roof pressing down on her and she longed to be outside underneath the cold grey sky. Her arms and shoulders itched inside the soft wool, and the urge to tear the gown from her body was so strong she clasped her hands together.

Brigid's mother, her attention turned to her own preparations, did not notice her discomfort.

"Now that you're ready, I must see to myself. Will you be well enough on your own for a little while? Clare promised me a hot bath in her tub before I get dressed."

"Yes," Brigid said, her voice sounding strange and faraway. "Tell Clare I'm so glad for her, and give Aoife a kiss for me."

"You may do both yourself at the wedding."

"Of course," Brigid murmured.

After her mother left, Brigid removed the crown of flowers and unfastened the Faerie woman's ribbon, which she put inside the bodice of her gown. She paced back and forth inside the cottage, wishing she'd not let her mother leave her alone. Now there would be no one to stop her.

At first she just opened the cottage door, hoping it would be enough to feel the cold air on her hot, clammy skin. But it was not enough. She wanted to run hard and fast underneath the morning sky until her body seemed to float above the ground. There was nothing to fear. The dark-haired woman told her to come on All Hallows' Eve, and it was still morning. The sun had not even fully risen in the sky. I will only go a little ways into the forest, she thought. Just far enough to let earth and tree and stone sink into her skin one last time. She would be back before her mother returned from Clare's. No one need know she'd been gone.

The cottage door shut firmly behind her, Brigid drifted along the familiar path as if in a dream. It was not until the ground beneath her feet disappeared into a tangle of moss and fallen leaves that she felt the weight of her next step. She saw her mother as she'd been that morning, her skin rosy with anticipation, and Connell's serious, determined face, his grey eyes bright with purpose. Neither of them would want her to go to the forest. Once she was married, Connell would take up her mother's warnings.

Brigid took one step inside the wood, and then another, and then she began to run. The promise not to go far forgotten once the gently waving branches closed behind her. She ran as though the ground were made of smooth, clear glass, uncluttered by stones and fallen branches. She ran until she came to the sacred well where she stopped to peer into its dark depths. "Shall I make a wish?" she said out loud. Brigid had never asked the well for anything because she had nothing of value to give, but now she removed the shining ribbon from inside the bodice of her dress. It twisted in her hand like a serpent until she let go. The ribbon shot into the well in a stream of silver.

"You give the well a valuable gift. What do you seek in return?"

Brigid spun around. The dark-haired woman stood before her, tall and proud, her beggar woman's cloak replaced by a gown of moss green silk. Yet when she stepped towards Brigid, the skirt of her gown rustled as though it were made of dried leaves.

"My wishes are my own," Brigid said.

The dark-haired woman laughed, a light musical sound that seemed at odds with the hardness glittering in her dark eyes.

"Don't tell me then. It matters not, for I already know. You asked the well to protect the safety of your child, Midir's child."

Brigid felt her spine turn to melting wax. "What do you want?"

"Only to help you."

"Why should you want to help me? I remember your face at the ball. You did not seem to like me much."

The dark-haired woman laughed again, this time with genuine amusement.

"You are not mistaken. When I saw you that night, I thought you another of Midir's conquests, an attractive human to be used and discarded. But I have watched you, Brigid. You are not like the others. You do not bend like a green bough in the wind. Midir wanted you and you refused him. This is not the way of your kind. I do not understand it, but I admire it just the same."

"The others?" Brigid thought of Eanna and her lost companions. They, too, had crossed into Faerie for love and spent the rest of their lives paying for the experience. Was Midir responsible for their fate?

"Do not compare yourself to them. You have nothing to fear from taking a Faerie lover."

Brigid stared at the other woman. "How did you—"

"Read your thoughts? Your voice is strong and we are in

a sacred place. Outside of the forest it would not be possible, but here we might understand one another without words."

Brigid tried to make her mind as dark and impenetrable as a starless night, but the truth about Midir clung to her like moss on a stone. He was Eanna's lover. Brigid recalled the Willow Woman's words of reproach that afternoon in the forest, words meant for Midir, the man who'd abandoned her, not Connell as she'd thought. She could still see the way Midir looked at Eanna, as though she sickened him, and yet he'd loved her once. All the pretty words he'd whispered in Brigid's ear when they lay together in the forest. Perhaps he'd whispered those same words in Eanna's ear, and countless others as well. Brigid shivered. If she'd stayed with Midir, would he have one day cast her out mad and weak like the rest of the Willow Women?

The Faerie woman gazed at her intently, her face devoid of any recognizable emotion. "You were not mistaken in Midir's regard for you. It is different from the love in your tales, but that is all foolishness. In Liradon, men and women share their desire freely. There is no mine and thine, and when it ends, as love is wont to do, there is no anger or sadness or bloodshed. Can you say the same of your world? Come with me now and you shall know a love truer than any you dreamed possible. A love that needs no vows to keep it steadfast, and that never grows old or weary of itself. A Faerie lover offers pleasure that never reaches its end."

The bemused arrogance faded from the dark-haired woman's voice. She spoke gently now, and her words caressed Brigid's ears like the soft-winged tips of dove feathers. Brigid covered her ears with her hands to shut out the sweetness of that voice, but soon dropped them again. The dark-haired woman took several steps towards her until they stood facing one another, silent and still. The breeze ceased to move through the trees and no birds sang. Even the morning sun seemed to have halted its ascent in the sky. A sweet lassitude filled her limbs, and for a moment she imagined herself taking hold of the dark-haired woman's hand and following her deeper into the forest . . . Brigid opened her eyes and dug her fingers into the skin of her arms until three crimson spots of blood appeared on her white flesh.

Pleasure that never reaches its end. Is that what Midir promised Eanna before she broke her family's heart and followed him to Faerie? If she found true love, then why did she return to Alainn Ross, sick and broken?

A flash of irritation crossed the dark-haired woman's face, disrupting the smooth, marble-like surface of her skin. "You do not see it, even now, and yet I know you've felt it more than once."

"I'm not as skilled as you at reading thoughts," Brigid said. "You must tell me what you mean."

"You are not like the others because you are one of us, or at least partly so. That is why I summoned you here. To bring you and your child to Liradon where you belong."

Brigid backed away from the dark-haired woman until she felt the cold dampness of the well's curbstone against her back. "You're wrong—I'm not . . ."

"You have Faerie blood in you. It is what draws you to these woods, the reason why the Faerie Queen showed herself to you, and why you were able to see Midir's true form through his glamour. It is why even now the urge to run from me is only slightly stronger than your desire to embrace me."

Brigid shook her head. "None of what you say can be true. My mother and father—"

"Are your true parents. There is no question of that. I do not know when the intermingling of our blood took place, or why it has taken this long to reveal itself. Time runs differently in Liradon. Fifty years or five hundred makes little difference to us. Your storytellers have gotten that much right at least."

"But I'm still human," Brigid said. "You said so yourself. 'I belong neither here nor there, nor anywhere.'"

"Listen to me, Brigid." The softness slipped from her voice like a lady removing her gloves. "There is more at stake than you know. Midir spoke truly when he offered you a place at his side. Here you are nothing, but among us you would be a great lady. The sadness and suffering you have known in this world will be taken from you as though it had never been. In time you will not remember what it's like to feel hunger in your belly or the chill of a winter's morning. Neither you nor your child will know a single day's hardship, I promise you."

An icy gust of wind swept through the clearing, and Brigid wrapped her arms around herself for warmth. "You promise a great deal, and yet I don't even know your name."

"My name?" the dark-haired woman asked, her delicately shaped eyebrows lifting in surprise.

"Who are you?" Brigid repeated.

"My name is Morgana, younger sister to the Faerie Queen, and Midir's wife," she added.

The chill in the air deepened until Brigid's bones felt as dry and brittle as the rust-coloured leaves scattered on the ground.

"His wife," she repeated, but the wind seized hold of her words and carried them away.

"Midir did not tell you so himself because he knew you would not understand. Faerie blood or no, you have lived too long among humans who do not understand our ways. We do not put chains on one another as though we're pieces of chattel to be bought and sold. There is no mine or thine among us. Midir is my husband but I will share him freely with you, and you will share your son with us. He will hold a place of honour in the Faerie Queen's court, far surpassing the coarse nobility of your world. Tell me, can you offer him as much?"

The pleading note that entered Morgana's voice startled Brigid almost as much as her words.

"My child will have all that I can give him . . ."

"The life of an outcast, you mean? Think, Brigid. Think about your future and that of your child. If you remain here, all that lies ahead of you are long, cheerless nights spent in the arms of a man you do not love, endless chores, struggle and bitterness, until you eventually grow old and die."

Brigid closed her eyes against the images invoked by Morgana's words. A life devoid of true love had been the thing she feared most. But now a greater fear pushed against her ribcage, making it difficult to catch her breath. Morgana's vision of her future was terrible to behold, but nor could she imagine spending her life as Midir's mistress, no matter how luxurious her surroundings. Morgana's words changed everything, and nothing at the same time. Faerie or human it didn't matter. She belonged nowhere.

"I must go," she said finally.

"Wait!" Morgana reached out her hand but made no move to touch her. "Are you so foolish as to refuse the gift I offer you? The gift of perfect happiness for you and your child?"

"Perhaps you are right. I have lived too long among humans. The place you describe is the stuff of tales, and yet I cannot imagine a place for myself there. Midir didn't tell me the truth about himself, and I do not think you are telling me the truth now."

Morgana stepped towards her, close enough for Brigid to see the flecks of gold in her eyes. "What does the truth matter, really?" she whispered softly. "Will the truth comfort you when are cold, lonely, and afraid? Think of your father,

Brigid. Did Michael O'Flynn not value the warmth and beauty of a finely wrought tale over the heartless cruelty of what you call truth?"

The sound of her father's name on Morgana's berry-stained lips made Brigid's head ache. She put out her hands, a slight, feeble gesture to ward off the other woman's words. "No, you're twisting things. My father never lied to me. He believed . . ."

"He believed in the power of his tales, just as you must believe in your own, Brigid."

Brigid pictured her father's face. She would never forget the way he held her mother's hands and looked into her eyes. It was all she ever wanted for herself. "You know nothing of me or my family, Morgana. I would rather embrace a difficult truth than be made a fool of by a lie."

"In time, none of what you say will matter. All the pain and ugliness of human mortality will pass from your mind like a winter storm, and you will know only perpetual spring where nothing ever withers or dies. What more could you want?"

For the first time Brigid detected an almost human note of puzzlement in the Faerie woman's voice. "I don't know," she said honestly. "But I can't go with you, not now."

"The chance will not come to you again. You must cross the veil before dawn breaks on All Hallows' Eve, or stay forever in this world of sorrow."

Brigid bowed her head, and allowed herself to think for a moment of all she might be giving up, but when she tried to summon the memory of her visit to Liradon, all she could see was Connell's sun-browned face creased in disappointment as he waited for her by the church door.

Brigid picked up her long skirts so she wouldn't trip on them. "I must go."

"Where?" Morgana demanded. "Back to the man who offers you his pity instead of the love you crave? Will such meager regard be enough to protect you and your child when the villagers come to your door with torches in their hand and hate in their eyes?"

Morgana's words ensnared her like a hunter's net. She sought to free herself, but everywhere she turned she was confronted with some new obstacle. A wall of thorns sprung up from a pile of leaves and the ground beneath her feet turned slick with mud, causing her to lose her footing. A sharp bolt of pain tore through her ankle, and Brigid clutched at the knotted branch of an oak to steady herself. The tree answered her touch with a shudder. She could feel the strength of its roots throbbing beneath her fingertips. Brigid tore her hand away and dragged herself forward despite the pain in her ankle that felt as though it had been stuck with a handful of embroidery needles.

"You will regret this day for the rest of your life," Morgana called after her.

She ran through the forest, her arms stretched out in front of her to protect her face from the branches that seemed to descend from every tree to block the way forward. Please don't let it be too late, she thought.

Chapter 24

When Brigid finally emerged from the forest, the sky was the colour of a fresh bruise. Only a glimmer of the sun's light remained. She had missed her wedding.

Brigid looked around her in disbelief. The day was still new when she entered the forest. Surely she could not have spent so long with Morgana? No sooner did the question form in her mind than she knew the answer. Her father's tales often told of men and women who returned home from Faerie to discover that a hundred years had passed, their loved ones dead and gone. She had lost only the better part of a day.

Connell. What must he think of her? She realized suddenly that this mattered to her more than anything else. He would think she abandoned him to be with Midir. She told Morgana she didn't know where she was going, but she did know. She would go to the mill and try to explain everything to Connell. How afraid she'd been. If Morgana were right about her future in the village there would be difficulties ahead, but it was Connell she wanted by her side, no one else. He was the one she trusted. Why didn't she see that before now?

The mill was dark when Brigid arrived. She stood panting in front of Connell's cottage, so exhausted it took all of her strength to knock on his door. No one answered. She went around to the window and pressed her face against the glass, hoping to see some movement within. After her day in the forest, even the sight of Maeve's frowning face would be welcome. But the cottage was still and silent, not even a mouse stirred in the front garden.

Brigid turned away, tears blurring her vision. It is no more than I deserve, she thought. She expected everything from Connell, and yet gave him so little. Even before Midir took Connell's place, it seemed she had lived half her life caught in the shadows between one world and another, and now it was too late . . . No. She would not give up so easily. There was no choice but to go into the village. She would go to Clare. Her friend would tell her what happened at the church, and perhaps where Connell had gone.

Brigid shivered in her wedding dress, wishing she'd thought to wear a cloak. The mottled blue and purple sky had deepened to soft black. Soon it would be dark as pitch and Brigid had no rushlight to guide her. No time to go home. Besides, she could not face her mother before she'd spoken to Connell. A thousand half-formed explanations grew in Brigid's mind as she made her way towards the village. She'd spoken the wrong words to Connell too many times. If he would agree to listen, this might be her last chance to get it right.

Consumed by her thoughts, Brigid did not notice anything wrong until she was upon the village square. The cluster of cottages around her was in complete and utter darkness. The entire village might have been covered in a thick blanket of soot and shadows. Not a single candle glowed in any of the cottages' windows.

Brigid pressed the heels of her hands against her eyes as if to clear them of the surrounding darkness. A sick feeling of dread gripped her insides like a giant's fist. What if she was wrong about how much time had passed? Maybe Morgana sought to punish her for her refusal? What if she had indeed been gone for years instead of hours? Brigid put her hands out in front of her. She could not see them clearly, but they still felt soft and smooth to the touch, and when she placed them on her stomach the gentle curve was the same as before. And then she remembered: All Hallows' Eve. The villagers bolted their doors and darkened their windows to keep away the spirits and any member of the Faerie Host that might visit them. No one would open their doors to anyone this night, and especially not to her. No one, she hoped, except Clare.

Brigid walked quickly across the green, her legs refusing to carry her in a run. When she reached Clare's door, her entire body trembled with hunger and fatigue.

Clare's husband, Aed, answered her feeble knock.

"Get away from here," he growled. "You've already tried to steal my son from me. I'd sooner have you strike me dead than let your kind near my family again."

"Aed, it's me, Brigid. I must speak to Clare."

"Brigid?" he asked as if the name were unknown to him.

"Yes, Aed. I promise you 'tis no demon come to your door. Only the girl who helped return your child to you. Please, I must speak to Clare."

"They said you returned to the Fair Folk," Aed whispered through the door. "That you are one of them now."

Brigid drove her hands impatiently through her hair, causing several strands to come away in her fingers. "I did not go with the Fair Folk. I am here, now, talking to you. Please, let me speak to Clare and I will explain."

The silence on the other end of the door told Brigid Aed was considering her request.

"I cannot let you come in, Brigid," he said finally. "But I will ask Clare to come to the door if you promise . . . if you promise to go away as soon as you've spoken to her."

"I promise. Now, please hurry."

Brigid listened as Aed's heavy footsteps were replaced by Clare's light and graceful ones.

"Brigid," Clare whispered urgently. "Is it really you?"

"Yes, of course it is. Please, Clare. You must tell me what happened today. My tale is too long to be repeated now, but I must find Connell and explain. I went to the mill but he wasn't there."

"What happened to you, Brigid? Your mother found your wedding flowers on the path to the forest. Everyone said you abandoned Connell for the Faerie. Your mother tried to tell them it wasn't true, that you must have been taken against your will, but no one believed her. No one except Connell."

No longer able to stand, Brigid kneeled at Clare's door. "Where did he go?"

"He went to the forest to look for you. Alone."

Brigid place her hands over her face. Connell was alone in the forest on All Hallows' Eve because of her. "Thank you, Clare. Now I must try to find him before it's too late."

"Wait! What will you do?"

"I must go to the forest and look for Connell. It's my fault that he . . ."

"You cannot go into the forest alone on All Hallows' Eve! The Fair Folk will take you for sure this time."

"I must go, Clare, but all will be well. I promise."

When Clare did not respond, Brigid wondered if she'd gone away, but then the door opened and she was greeted by the sight of her friend's freckled, anxious face.

"Here, take these. You'll have need of them."

Clare handed her a generous hunk of bread and cheese wrapped in linen, a freshly lit rushlight, and a small broken piece of horseshoe. "You can't go into the forest without a bit of cold iron about you," Clare said when Brigid looked at her in askance. "It's the best I can do."

"Thank you, Clare."

"Be well, Brigid, and God bless you."

Brigid longed to run back to the forest, but the darkness forced her to tread carefully. If she fell down or accidentally dropped the rushlight, she would be blind before she left the village, and she had to find Connell. No matter how he felt about her now, she must tell him she did not abandon him, that she still wanted to marry him if he would have her.

What is love? Eanna's question came back painfully to her now. Finally, she understood the older woman's disappointment at her answer. It was the answer of a girl, not a woman. Love was not the unending ease and pleasure of a Faerie song, but a complicated dance between two people. From the beginning, she and Connell were woefully out of step, but in spite of their awkwardness Connell was the partner she wanted.

The forest loomed before her like a heavy dark cloud, the outline of the trees barely discernible in the darkness. No matter how many times she left its leafy borders, the forest always found a way to summon her back. A few more steps and she would be swallowed up by its yawning mouth of leaf and bark. She fought a sudden urge to turn around and run back to the safety of Clare's cottage, but there was no choice but to go forward. She would not let the Faerie take someone she loved a second time.

Brigid held the rushlight out in front of her. If the Faerie Host meant to ride this night, there was no sign of them yet. The ground was soft and unmarked, and no lingering enchantment hovered in the air. The forest was only a forest, filled with the ordinary dangers that awaited a lone traveller at night. The claustrophobic tangle of trees, jutting rocks, and sudden drops in the forest floor, to say nothing of the wolves, required no Faerie magic to cause her injury. She might easily lose her way as she'd done before, and this time she doubted Midir would come to her rescue.

The trees stood motionless. Not a single breeze disturbed their branches, and yet the rushlight in Brigid's hand flickered and went out. She was alone in the dark, unable to see the way ahead or behind.

"No," Brigid cried out. "Please, do not keep me here. All my life you have given me welcome when others turned me away. Do not betray me now. Why should the Faerie command you in everything? Do you not possess powers of your own?"

Brigid held her breath, hoping for a sign that her words did not go unheard, but there was no answering rustle of leaves in the trees overhead. She turned around slowly, looking for some glimmer of light beyond the wall of trees that surrounded her in every direction. Without even the soft glow of moonlight to guide her path, she would be trapped in the forest until morning, and by then it would be too late.

There is more at stake than you know.

Overwhelmed by all that she had learned, Brigid did not stop to think what Morgana's words meant. But now she was certain. Something was meant to happen that night— something more important than Brigid's decision to remain in Alainn Ross.

A flicker of white passed through the corner of her eye. She turned around sharply, but whatever it was disappeared amongst the trees. Could it be the same lights that led Connell into Faerie? She stood so still she might have been mistaken for a willow with her tall slender body and wild silver hair. She stared at the line of trees in front of her until her eyes teared. And then she saw it. A flash of white between the trees, followed by a rustling in the underbrush.

"Is someone there?" she whispered.

The answer came in the form of something wet nuzzling the back of her neck.

Brigid froze, every nerve ending in her body jangling in alarm. Unable to move, she endured the creature's gentle, but increasingly insistent pressure upon her skin. Surely a wolf would not behave in such a leisurely fashion? Unless, of course, he hoped to play with his dinner before eating it. Finally, movement returned to her limbs, she turned around slowly, hoping not to startle whatever it was into further action.

The white hart. The sight of his shining dark eyes with their human-like expression made her dizzy with relief. She resisted the urge to press her face against the animal's silken flank and weep like a lost child.

"You found me," she said to the hart, for she was certain she'd been found and not discovered accidentally. The hart sensed her need and came to her just like before. "I must find Connell. Do you know where he is?"

The animal gave no indication that he heard her question, but when he turned away Brigid understood he meant for her to follow.

The hart moved quickly through the forest, his long, graceful legs easily traversing the uneven ground and leaping over fallen tree trunks. Brigid did not move so easily and was soon panting with the effort to keep up. Sometimes she lost sight of him altogether, but then he would reappear, his antlers a beacon of white light in the darkness. He paused just long enough for her to catch her breath, and then he was off again.

When the hart finally came to a halt, her injured ankle throbbed painfully and her sides felt as though they'd been pierced with a hot poker. Unable to summon breath to speak, she looked questioningly at the hart. They appeared to have arrived nowhere. Barely distinguishable from one another in the dark, the surrounding trees resembled the same dark cloud they'd been walking through for what felt like hours. A strange, fluttering sensation invaded her limbs and she sank to the forest floor in defeat. She was no closer to finding Connell than before. A moment later, she felt the hart nuzzling at her face and gently prodding her with his forelegs.

"I can't," she whispered into her hands. "I can't go any further."

And then she heard it. Harp music. The melody was even more beautiful than she remembered, but now it possessed a darker, more insistent quality, as if each note was drenched in sorrow before being released into the night air. No longer soft and lilting, the music demanded some stronger emotion.

Brigid lifted her head, straining to listen. The music grew slightly louder and she rose to her feet. The harpist must be somewhere nearby. She walked carefully towards the sound, afraid that if she made too much noise the music would stop. She'd only taken a few steps when she saw the soft gleam of lights up ahead. "This way," she whispered behind her, but when she turned around the hart was gone.

Brigid pressed forward, certain the hart wouldn't have abandoned her unless he brought her to the right place. She half-expected the lights to disappear, but they grew steadily brighter until the surrounding trees seemed to emit a soft glow. The music was stronger now, but she could also hear the low murmur of voices. Afraid of being spotted, she crouched behind a thicket of brambles. In the space of a sigh, someone grabbed her from behind and clapped a hand over her mouth.

Chapter 25

"What are you doing here?" an angry voice, Midir's voice, whispered. "If Dania were to discover you . . ."

"Who is Dania?" Brigid asked once Midir removed his hand from her mouth.

Midir looked at her uncomprehendingly. "The Faerie Queen."

"She's not my Queen," Brigid whispered. "I've come to find Connell."

Midir placed one hand gently on her shoulder and ran his long fingers down the length of her arm. "I'm sorry if I was harsh. My only thought is for your happiness. There is much about this night you don't understand. In time I will explain, but now you must do as I say. I will take you somewhere safe. You can wait there until I come for you."

"Why did you send the Dark Rider for me? You said the choice was mine."

Midir looked at her in surprise. "I never sent the Dark Rider. I meant what I said. You must come to me willingly or not all."

"Then nothing has changed. I must find Connell. It's my fault he came to the forest . . ."

Midir stared at her, and once more she felt the pull of his nearness. The intensity of his gaze lit up the surrounding darkness.

"Connell is gone," Midir said flatly. "You and our child must return to Liradon, where you belong."

"No, I cannot."

Midir pulled her close. He smelled of sunlight and fresh grass. "How can you refuse me?" he murmured into her hair. "Were we not happy together? When I played for you in the forest, you told me our time together was like a dream from which you hoped to never wake. Come with me now, and I promise our life together shall be sweeter than any dream you've ever known. Each day will be like a dance for which the music never ends . . ."

Midir's words were like a tapestry woven with threads so fine and bright that she could not help but admire their beauty, but even as she admired them she did not believe in them. Faerie blood or no, she could not live in a dream forever.

Brigid lifted her face to Midir's. "I will love our child well, but I cannot do as you ask. My life is here and nowhere else."

Midir shoved her roughly away from him. "Twice I have offered myself to you and twice you have refused me. I will not make that mistake again, but know this: If you leave the forest this night, you leave alone."

"What do you mean?"

Midir shook his head. "I will speak no more of this to you."

"Midir, please. If you have any love for me at all, tell me where Connell is."

But Midir was already walking away from her, his tall, straight figure becoming less substantial with every step until she could no longer make out the shadowy outline of his body. The Faerie lights in the trees above echoed Midir's departure, dimming before they finally went out. Brigid was alone in the darkness once more.

"You have wounded him," a familiar voice whispered behind her.

Brigid whirled around. "Morgana."

"I tried to warn you, but you wouldn't listen."

"You meant for this to happen! Connell came to the forest to look for me, and now . . ."

Brigid couldn't see Morgana's face, but she imagined it would be as maddeningly calm as her voice.

"Blame me if you wish. Connell has been chosen, and nothing that either of us say or do can alter that fact."

"Stop talking in riddles! If we are truly kin as you say, then tell me the truth. Where is Connell?"

Morgana seized her by the arm. "Come with me. We cannot speak freely here. Even the trees are listening."

"Where are we going?"

Morgana tightened her grip on Brigid's arm. "The answer would mean nothing to you. Humans cannot find their way in or out without the aid of a Faerie guide."

Morgana's step was so light and quick she seemed to fly amongst the trees. Brigid struggled to keep up, her gown snagging on every root and tree branch before the ground shifted and she felt her body lurch forward. They continued downhill at breakneck speed before coming to an abrupt halt.

Suddenly the sky disappeared and the night drew instantly darker and chillier around them. They were somewhere underground. Instead of earth and trees, she smelled rot and damp. Brigid shivered violently. "Please . . ."

Morgana pulled her sharply to the right. "You'll soon be warm enough. We're almost there."

Brigid stumbled after Morgana in what seemed to be a dark, airless tunnel. When they finally reached the end, Morgana placed her hands on the flat stone wall. It gave way underneath her touch and Brigid found herself entering some kind of cave.

"Where is this place?"

Morgana folded her arms across her chest. "No one will look for us here. That's all you need to know."

"I need you to tell me about Connell."

"If I were to tell you, what would you do when you found him?"

She turned away from the intensity of Morgana's gaze that never seemed to waver. "I don't know."

Morgana laughed, the sound as empty and as hollow as the cave itself. "At least you're honest. Most of your kind would make a lie if they could not find an answer to serve them."

"My kind? So you see me as human after all? In spite of what you said in the wood?"

This time it was Morgana who looked away. "I call you human because your feelings are strange to me. I could not live as you do even if I wished it."

"Midir thought he could."

"Perhaps for a time, but he could not have endured it for long. None of us could. And yet . . ."

"What?" Brigid asked, curious despite herself.

"We are a dying race. Save for a precious few, our women are barren, and yet your kind continues to grow in strength and number. For all your clumsy weakness, you possess some deeper magic that even I do not understand. What do you have to look forward to except hunger, poverty, and disease? And yet you bring children into the world as if certain some fresh paradise awaited you. Our Queen tells us it is only further proof of human foolishness, but I wonder if she is wrong. Perhaps it is something more than foolishness that drives your kind to pursue each day, no matter how dark and cheerless it might be."

Morgana seemed bemused, as if speaking her thoughts out loud, but now she fixed her dark, burning gaze on Brigid's face, and when she spoke again she sounded almost human, shades of puzzlement and fear flitting through her voice like a shifting rainbow. "How is it that a peasant woman, who possesses neither wealth nor status, thinks to refuse our offer to live as we do? Such a thing should not be possible, and yet . . ."

Brigid felt the weight of the earth above pressing in on her until she couldn't catch her breath. "What are you telling me?"

"I lied when I said you had a choice: Remain in your world or cross the veil to begin a new life in Liradon. But there is no choice. You will join with us this night whether you wish it or no."

She closed her eyes against the chilly perfection of Morgana's face.

"And if I still refuse?"

"You will not." The colour drained from Morgana's voice until it was grey and flat like the stone beneath their feet.

"How can you be so sure? You say that I am a wonder, my feelings incomprehensible to you. Why should you claim to know what I will do?"

"I saw the way you looked at him, and the way he looked at you in return."

"Midir?"

"Connell. I watched you in the churchyard, both of you, and later in his cottage. Even now you do not understand the depth of your feeling for him. But you will—when you are forced to choose."

The sides of the tunnel began to soften and blur, and Brigid was overcome with the sense that the whole world had swiftly fallen out of her grasp. "Connell."

"He will pay the tenid. The Faerie Queen chose him herself, with some help from Midir, of course. So you see, everyone will get what they want. The Queen has her payment and Midir shall have you and his child."

A vein of colour returned to Morgana's voice when she

spoke this last, and Brigid wondered if she did not detect a note of bitterness in the Faerie woman's words.

"I don't understand. What is the tenid?"

Morgana smiled. "You should understand better than anyone. Does your lord not demand a share of the villagers' labour? Our tenid is much the same as your village tithe. The servant pays the master for his care. Life in Liradon has a cost. Every seven years we must offer a sacrifice to the land. The payment of the tenid allows us to remain here."

"Here meaning Alainn Ros?"

Morgana shook her head in a gesture of impatience. "Yes and no. Liradon cannot exist on its own. Your world is tied to ours like an anchor to a ship. If our connection to Alainn Ros is severed, we lose Liradon as well, at least until we can find another place to bind ourselves to."

"Then why don't you find another place? Surely it would be easier to find another village, another forest, than to murder an innocent man?"

Morgana cocked her head to one side, and Brigid was struck by how the simple gesture marked her Faerie nature more strongly than her burning, slanted eyes or impressive stature. Morgana's indifferent expression told Brigid that the idea of murder was as incomprehensible to her as the notion of work was to Midir.

"The tenid is a noble sacrifice," said Morgana. "We are grateful to the one who pays."

"You're talking about a human life as though it were a loaf of bread or bolt of cloth! How can you not see that forcing someone to pay the tenid is wrong?"

Morgana looked at Brigid thoughtfully. "No one is forced to pay. They must do so of their own free will, or the payment will be refused, and even if what you say is true, what is a single human life against the survival of an entire race?"

Brigid was seized by an overwhelming sense of hopelessness. How to convince Morgana to see beyond her people's desire? "The Fair Folk are foolish to set themselves above humans. You are just as grasping and greedy, perhaps more so. The villagers left me in the forest to die because they thought to protect their families from ruin, but what you do is worse. There is nothing noble in a sacrifice that ensures nothing but the continuation of Faerie feasts, music, and dancing. A peasant collapsing in the field dies for a far better cause than yours."

Morgana shrugged. "I do not expect you to understand our ways, but in time . . ."

Brigid's mind raced frantically. Where was Connell? Was she already too late to help him? Knowing Morgana would have no patience for tears, she forced a calm she did not feel.

"You said I must choose. If Connell is to pay the tenid, what choice is left to me?"

"Only that if you come with us willingly you might spare his life."

"I don't understand," Brigid said.

"Connell must pay the tenid. But if you release your claim on him and surrender to the will of the Faerie Queen, he will live."

"He will not be harmed?"

Morgana paused, and in that moment Brigid felt the weight of every sorrow she'd ever known dragging her towards the floor of the tunnel.

"Tell me," she said.

"The tenid ceremony will take what it may, the strength and free will of a young human man, but it will leave his body intact. He will feel no pain, but he will be . . . altered."

The bile rose in Brigid's throat until she thought she might choke on its bitterness. "There is nothing to choose in what you offer! The Faerie Queen means to take away Connell's mind the same way Midir took away Lord Osin's. What kind of life would Connell be left with? Do you think I would have him spend his days wandering Alainn Ross babbling nonsense? The villagers would not suffer his presence among them for long. Connell would rather be dead than to suffer such a fate!"

Morgana remained silent, and Brigid tried to read her thoughts, but she could not quiet her own mind long enough to enter into someone else's.

"You have more than Connell to think of now," Morgana said, not unkindly.

She turned away, wild with the desire to smash, tear, or throw. To do something that would shatter Morgana's calm acceptance of something so evil, but Brigid could find no weapon. Her hands slid over the walls of cave, unable to find even a tiny piece of loose stone. It suddenly occurred to her that this was the real Faerie. Not gilded floors or glittering chandeliers suspended from the sky, but a cold, dark cave.

"Do not exhaust yourself. There is nothing to be done." Morgana removed a slender ivory horn from the sleeve of her gown. "Shall I play for you? The music will help to ease your mind. Or perhaps you would like a cup of warm wine? Either one will put you to sleep, and when you awaken it will all be over."

Brigid clamped her hands over her ears like a child. "I don't want my mind eased! I will never forget this night, no matter how many songs you play, or how much Faerie wine you force down my throat!"

"Very well. I shall leave you and tell the Queen that you have made your choice. I expect that when I return, you will have changed your mind about the music. I've never met a human who did not choose oblivion over pain when given the choice." And then in a gentler tone, she added, "You've shown great strength, Brigid. You may not care to hear it now, but this night marks a new beginning for you. You will be happy in Liradon. It is not possible to be otherwise."

Brigid heard the rustling of Morgana's gown as she turned to leave.

"Wait," Brigid said.

"Have you changed your mind?"

"Is there really no other way?"

"No."

A thin sob escaped her throat. "You wouldn't tell me if there were was, though, would you? You're one of them, after all."

"The tenid must be paid. When you live among us, you will understand its importance."

"I don't want to understand! My father's tales were wrong. The Fair Folk are not noble or honourable. They are as cold and heartless as this cave."

"Your father," Morgana murmured as if remembering him herself. "He was a storyteller with a fondness for tales of love."

She stared at Morgana, whose green eyes blazed back at her in the dull light of the cave. "That is what I asked him for - stories of true love."

"And what did you learn from these stories?"

Brigid shook her head. "I can't remember them all, there were so many, but they all ended the same way, happily. Not like this."

Morgana closed her eyes briefly, and when she opened them, they were empty and cold. "Farewell, Brigid."

Brigid sat down on the floor of the cave and pulled her knees up to her chest. Had the tenid ceremony already begun? Did Connell know what was meant to happen? She was sure of one thing. If the Faerie Queen offered to ease his mind, he would refuse. Connell would face his death as a man, with no Faerie magic to aid him. His death. Connell's death. Her stomach wrenched painfully. She moved onto her hands and knees and vomited what little food she'd eaten that day. Morgana will be disgusted when she sees the mess, she thought, a harsh burst of laugher escaping from her throat.

She sat back on her heels, and felt something cold stab at her breast. Clare's horseshoe. She'd forgotten she still carried it. Not that it would do her much good alone in this cave. She ran her hands over the horseshoe's rough edge. If iron was meant to repel the Faerie, it seemed to have had no effect on Morgana. The other woman had been only a few feet away from her and shown no signs of discomfort. Still, the iron felt comfortingly real and solid in her hand.

Brigid stood up and felt her way along the sides of the tunnel until she reached the entrance. Morgana said she couldn't find her way out without a Faerie guide, but that need not stop her from trying. She regretfully thought of the white hart. Even he could not find her underground.

To her surprise, the wall gave way when she pressed on it. Was Morgana so sure of herself that she'd not bothered to seal it? Brigid moved slowly but steadily forward, her hand pressed against the side of the tunnel for support. Surely she could not be far underground? It seemed to have taken only moments for Morgana to bring her here. But of course that meant nothing if magic was involved. Brigid forced herself to keep moving even though she could not see the way ahead. Without the light of a single star to guide her, her progress was agonizingly slow. The low ceiling and close walls gave her the unpleasant sensation of being buried underground. Several times she felt the air being sucked out of her chest, and she had to remind herself to breathe slowly in and out.

When she finally came to the end of the passageway, she paused for a moment before turning instinctively to her left. Another opening. She'd only gone a little ways when the surrounding blackness seemed to soften. At first she thought it was only her eyes adjusting to the dark, but eventually she realized it was more than that. She could see the outline of the cave walls, their uneven surfaces marred with deep cracks, and the greyish-coloured moss growing in between. Smokey black soon lightened into grey, her breath came more easily now, and she began to move freely through the passageway that gradually became less narrow. Suddenly the tunnel flooded with bright yellow light. Brigid put one hand in front of her eyes, blinking painfully. When her eyes adapted, she took several tentative steps forward. The light was coming from outside. Torches. Too many of them to count. She hesitated in the mouth of the tunnel. So intent on escaping from her underground prison she'd not thought what to do next. How long would it be before Morgana returned and found her missing? If she or any of the Fair Folk saw her, they would shut her away again and she would never be able to find Connell.

"Do not hide yourself in the shadows, Brigid," a melodious voice called out. "Come and join us. We've been waiting for you."

Chapter 26

The Faerie Queen had spoken to Brigid only twice in her life, but the sound of that rich, languorous voice was forever etched on her brain. No one spoke with such voluptuous slowness, as though each word was a caress meant for the listener alone. And yet, underneath the melting honey of that voice was the unmistakable glint of iron.

Brigid emerged slowly from the tunnel and found herself standing in a large clearing that was both strange and familiar. The trees surrounding the clearing were ordinary enough. She recognized the thick, sturdy oaks, diminutive hawthornes, and graceful sway of birch, and when she looked up, she was comforted by the sight of the stars glowing overhead in a moonless sky. But the clearing itself was obscured in a thick, dark mist that smelled of earth and wet leaves. Relieved to be back above ground, she breathed deeply, but the smoke-like quality of the air made her lungs rebel.

"Don't be afraid," the Faerie Queen called from somewhere inside the mist. "Enter the circle and join us."

She took a blind step forward, the veil of mist lifted and the long graceful lines of the Fair Folk began to solidify in front of her. Shedding their spectral quality like a swan shaking the water from its feathers, they stood in a close circle, their long necks arched slightly forward as if guarding something precious. Although still pale and beautiful, their appearance was completely altered from what it had been at the Faerie ball. The women's opalescent gowns had been replaced by shapeless black shifts that seemed to be woven out of shadows, and their wheat-coloured hair swept down their backs in a simple unadorned wave. Not a single jewel glittered at their naked white throats. The men were equally plain in soft black tunics, devoid of buttons or brocade, and dark-coloured hose. And yet, in spite of their sombre dress, their eyes shone. A feeling of barely suppressed excitement permeated the clearing. Every leaf on every tree, every scattered twig and stone underfoot seemed to be holding its breath. Midir had told her one truth at least. There would be a ceremony that night, and somehow Brigid understood her attendance was required.

No one turned to look at her or acknowledge her presence in any way. For a moment, she wondered if it were not all some strange dream and she was still alone in the cave. But underneath the preternatural stillness of the clearing, Brigid heard a low, anguished moan that cut her to the bone.

Brigid put one hand on her chest and felt the unyielding hardness of the horseshoe before pushing her way inside the circle. There was a roaring in her ears followed by a death-like quiet. A hundred pairs of wide, slanted eyes, their centres glowing like candle flames, were fixed on her face, waiting for . . . what?

And then she saw him. Connell lay on a smooth, flat stone in the centre of the circle. His hands and feet were bound and a blindfold covered his eyes.

"Connell!" Brigid rushed towards him, but the Faerie Queen seized her by the arm with surprising force and dragged her back to the edge of the circle.

"He cannot hear you." The Faerie Queen's loose-limbed grace vanished. When she released Brigid's arm, she looked taut, ready to pounce, like a cat that'd awoken from its nap and smelled a rat. "The tenid ceremony has already begun. This man has accepted his part as our saviour, and released his claim on this world. All that remains is for us to give him our thanks and speed him on his journey."

The Faerie Queen spoke gently now, almost kindly, but when Brigid removed her eyes from her too radiant face she saw the knife glinting in her hand.

"No," Brigid said.

The Faerie court was silent while the Queen spoke, but now Brigid could hear their low angry murmurs.

"Take her away," one of the Faerie women cried out, and Brigid felt a talon-like grip on her shoulders.

"Leave her," the Faerie Queen commanded. "She will remain until she has fulfilled her part in the ceremony."

The Faerie Queen turned cold eyes on Brigid. "Morgana told you what is to happen?"

Brigid searched for Morgana's dark hair in the circle of golden tresses, but did not see her. "Yes."

"Then you understand what you must do. The man who pays the tenid must be released from his earthly ties. As his betrothed, you must release your claim on him so he will be free to fulfil his destiny. Our time grows short, so speak now. Do you release your claim?"

"No, I do not," Brigid said.

The Faerie court exploded around her. A scarlet ribbon of anguish slipped through the circle culminating in a high-pitched shriek of rage. Brigid placed her hands over her ears to cover the sound, but Connell did not stir.

The Faerie Queen raised a slender white hand and the court fell silent once more. "Do not be angry. The woman who stands before you is one of us. Her refusal is no more than ignorance, a simple misunderstanding. We must help Brigid let go of her world of sorrow and pain and embrace the world that awaits her. Only then will she able to learn our ways, the true faith of this land. One of our own great lords has already proclaimed his love for this woman. Is this not so, Midir?"

Midir emerged from the shadows and stood before her, the beauty of his face made more dazzling by his simple attire. He stared at her long and hard, and Brigid wondered if he were not trying to reassure himself that she was worthy of his claim.

Finally, Midir took her hand in his own. His skin was as soft and smooth as she remembered, but it held a chill that made Brigid want to yank her hand away and press it against her chest for warmth. Had he always been so cold? Why had she failed to notice it before?

"It is true, my Queen. I have offered this woman my love and a place at my side in Liradon."

The Faerie Queen's lips curled into a satisfied smile. "Do you see what happiness lies ahead of you?" she said to Brigid. "When this is done, we shall celebrate your return to us. There will be music and feasts and dancing. All that you desire shall be yours. Tell me, is this not the happiest of endings for one who has suffered many wrongs?"

Brigid closed her eyes and tried to imagine what it would be like to finally belong, to bask in the warm glow of acceptance instead of standing alone in the shadows fending off the villagers' barbs of fear and hatred. She opened her eyes. The Faerie circle gave her glimpses of herself, a slant of bone, a gleam of silver hair, a cheek so pale it revealed the delicate tracery of veins beneath the skin. But it was not until she looked at Connell's face, his sun-browned skin and furrowed brow, that she felt a shock of recognition that made her gasp.

"No, I do not," she said again, startled by the strength in her voice. "This man is my betrothed and I will accept no other in his place."

Connell stirred slightly. Wake up, she pleaded silently. She needed him to know that she hadn't abandoned him before they took her away.

"Look at me," the Faerie Queen demanded.

Brigid obeyed, her body stiffening under the Queen's penetrating gaze. She felt naked, as though every doubt, every disappointment, every shaming thought were engraved on her skin for the Faerie Queen to see and judge. The strength slipped from her limbs like petals from a dying flower, but the Queen was the first to look away.

"What more do you want?" the Faerie Queen asked, and for the first time Brigid detected a note of weariness in her voice.

"I want nothing but Connell's freedom."

"You would give up immortality for yourself and your child to spare the life of a man you do not even love?"

Brigid looked at Connell's lifeless form on the slab of stone. "I do love him," she said, realizing it was true.

The Faerie Queen laughed, a harsh, rasping sound, and turned towards Connell, the knife raised in her hand.

Brigid lurched towards the slab, but Midir seized her from behind and held her fast. He whispered something in her ear, but Brigid did not hear what it was. Every ounce of her attention was focused on the shiny blade the Queen held poised above Connell's chest.

In one swift movement, the Faerie Queen replaced the dagger in the diamond-encrusted belt she wore around her waist and swept over Connell's body so that her lips brushed against his ear. When the Faerie Queen raised her head, Connell sat up slowly, pressing the heels of his hands against his eyes as though waking from a deep sleep.

Brigid struggled in Midir's arms, never once taking her eyes off the Queen, whose glittering eyes regarded Connell as watchfully as a jealous lover.

"Connell Mackenna, have you pledged your life to pay the tenid?" the Queen asked.

"Yes." Connell's voice was barely above a whisper, but its certainty made Brigid's blood run cold.

"There is a woman here who claims you for her own. What do you wish to say to this woman?"

Connell raised his hands to the blindfold and then let them drop. "Brigid?"

"Yes, Connell, it's me." All of her carefully planned words turned to stone in her mouth. "I've been looking for you. I wanted to tell you I'm sorry about our wedding. I didn't mean to . . . I swear it."

"This is what you call love?" the Faerie Queen interrupted. "You deserted your betrothed because you were afraid of joining your life with his, afraid of the drudgery that lay ahead of you in his poor, dingy cottage where you would fill your days scrubbing pots and carding wool. A life without music or dancing . . . You ran into the woods to meet your lover, but really, who could blame you?"

"No!" Brigid cried. "That's not true. I swear to you . . ."

"How can you believe her, Connell?" the Faerie Queen asked, and even Brigid was struck by the genuine puzzlement in her voice. "This woman who calls herself your betrothed has lied to you before. Did she not betray you with another man? A man whose child she now carries in her belly. A man who even now holds her in his arms?"

"No, Connell. It's not like . . ."

The Faerie Queen caressed Connell's bare cheek with her long white fingers. "Tell me, did you believe her when she said she thought it was you she lay with on the forest floor?"

When Connell made no reply, she continued, barely able to conceal the rising excitement in her voice. "How many years have you loved and protected this woman? And yet she's never loved you in return. So what do her words of love mean now? Nothing. They mean nothing. She does not love you as a woman loves a man. She only wishes to spare herself the guilt and shame she expects to feel upon your death. But there is no shame in what you give tonight, only glory. A glory she thinks to steal from you with her empty words of love. Tell her you do not want her pity. Tell her to release her claim and set you free."

Connell parted lips that Brigid saw were dry and cracked. "Brigid, you must do what she asks. I promised to pay the tenid so that you and the child would be safe."

"I will not let you, Connell Mackenna! You made me a promise."

"Listen to me. The Faerie Queen promised . . . You will live like a noblewoman, and your child will be as good as a lord. What can I offer you? A snug cottage with a dry roof and a plentiful garden? I would have loved your child well, but he would be no more than a miller's son."

"I don't want to be a noblewoman. I only want you. Neither my child nor I could ask for more than that."

"Enough!" The Faerie Queen slapped Brigid hard across the face. "You are only human after all. I should have taken your mind that day in the woods, but I spared you because I saw the mark of my people on your face. It is a mistake I will not make again." She turned to Midir. "Remove her from my sight. The Tenid ceremony will continue."

Chapter 27

Brigid allowed herself to be dragged to the edge of the circle before she raised her right foot and kicked backwards as hard as she could. Midir released his hold long enough for her to remove the horseshoe from her bodice. When he tried to seize her again, she shoved him away, the object gripped firmly in her hand.

Midir stumbled backwards, and the smell of burning flesh filled the air. A desperate, keening sound rose up from the circle before it broke apart and every Faerie man and woman rushed towards her. Long slender arms grabbed hold of her arms and legs, and Brigid felt certain they intended to tear her to pieces. A violet-eyed woman sat on top of Brigid's chest, crushing the air from her lungs. Brigid watched the beauty leak from her face until it was a hollow masque of rage.

"Release her," the Faerie Queen screamed.

Whining like disappointed children, the Faerie reluctantly retreated, and Brigid rose shakily to her feet.

The Faerie Queen's eyes flashed cruelly. "If you want him, come and claim him!"

Connell's body began to writhe in agony as though he were being tortured by an invisible assailant. Brigid screamed. His head reeled from side to side, crashing against the stone, and his legs twisted underneath him. Brigid threw herself at his body, and struggled to untie the rope that bound his hands and feet. When she finally managed to free him, his body went still. Relief surged through her veins. Connell lived. She could hear his breath moving in and out of his chest. But then something else began to happen. The taut muscle in his bare arms and legs melted into soft folds of sagging flesh, his abdomen turned into a hollowed cave, and Brigid could see the rapid beating of his heart in his now skeletal chest. A cry rose from Brigid's throat as her eyes travelled up the length of his body to his face. The skin fell away from his cheekbones until they resembled sharp daggers, but worst of all was the horror in Connell's eyes, which turned milky white.

"Look at him now, Brigid. Look closely at the future that awaits you. Look at him and think about what you've given up. Is this your choice? Human mortality brings decay and ruin to everything it touches. It steals youth and beauty and replaces it with age and ugliness."

The Faerie Queen stood over Brigid and gently smoothed her hair, the gesture a cruel parody of a mother's reassuring touch. Tears burned her eyes, blurring her vision of Connell's wasted body.

"Embrace him now if you will for this is what you have chosen."

Brigid laid her head on Connell's chest and wrapped her arms carefully around him. And then he began to change again. She felt his body grow damp until it was so slippery with sweat she struggled to keep hold of him. His skin broke out in a fevered rash that quickly erupted into large black pustules. Tears squeezed from Brigid's eyes as she held onto his body that was now covered with oozing, open sores.

"Disease," the Faerie Queen whispered in Brigid's ear. "Human sickness that you would never know in our world. We are untouched by such indignities of the flesh. Our bodies do not betray us; do not grow old or weak or ugly. But human bodies are as fragile as spun glass. A whiff of plague and Lord Death is at your side." The Queen waved her hand across Connell's body. "Is this what you're so eager to join yourself with? Will you forsake him now?"

"No, I will not," Brigid said.

The Faerie Queen lowered her gaze, and Brigid saw the rapid movement of her eyes beneath their closed lids. "Very well," she said softly. "Can you hold him now?"

Screams of agony filled Brigid's ears, but this time she did not know if they belonged to Connell or herself. Tiny blue flames licked around her arms that were still clasped around Connell's chest. She watched in horror as the flames grew taller, gathering strength and colour until she and Connell were engulfed in angry red fire. A searing pain spread across Brigid's back, her skin blistering from the heat. She could not see through the flames, but she imagined the pale beautiful faces of the Faerie lit by the glow of the fire as they watched her and Connell burn. But it was not only her and Connell. "No," Brigid whispered against Connell's blackening chest. Her child would not die. She would not let this be the ending of their tale.

Despite the searing pain in her arms, she held Connell tighter. She imagined herself back in her cottage, sitting with her mother and father while the rain fell gently outside their door.

Her father was telling a story just for them, a tale of true love, and she leaned against his shoulder so as not to miss a single word. Brigid's mother sat back on her heels watching them both, her face radiant with happiness.

"Is that the end?" she asked when her father fell silent.

"Yes."

"And did they live together in perfect happiness for the rest of their days?"

She couldn't see her father's face, but she heard the smile in his voice when he said, "No, but they loved one another so well it was enough to sustain them when they faced life's sadness."

"That doesn't sound like a happy ending," she said.

Her father kissed the part in her hair and reached out for Brigid's mother. "It is the happiest of endings. If they did not have trouble and sadness, they would never know the strength of their love."

"But how does that happen?"

"When there is no choice but to hold on tight and never let go."

Brigid opened her eyes. Her arms were still clasped around Connell's chest but the flames had disappeared. The air was fresh and clear with no trace of smoke or mist.

She sat up and began to search Connell's body for the wounds he'd surely suffered, but she saw no blemish save for the rough and reddened skin on his shoulders, the mark of hard work he'd carried since he was a boy. She touched his lips with her fingers. "Connell?"

Connell opened his eyes. "I'm alive. I don't understand it, but I am." He sat up slowly and drew Brigid close to him. "Where did they go?"

"I don't know, but the night has ended. Look at the sky."

Brigid and Connell looked up to see the first rays of dawn filtering through the trees.

"Brigid," Connell said hoarsely, and in that one word she heard all she needed.

Brigid pressed her lips against his. "I know."

"I hope that you will never regret it."

Brigid raised her head so she could look into his grey eyes, eyes that did not pierce or burn, but a gaze that was steady, bright, and true.

"How could I regret finding my one true love?"

Brigid and Connell stayed in the clearing for a long time, neither one willing to move apart, until finally Connell said, "We must make our way back. We have much to explain before we can ask Father Diarmaid to marry us."

Brigid smiled at her betrothed, whose strength of purpose seemed almost as preternatural as the Faerie. "Let us go then."

Brigid was never able to recall afterwards how she and Connell became separated. One moment they were walking hand-in-hand through the forest, and the next, a fierce gust of wind blew across their path stirring up twigs and piles of fallen leaves. Brigid released Connell's hand to shield her face from the sudden assault, and when she removed it, Connell was gone.

Brigid did not see her at first. She was as beautiful as before, but when she stood in front of her, Brigid could not tell where the forest ended and the Faerie Queen began. Her impressive figure appeared somehow less substantial. Brigid could see the outline of the trees behind her through her rust-coloured gown.

"Where is Connell?" Brigid asked.

"Not far. In a few moments he will return to you with no memory of your separation. It is you I wish to speak to."

"Whatever revenge you wish to take on me, do not harm Connell or my child. It is I who stole your sacrifice."

"You have nothing to fear from me. I will not harm you or those you love."

"Then what do you want?"

The Faerie Queen looked at her thoughtfully. "My revenge grows slow and strong like these trees. I will have my victory when I look into your son's eyes and see my own reflection there."

The breath fled from Brigid's body. "What do you mean?"

"Only this. You have chosen to age like them, die like them, and in time all memory of you shall pass from this world. This you have chosen, but what of your child? When he learns the truth, and you can be sure that day will come, will he think you chose well? Or will he despise you for giving up his chance to live as we do?"

"He will understand," Brigid said. "He will know that I . . ."

The Faerie Queen bowed her head, and for a moment it was as though Brigid were the Queen and she, Dania, the peasant. "Perhaps he will. Only time will tell."

When she returned her gaze to Brigid's, the expression in her eyes was a mixture of anger, disdain, and inexplicably pity. She whispered softly in Brigid's ear and then she was gone.

"Are you tired? Shall we rest a little?"

Connell. There, beside her, as if he'd never left. Brigid drew him into a tight embrace. She wanted to press her body against his until she, Connell, and the child inside her were melded together as one. Only his warmth and solidity could ease the chill and unearthly sensation of lightness that made her what she was. What did that mean for the child inside her growing strong on Faerie blood? But Connell held her tightly, and as she drew the heat of his body into her own the fear slowly began to fade.

"Let's go home," she said.

Epilogue

The village gave Connell a hero's welcome. The fact that he returned from the woods unharmed, and with Brigid beside him, was proof enough of his goodness. Although at first suspicious of the village's unexpected kindness and generosity, the resentment Brigid had carried for most of her life began to slip from her shoulders like a mantle of Faerie mist. In time, the villagers would tell the tale of fair Connell, who battled the Fair Folk for his bride and won. Her part in it all would gradually shrink and blur until no one was sure if she was there at all. But she and Connell knew the truth of that night and it was enough.

Brigid married Connell by the church door, and none but her husband detected the slight swell underneath the cream wool gown that Maeve had mended for her. "He or she will be the most loved child in all the world," Connell whispered to her on their wedding night once the guests dispersed and they were finally alone.

Everything was as it should be and yet . . . When the birth of her child drew near, she could not stop herself from entering the forest one last time. It was the kind of impulsive, foolish action she thought she'd put behind her. After all, she was now a wife, soon to be a mother, but still she had to make certain. Did the Faerie Queen tell her the truth? Was the village now safe from the Fair Folk's interference?

Her heavy body moved lightly over the forest floor, her feet never once tripping over an overgrown root or upturned stone, until suddenly she found herself beside the sacred well.

Listen underneath, the Faerie Queen had told her all those years ago. Brigid listened, her body as still and silent as the trees. She waited, scarcely daring to breathe. Did the willow mutter something to her? Or the birch reach out its silver branches in silent entreaty? The child pressed sharply against her ribcage, making her gasp for breath. Nothing. The wood was just a wood. The trees confided no secrets, and the ground was solid and sure beneath her feet. Tiredness overwhelmed her. She picked her way over the scattered leaves and fallen branches until she came to the stream. Brigid knelt down and lifted handful after handful of the cold clear water to her lips.

Not ready to return home where the vegetables for supper wanted washing and Connell's tunic needed mending, she lingered by the stream where she caught sight of her rippling reflection. Despite the changes in her body her face remained the same, and for the first time she wondered how long this would be true.

When she finally got to her feet, the day had grown old, and with the fading of the sun came the promise of twilight's chill. She wrapped her arms around her body for warmth, the gesture reminding her of the shawl she'd forgotten to bring with her, and then she remembered another shawl. A gift from Midir that she'd put away with the other treasures he'd given her.

Brigid found her old hiding place easily. She reached inside the gnarled Oak's hollow and pulled out the linen bundle that was only slightly damp from the earth. She undid the wrappings with trembling fingers, but when the material came away there was nothing inside but a handful of dried leaves and a single wizened berry.

On the way home, she felt the weight of her body as she hadn't before. Her feet felt thick and heavy, and her back ached with strain. But she walked faster, eager to be out of the woods even though she no longer had cause to fear them. When the dark overhang of trees finally gave way to a silver sky, just beginning to darken at the edges, Brigid allowed herself to rest. She lowered herself to the ground, lay her head on a clump of grass, and wept as she'd not done since the day her father died.

Not wanting Connell to see her tangled hair and reddened eyes, Brigid stopped at her mother's cottage on the way home. Her mother greeted her warmly and led her to sit in front of the fire. Once Brigid took her old place beside the hearth, she said, "The Fair Folk are gone."

She expected her mother to be angry that she'd gone into the woods, but her voice was gentle when she said, "It is all behind you now."

And so it was. She had her baby, a beautiful boy they called Aiden. A good solid name, a name of earth and fire. A name you could grab hold of and never let go. She devoted herself to his care until the days blurred together like a long, sweet ballad. More and more the Faerie seemed like a dream.

But one night she awoke to the sound of music, achingly lovely, and so faint she had to strain with every nerve ending in her body to hear it. She got out of bed, where Connell slept deeply beside her, and rushed to the window to better hear the music. Not daring to open the shutter for fear of waking Aidan in his cradle, she pressed her head against the opening. For a moment, the music swelled and her body was flooded with pleasure, her feet tingling with the familiar urge to dance until she felt her very soul underneath her feet. But as quickly as it began the music ended, and she stood staring at the window, trying to remember the tune that only a moment before seemed engraved on her memory forever. She went back to bed and lay staring at the ceiling until dawn, hoping for the music to return. But in the morning it was as far away as though it had never been.

When Aiden cried for his morning feed, she picked him up and pressed her lips against his soft skin. She needed his warmth to remind her that she, too, was made of flesh and blood and not wind and sky. Brigid breathed in her son's scent, a heady mixture of sweet and sour, and remembered what the Faerie Queen whispered to her that morning in the forest.

"You will never forget us, not for the rest of your life."

CPSIA information can be obtained at www.ICGtesting.com
Printed in the USA
LVOW100241280613

340394LV00006B/11/P